The Heart of the Romanovs

By Kristin Shaw Amrine

Edited by Val Serdy with Egg and Feather

Published by Kristin Shaw Amrine

©2014

All Rights Reserved

Dedicated to

The girls that live under my rule

Ashley, Bryanna, Caitlyn and Drew

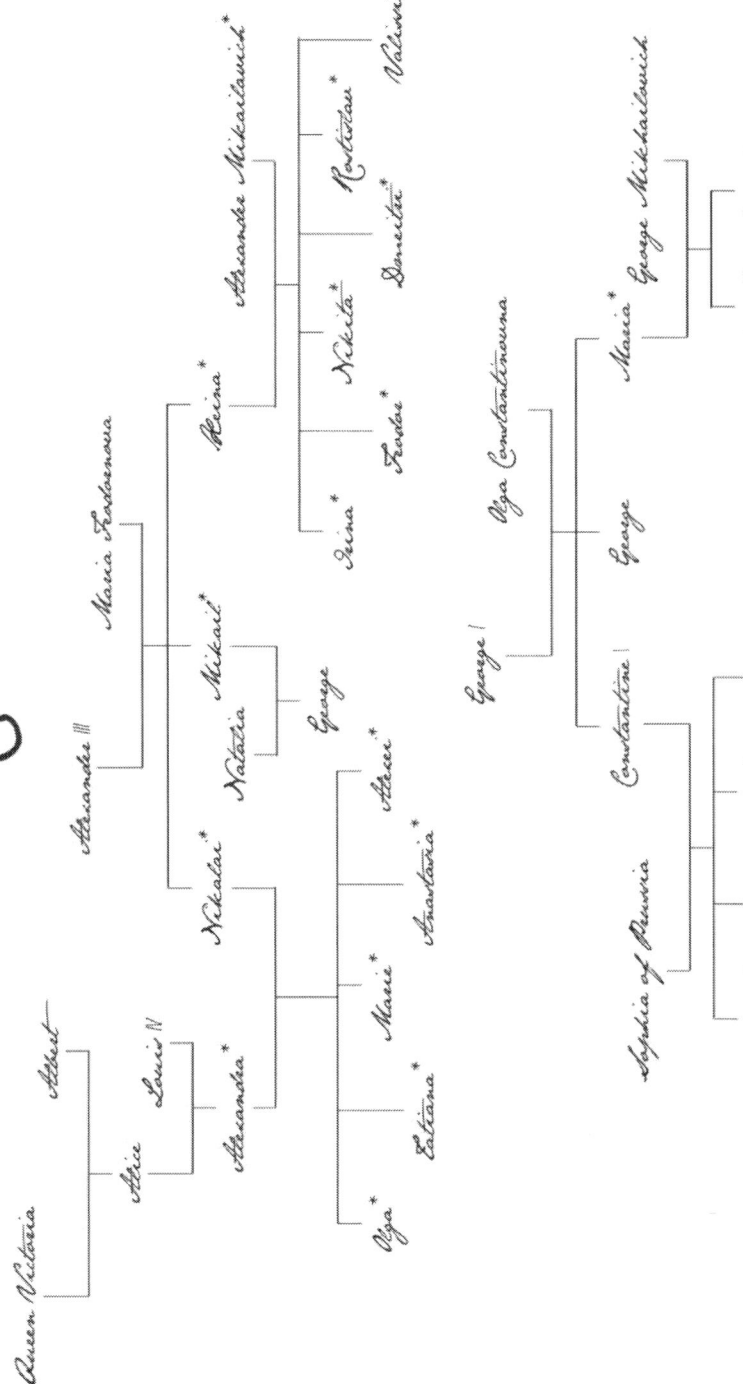

Prologue/Author's Note

Dear Reader:

After reading a lot of historical fiction novels myself, I had a desire to write one for young adults. I was pondering on what era to write about, when one day the TV in the background of my house was turned to the History Channel. It was a program about the daughters of the last Tzar of Russia. The show painted an image of the four girls as beautiful, cultured, flirtatious, and highly sought-after young ladies. I wondered why none of them ever married, especially since they seemed quite old to be single for the time period when they died. Also they were the great granddaughters of Queen Victoria, the greatest match-maker of all time. Having four daughters of my own, I could imagine their strong connection to each other, and my heart ached at the hardships they had to go through.

There are a few tales in history as tragic as the story of the family of the Tzar Nikolai II. The last of the reigning Romanovs, Tzar Nikolai, his wife, the German Princess Alexandia, his four daughters, and one and only heir, his son Alexei were thought by some to be only extravagantly rich and unsympathetic to the needs of a Russia at a desperate time in their history: the time proceeding World War I and ultimately the Russian Revolution. But the more I researched the family, the more I came to believe that they had been misunderstood. The father, Nikolai, never seemed to have ambitions of power, instead he cherished his children and the time he was able to spend with them. Yet as the leader of one of the most powerful, albeit barbaric, nations of the world, he was expected to rule with an iron fist. Something I believe went against his character. His wife was hated for her background as a princess of Germany, but in reality her connections were more with her Grandmother on her mother's side, Queen Victoria of England. I believe she was a little shy, and though she loved her husband, found it difficult to fit in with his family.

Though some of the characters in this story were invented by me, most of them are in fact historical figures that lived during this time and were connected with the Romanovs. Some of those connections were also stretched to serve my purposes.

In fairytales, the terms prince and princess usually refer to the children of the monarchy. But during this time period, those terms were used more loosely and referred to anyone of noble birthright. The children of His Imperial Emperorship's official titles were Grand Duke and Grand Duchesses, but they weren't used as frequently. Also nicknames seemed to be prevalent in Russia. Each of the girls, excepting Olga, had a nickname. Also the tzar and his wife had nicknames for each other.

Sometimes you will see the tzar referred to Nicholas II. That is also his name. I just chose to use Nikolai because I liked it better. His brother Mikhail was also Michael. Again, I prefer Makhail. As I prepared to write this novel, I read Tolstoy, and as a reader, had a little trouble with the character's names, nicknames, and surnames. Surnames are the father's first name with a suffix of some sort. Women's surnames have a female suffix. In my reading, I got quite confused by this. I was a third of the way through Anna Karenina before I realized that two character names referred to one character. That was about 300 pages into it. To make this story more authentic, I included these names as well as some nicknames, but for the sake of my readers, I tried to use them only when I felt it was necessary.

Nikolai was well versed in linguistics and he and his wife both spoke English and French fluently, but German wasn't one of the tzar's specialties and Alexandra had trouble with Russian, which probably had something to do with why the she felt so disconnected from the Russian people. English was the main language spoken in the home, and French was the official language of the Russian court. Of course Russian was used outside the home.

My purpose in writing this story is to show the softer side of the family of the last tzar of Russia. I hope to help you create a picture of the Russian court at this time. A time where Russian traditions were still strong, but there was also a big push to be more "European." The lives of the children of Tzar Nikolai were very difficult, but their spirits were strong. This Russian family was willing to pursue happiness, even until their tragic ending. In the end, death was the only way they could be free, and was indeed their only way to find true happiness.

I hope you enjoy reading about them as much as I enjoyed writing about them.

Kristin Shaw Amrine

The Heart of the Romanovs

By

Kristin Shaw Amrine

6 October 1912

Bialovezh, Russian Poland

I

The doctor's shoulders sag from exhaustion as he steps into the hallway outside my brother's room. With hands clasped behind his back, he slowly approaches my father.

"The prince's stomach is hemorrhaging, and his fever has caused him to slip into a coma." He slowly breathes in, and softly exhales his next words. They are almost inaudible, but everyone waiting in the room hears as though he's shouted. "I'm afraid death is inevitable." Dr. Fedorov hangs his head, truly grieving with us. He wrings his hands and whispers aloud the words we are all thinking. "At least now, he may get some rest."

My brother, the Prince, at only eight years old, is the strongest person I have ever known. Alexei's illness causes him to face death every day, yet he never acts fearful. But this time, I am afraid that even he cannot endure the pain any longer. The past months have been excruciating for him. He has suffered in ways I can't even imagine while my sisters and I are forced to listen to his anguished cries and watch as our mother's spirit dies inside her. She feels his hurting deep in her heart.

The sun still hovers in the sky above the dense tree line that surrounds the Bialovezhian hunting lodge, but it doesn't share any of its warmth. Father shivers and puts his hand to his face to disguise his emotions. "We begged God that he would bless us with the birth of this boy, but now, just eight years later, we can only pray that his death will come quickly so that he might be spared from the pain. I can no longer be at his bedside. I cannot bear to hear his cries."

"It's time we let your subjects know what has happened to your heir." My Uncle Makhail comfortingly takes my father's arm. Our uncle too, is grief-stricken. He has always had a soft spot for my brother, but now he must stay stalwart and act in the Tzar's behalf. This will be the first time Russia has heard anything about Alexei's illness. "I will give Count Fredericks word to begin releasing a medical bulletin." Father nods acknowledging his words. Makhail, his only living brother, has stood by him through these last horrible days.

We have always been so careful. Alexi wanted to be out hunting with Father. But hunting is far too dangerous, so he went sailing instead. Sailing is supposed to be safer for him, but this injury to his leg is the worst he's ever had. It was caused by simply jumping from the boat to the dock. For most boys his age, a cut, a bruise is expected, but for Alexei it can mean infection, internal bleeding, even death.

The room goes silent as his door slowly opens. Mother silently comes out of his room. It seems as if she hasn't stepped outside of it since we arrived here in Spala. Her dress sags and her hair hangs in strings of grey. She hasn't eaten or slept in days.

"Is there any word from Rasputin?" Mother asks in desperation. Father goes to her side, puts his arm around her waist and pulls her to him.

"It is too late, my love. Rasputin was notified of Alexei's accident weeks ago. He hasn't answered and now it is too late."

It seems that Father and Uncle have finally found a way to draw Mother away from her beloved healer's hypnotic powers. Father's advisors tell him to stay away from Rasputin, but he has become our family's savior.

"He has been sent by God," Mother tells us continually. Though the man frightens me, I am grateful that he has been there for my brother and my mother.

I can no longer disguise my emotions as my sisters and I are herded out of the room by servants. With tears streaming down my cheeks, I pull at my hair and hug myself beneath my sweater. Olga, my older sister, comes to me from behind and wraps her arms around me. I turn to face her and we hold each other until our sobbing quiets. Then we turn to comfort our younger sisters.

Anastasia, at age eleven, is closest in age to our brother, and I expect this to be hardest on her, yet she seems to have matured beyond her years in the recent weeks. She has gotten control of her emotions already. Marie hides her grief, as she does most of her emotions, and we allow her to deal with her sadness privately.

The remainder of the day is spent making arrangements for our brother's impending death. My sisters and I are allowed to go in his room, one at a time, to say goodbye. As I wait my turn, I look out of the plated glass window of the cabin. It is snowing heavily outside. The trees surrounding the lodge seem to sigh as if they can no longer hold up their weighty branches. Men dressed in fur and boots work on a makeshift chapel my father has commissioned to be built outside the hunting lodge, so my brother can receive his last rights. Though stinging ice blows sideways against their faces, no one inside notices the storm.

When it's my turn to go in I see Mother, sitting at Alexei's bedside, looking like a ghost herself. I think she will never forgive herself for this bleeding illness—this hemophilia—she has inadvertently passed on to her son.

I take a couple of deep breaths to be sure I can keep my emotions in control. I don't want my mother to see me upset. She already knows how hard this is on all of us; I don't want her to feel anymore guilt. I try to think of happy times with my brother, long before this all started. I put my face to my brother's cheek so that I can feel his hot, weak breath. I am stirred by the depth of love I feel for this boy.

"Brother, it's me," I whisper softly into his ear. "It's Tatiana—Tanya, your favorite sister." I look over at Mother to see if she can see my smile, but she only stares at the Bible in her lap and clasps her hands in prayer.

Convinced that my mother is barely aware of my presence, I refocus my attention on the boney body that lies before me. It's almost unrecognizable as my little brother, and his fever induced coma doesn't seem to have allowed him any rest at all. His face is tight with pain, and his body is racked with tremors. It hurts me to see him like this.

Our family is very close. My sisters, Olga, Marie, Anastasia, our only brother, Alexei and I, we have grown up with only each other to play with, go to school with. We are isolated most of the time and constantly guarded when we are in the public eye.

My brother's illness is strictly a secret. He is the one and only heir to the Imperial Russian Dynasty. If word were let out that he was sick, his power would be diminished. As the children of the tzar, we are in constant danger, depending on Father's popularity or the direction the wind is blowing, it seems.

A tear falls from my eye, as I try to imagine life without my brother, but the tender moment is interrupted by a knock on the door. Mother sits up with a start. Dr. Fedorov slowly raises his tired body from the chair and painfully crosses the room to see who is there. A servant stands holding an envelope. Before Mother can get up to see, Father comes in. He and the doctor have a hushed conversation, but

Mother's face flows with color when she hears them whisper the name of the man she thinks has been brought to her from God.

"It's from Rasputin. Let me see it."

Before the physician or Father get a chance to reason with her she has the envelope in her hand. "A telegram," she sighs. "I knew he wouldn't forsake us."

Standing at Alexei's bedside, no longer aware that I'm here, she reads it softly out loud.

> *"God has seen your tears and heard your prayers. Do not grieve. The Little One will not die. Do not allow the doctors to bother him too much.*
> *Your Dear Friend, Greggori Rasputin*

She sighs, sits slowly back in her chair, and places the telegram to her heart. Father and the doctor look at each other, trying to find words to console her, but with Alexei's hand in mine, I can feel an immediate change in him. As if the words from the telegram have drained the pain from his body.

"Father," I exclaim. "Come look!"

"Tatiana my darling, don't let your hopes..." But he can see it too. My brother's face is no longer distorted in discomfort, his breathing has slowed, and the tremors have stopped.

I hear Mother whisper a grateful prayer. The doctor looks at my father and shakes his head. "He must be close to Heaven now. It's the only explanation."

But my father's hope is renewed. "His heartbeat is strong." With his head on my brother's chest, he calls to the doctor. "Listen."

The doctor grabs his stethoscope as a servant, scoots me out of the room. I immediately run to share the news with my sisters.

Father and Mother stay in Alexei's room all night, but Father meets us in the dining hall for morning tea wearing a smile that I haven't seen since we left Livida.

"The fever has broken. Alexei opened his eyes early this morning and asked for some water. Thanks be to God, and your mother's faith in His healer. Today is a joyous day. We have seen a miracle at the hands of Rasputin!"

Alexei has been healed and the Russian people may never need to know of our family's secret.

Winter 1913

The Winter Palace—Petersburg, Russia

We don't usually stay in the old Winter Palace anymore. The living area of the Palace in Tsarskoe Selo, where we usually live in the wintertime, is upstairs, and since Alexei's accident three months ago, Rasputin insists that Alexei must not be moved around too much while he heals. Mother always heeds her friend's advice, so this year we have to winter in this dark, dismal place with miserable memories, especially for Papa.

Aside from our private chamber, I know very little of the rest of the palace. It was built centuries ago by Peter the Great. Its majesty is almost primeval. Monstrous in size, it has a hundred unknown rooms used for government and diplomatic purposes. It might be exciting to explore, but because of Father's trepidation, he has guards posted at every hallway—for our protection.

As children of the tzar, we are to be seen and not heard, and very rarely seen. When we are forced to stay here we spend most of our time imprisoned in our private apartment. But Father is haunted by nightmares. At this very palace thirty years ago, he watched his grandfather, his body nearly blown to shreds by an assassin's bomb, breathe his last breath.

As if that weren't enough to make him sleep restlessly, in front of this palace, just seven years ago, when I was eight, Alexei's age, a bloody massacre of Russian common men took place, seemingly at Father's command. It was to be a demonstration. Hundreds of workers parading onto the castle grounds on strike, demanding fair treatment, but as the crowd got louder more and more advisors told Papa he must put a stop to it. He finally agreed, but seemed shocked by what means this had been done. Over a hundred and fifty innocent men were shot to death by father's police force—workers, fathers, sons. My father became known as "Bloody Nicholas" and he sadly felt that the nickname fit. Our family could see how devastated he was, but when explaining it to his men he said, *"I must assert my power. I must show the people that God has given me this station and I can only protect them if I rule absolutely."*

The palace haunts Father, but to me it's a prison, a constant reminder that I my life is not my own. I must do what is expected of the daughter of the tzar. Also, the unrest in Russia and the hostility towards my father has made being seen outside the palace walls hazardous, possibly even life threatening, even if I feel it is necessary to my sanity. I can't take the isolation any longer. We aren't usually allowed off the palace grounds, but I have a plan and I can be very persuasive. I wait until his belly is full and the warm fire in the den has softened his heart. After a hard day, nothing relaxes my father more than dinner with his family in the palace's private chamber.

With a saddened expression on my face, I kneel at his chair and look longingly into his eyes. "It would please me more than anything, Father, if my sisters and I could go ice skating just once this winter. Oh please Papa, here we are like prisoners locked in a dungeon. How are we to grow to be the leaders of Russia if we don't even know what the outside of the palace looks like? Our muscles are getting weak and I fear our beauty will be next."

I demonstratively flip my hair off my shoulders. I know that Father values good muscle tone and, as the father of four girls, he knows, if we don't have beauty, we have nothing.

His hazel eyes get big as he takes my face in his hands and laughs with his full belly.

"Skating ey?" He pauses and looks around the room, maybe to see if Mother is in listening distance, but I have already made sure she is occupied in the kitchen. "I was a very skilled ice skater as a boy," Father continues in a whisper, his eyes gleaming with amusement. "It certainly is a noble undertaking, and good exercise. How long has it been since we've been? Four, maybe five years?" He chuckles as he remembers. "You and Olga were always so competitive, always trying to out-do one another. But now look at you, best friends. 'The Big Pair.'"

He calls us by the nickname we have been given by the household. My younger sisters,
Marie and Anastasia are "The Little Pair."

"We should go skating, Tatiana. Yes, we will go. It will be wonderful!" His face lights up like a boy, but then it falls quickly.

"Ahhh….but it cannot be, I forget myself. There is too much work to be done, men to see, advisors to meet with, and it is far too dangerous for you to go on your own."

I jump in before the school boy in him is completely taken over by my father. "We won't go alone, Papa. Your men can supervise us. Choose anyone you wish. We will sneak out, before the sun rises. No one will see, I promise. We'll bring lanterns to light the ice, skate quietly, get some exercise, and come home before the sun even rises. No one will ever know."

Father's eyes twinkle with delight. "How long have you been planning this, my little Tanya? I can see where your hearts is. I will send my guards to hold the lanterns. What I wouldn't do to be free of all of the cares of Russia; free to join my daughters on the ice."

"What about Mother? She will never let us." My shoulders sulk, but I know that once the idea is Father's, he will handle the delicate task of telling her.

"Don't worry about your mother. She will not be happy about this, and it would be better to not mention our plan to your brother either. Alexei will be disappointed even though we all know it would be impossible for him to come along."

I'm sorry for my brother too, but this was also part of my plan. Mother is occupied with Alexei's treatments most of the morning, and she will be too busy to notice.

So with Father's blessing and Mother unable to stop us, we wake before dawn and load in the sleighs. I do not take this opportunity lightly. I have already picked out a dazzling blue dress to go with my parka. My sister's too, are dressed in their best skating attire. The pond, though it will be too dark to see, will be dotted with color, the pink and blue hues of our dresses.

It's a cold, dark morning, as it always is in Russia in February, as my sisters and I ride the gold trimmed, royal sleighs to the skating pond just outside of the village near Petersburg. Bundled in the sleigh, with fur draped across our laps to keeps us warm, I breathe in the frozen winter air, and I can smell freedom. The morning is glorious. The moon can still be seen low in the western sky and my sister's eyes reflect the lantern light shining against the silvery background of the snow and ice.

"Tatiana," Anastasia, calls from across the pond. "It's wider at this end. You'll have more room for your axles." She chooses to skate with me in an area where I can practice my jumps and turns. My heart is pumping the blood to parts of my body that seem as if they haven't been used in ages, causing a tingling sensation all over. My lungs stretch to their full capacity filling with fresh open air. As I spin in circles, I flare out my arms and legs and relish the cool breeze. I don't know how long this will last, and I don't know when I'll get the chance to do this again.

My youngest sister stands by and cheers every time my skates lift off the ground. There was a time when Anastasia would have been copying, trying to outdo me, but since contracting measles a few years ago, she has become much more reserved, though her smile is still a ray of sunshine.

"Olga, come here," I shout enthusiastically. "There is more room." I long for her to share in my joy. Several years ago, we were allowed to come here daily. Back then, the pond was surrounded by villagers. My sister and I were quite competitive. The bystanders made bets as we engaged in contests to see who could jump the farthest or twirl the longest.

"Oh there is plenty of room at this end. I don't need to skate fast." Instead Olga chooses to skate in an oval with elegance and grace, at the opposite end with my younger sister Marie, who is always slow and cautious. Olga has forgotten how to have fun. At seventeen, she is old and boring. It seems the only thing on her mind is whom she will marry and what her status will be.

At first, the pond is vacant. The guards standing around look intimidating, with stern faces. Maybe no villagers will dare come near, fearing the guards.

I attempt to get them to relax.

"You're doing such a fine job, Felix!" I call out to amuse myself." The men that guard the palace, and in this case, the tzar's daughters, are all young and handsome. Not much older than Olga and I.

"I will tell my father to slip an extra ruble in your salary," I wink.

"I'll believe it when I see it," he grins back. Our interaction with the guards is always light hearted. We have to find some way to amuse ourselves at the palace.

As I'm thinking of something else to tease Felix about—or maybe George, George has a dimple in his cheek and long eyelashes—the guards suddenly stop smiling and stand taller.

Nervously, I look in the direction their eyes have turned. Approaching in the shadows, a single man can be seen in the distance stepping onto the ice. He's tall and lanky, wearing a suit and tie, attire that doesn't seem suitable for skating, but he is indeed wearing skates. He glides in my direction. Curious, I abandon my figure eight and slide towards the brave young man with Anastasia in tow. As he comes into the glow of the lanterns, my eyes light up with recognition.

"Stepan Karenin! You are shameful. To what extent will you go to seek after my sister?" I chide. "How is the Dumas to be run without you?"

"I'm sure they can do without me if only for the morning." His green eyes lock into mine and his smile stretches across his face so that his sparsely grown, reddish beard looks like he has penciled it on himself and missed a few places. Stepan is only a few years older than Olga, but his father is a dear friend of my father. The grand Duke Andrei Karenin's connections have already won his son a prominent position in the in the Dumas. The Dumas was created by my father, it consists of a body of elected officials that help to govern Russia. Though the representatives are "elected," my father still has a large say on who runs for election. Stepan Karenin is charming--charismatic and bright—one of my mother's favorite suitors for Olga.

"Tatiana, you are amazing. I was watching from the road. Show me again how you did that last stunt." He reaches down affectionately for eleven-year-old Anastasia's hand and I do a few easy jumps, to humor him, some of my less difficult skills. Soon he has seen enough.

Leaving my sister without a hand warmer, he speeds across the ice, leaps in the air, twists
his body around, and clumsily comes to a landing just feet from where I stand, spraying me with shavings from the ice.

"You oaf," I laughingly complain as he apologizes profusely and attempts to brush the snow off my coat. He tenderly wipes the melting ice dripping off my face with his gloved hand. My cheeks redden as his mouth softens into a warm smile.

Stepan's bravery seems to have started a trend. Though the guards are still valiantly holding their posts, the pond is soon dotted with gentleman willing to don skates and relive their boyish stunts. I have grown quite accustomed to the consideration royalty gets me. The longing glances, the flirtatious smiles, men falling over themselves trying to get my attention, and young Anastasia is thrilled with the young men's curiosity. Stepan doesn't join the others in their attempts to better each other. Instead, he does as I supposed he would, and skates with dignity to Olga and Marie's side of the pond.

The guards become nervous as the number of skaters increase. The sparse lighting gives them a limited view of the pond, so they quickly begin to collect us like hens gathering their chicks. Before the beginning of the next hour, our sleigh is loaded with four girls in beautiful dresses and fur blanket leaving for the palace and ending our short bit of sovereignty. I must plan another outing—soon.

At tea later that morning, Mother growls her disapproval. "I don't understand why you girls are willing to put yourself in such danger. What if a rebel from the Marxist party had seen you? Terrorism is heroism to those men."

It's this palace that invokes my mother's fear; my father's as well. Of course Mother is afraid of another raid on the castle grounds or even a single disgruntled workman with a score to settle. I was seven at the time, and though my sisters and I were hidden away in the palace and carefully sheltered from the aftermath, I remember well the constant frown on Father's face and the fear in my mother's eyes. But that was a long time ago.

"Or worse," Mother continues, "what if you were to contract a disease and bring it home to your brother?" My sisters and I glance at each other across the table. We have gotten used to our mother's priorities regarding our brother—the one and only heir to the throne. The Prince Alexei, is seated at the table, his wheelchair parked in the corner, smiling and bouncing out of his seat. He hasn't been privy to this much excitement in weeks.

Father overhears the conversation from the other room, comes in and snatches a roll from the table. "My children will not be held captive in their own home," he proclaims in the voice of the tzar. "But this will be the last outing for a while." His eyes become sad, and he continues in a softer, more fatherly voice. "Things will be better soon. There are changes that must be made first, but things will be better." Then, he kisses Alexei on the head and ruffles his hair. This is why we are in the Winter Palace, so that we can have Alexei near us. Mealtime is a very important time for my father. He wants his family together.

Papa's childhood was much different than ours. He grew up away from home, attending the military academy when he was younger than Alexei, just like any other noble boy in Russia. As tzar, Grandfather Alexander wanted to raise hearty boys. His sons didn't live in a luxurious palace; they slept on a cot, killed their own meat and took cold showers in the dead of winter. Father is not used to the riches that have come with his responsibilities. In his eye, those riches are one of the burdens that accompany the title. But he feels it is important to show his followers that he is as powerful as the royals in Europe and that he is God's anointed ruler. He has learned to behave as my English bred mother sees fit, but he likes to have his children close around him. I am grateful that Father puts so much emphasis in family, though I tire of them occasionally.

Mother speaks up, changing the topic of conversation.

"Life in the palace won't be dull much longer." Mother pauses to see if she has our attention. "There will be some excitement around the palace come Saturday." Her announcement comes as a surprise, and certainly changes the tone at the table. Marie and Anastasia at least, look up with hopeful eyes.

"We will be hosting a grand ball in the West Ballroom. It's sure to be the finest yet this year."

Olga rolls her eyes. This gesture does not go unnoticed. The Empress turns to her oldest daughter. "You, my dear, should be most appreciative. You are months past your seventeenth birthday and you have not yet chosen a suitor. Your Great Grandmama Victoria would have had your prince chosen for you before you were sixteen. Your father's heart is too soft, letting you chose your own husband, but I will not let this continue past your next birthday."

"But Maman, you and Father were in love when you married," little romantic Marie brings a spark of memory to our mother's eye. My mother's mind seems to go back to when she was Marie's age. She thought she was in love with our father, the handsome young Russian prince whom she called "Nikki," even as a young girl.

"Your father and I were chosen for each other by God. I will find the man God has chosen for you, if you do not find him yourself soon."

I jump in, saving my older sister from having to answer to mother. "Why must the ball be here?" I sigh. "I remember when the Predoviches and the Gorbachavs hosted the most wonderful balls."

Mother puts her thumbs on her temples, but I go on. "Wouldn't it be glorious to make an entrance pulling up in our sleighs and being announced at the front gate?" I stand to demonstrate, waving my arms and drawing a laughter induced cough from my brother. But my attempt to draw a picture that would sway my mother seems to be in vain. Her expression does not change.

After tea, my sisters' and I are excused go to our suites and begin our tutoring. Mother takes Alexei to a room at the end of the long hallway where he is to receive a treatment from his healer. Olga is busy getting ready to inspect her regiment. Last year, she was made colonel over a regiment of soldiers—her first duty as the daughter of the tzar. Though the idea was not popular with the men, they have learned to respect her as a strong, distinguished woman. Now it seems inspecting her regiment is the only thing that brings her any pleasure in the day.

Though the inspections are done on the West end of the palace grounds (still walking distance from the palace) it must be good to get away from the palace every day.

Olga still seems upset. I decide make my tutor wait as I follow her to see if she's ready to talk. I find her in our suite, angrily attempting to do up the buttons on her boots. I take the fastener out of her hands and sit at her feet. Olga straightens and fusses with the epilated sleeves on her jacket.

"Oh, how I wish I could command a regiment," I swoon as I manipulate the loops for the buttons on her boots. "It must be difficult to keep a stern face while you 'inspect' the soldiers."

Olga puts her gloved hand to her mouth to stifle a giggle. Despite her foul mood, she smiles affectionately. "It is necessary to make sure our soldiers 'flanks' are firm." She swats her hip, and flashes me a wicked smile. We fall laughing, into each other's arms.

"Why are you not excited about the ball on Saturday?" I question as I work on her boots.

"I'm tired of it Tanya. Tired of being told what to do all the time."

Frankly, I'm surprised hearing these sentiments being made by my sister. This is how I have always felt, but I thought she was quite satisfied in being the oldest and setting the example for obedience."

"Aren't you anxious to get married? To get out of here and see how the rest of the world lives?"

"Anxious? Yes, but not in a good way. I don't want to be pressured into choosing a husband so soon."

Upon finishing the last button, I decide to change the subject. I put my arm on her shoulder, and speak softly in her ear.

"What I wouldn't do to be colonel of a regiment of my own. I would find the most handsome soldier, run off with him, and have twenty children."

"You would be the mother of all of Russia if you were given your way." She sighs, "and what I wouldn't do to be in your place, so young and unconcerned of your position in the hierarchy."

Being in the situation we were born into, daughters of his Imperial Highness, the tzar of Russia, we are expected to marry a man of high standing with strong military positioning to help protect our family's allegiances. Great Grandmama, Queen Victoria of England, was the best matchmaker of all time, placing her family—especially her children and grandchildren—in high stations all over Europe.

"Oh, so that's it, my dear. You're concerned about your future standing. Waiting for an invitation of marriage from one of the princes of England, maybe? Maybe even Prince Edward himself." I raise my eyebrows. "Wouldn't it be just like you to have such ambitions—Olga Nikolaevna, the next Queen of England."

"And get out of here? Yes—without hesitation," she quickly answers. "But it will be your turn soon, Tanya. I was given my post at age sixteen. You have less than a year, but good luck finding a soldier who doesn't look on you with disdain." She reveals with a frown.

"You mean your regiment is not loyal to the royal command?" I say sarcastically.

Olga can only answer my question with a crooked smile. We are not unaware of our family's unpopularity. We have been blessed in abundance, while most of the Russian population falls into the class of peasant. Peasants all over Russia have abandoned their farms in the country, and are now roaming the streets of Petersburg in poverty. A group of peasants were trampled and killed in a riot that began on Mother and Father's wedding day. It was seen by many as a bad omen—that the marriage would be cursed.

That was long ago and mostly forgotten, but the Dumas still cannot come to an agreement on what is to be done about the economic situation. Our family's massive wealth doesn't make us appear to be sympathetic to the problem. Everyone has a different view of what is to be done about Russia's economy, and it seems that no one's view includes loyalty to royalty.

I hear Mother coming, so I slip out the back passage-way and follow the corridor back to the classroom. I don't want to give my tutor anything to complain to her about.

II

My younger sister Marie seems especially excited for the first ball to be held in the Winter Palace this year. It is to be held in the ballroom in the West Wing, and she has found that through the floor to ceiling windows the moon is in full view. After sneaking a peek, she comes running into our suites to tell us, "It hangs low in the sky and looks like it has been placed there just for our enjoyment."

I always enjoy balls, or rather I enjoy being doted on by all of the young men, one of the privileges of royalty. But at thirteen, Marie is just old enough to appreciate it for all its majesty and beauty: the extravagant gowns, the orchestra, the sense of anticipation in the air.

Would tonight be the night that she, or one of us, will meet the man that will love us forever?

She enters our suite while we are still dressing. Marie has been dressed for an hour and has been asked to bring the jewels mother has selected to our rooms. I frown when I see what has she has brought. They are stylish and elegant, but extravagant, and I know that there are those attending the ball that will think we are flaunting our wealth. It would be disgraceful to appear proud. But knowing that mother has sent them, I feel obligated. I select the most unassuming pieces I can find, a string a pearls, to go with my dress. It's cream colored, mostly lace over chiffon, fitted at the hips and flared at the bottom. It has become fashionable to wear white. It's the color of purity and wealth. Simplicity that looks costly. Olga's dress is a sharp ivory that drops at the waist. She selects a pair of diamond drop earrings that will compliment her glimmering hazel eyes and the tiara that sits on her ash blond chignon.

My dark hair is not set as high, and loose curls frame my face. I am also wearing a tiara, as is the fashion, but especially expected of the daughters of the tzar. I am the only one in the family with dark skin and hair, but my eyes are light like my sisters. I'm also the only one who has inherited any height (from my mother's side), which makes me feel lanky and skinny standing next to them.

"Marie, your tiara makes you look very grown up." Olga compliments our younger sister as she selects earrings similar to her own. "You are sure to catch the eye of a few gentlemen looking so elegant." Marie is nicely plump, and has filled out well for her age. She has a sweet angelic face—the prettiest of all of us.

Marie may be growing into a young woman, but Anastasia still looks very childlike in her delicate pink dress with her golden hair worn with curls cascading down her shoulders. The diamonds she has chosen don't sparkle as much as the blue diamonds set in her eyes.

Not long after the jewels are selected, mother comes to present us with our dance cards. The Empress personally approves every dance partner. The ball is not a social event for my sisters and me, it is our duty. I enjoy the men's company, but it's hard to enjoy one's self with mother's eye on us every second. Looking over her shoulder, I inspect Olga's card. Stepan Karenin is the first name on her list. The song is a waltz.

"Maybe Stepan Karenin will get his wish." I say quietly, so only Olga can hear.

Olga turns to me with questioning eyes. "Stepan? What do you mean?"

I chuckle at first, but then realize my sister doesn't understand. "Don't tell me you haven't noticed the look in his eyes when he comes 'round you? And he is always around."

Olga's eyebrows furrow, as if she is contemplating my observation, but then throws her head back and laughs. "He doesn't look at me differently than he looks at anyone else. He's just a boy, a childhood playmate."

Upon considering this, I question the conclusion I have made regarding, Stepan's, or any man's intentions. Could I have been reading them wrong all this time? No, Olga is only in denial, I soothe myself.

With my dance card in hand, I line up with the rest of my family for inspection. We are now the regiment, and Mother is the colonel. Alexei's wheelchair is parked in his private chambers tonight. It's mostly just to ease Mother anyway. He can walk, gingerly, while his leg is still healing from his accident in Spala, but he must join the ranks tonight. His dirty blond hair is cut short like the students at the military academy, and his grey waistcoat and narrow neck tie make him look older than he is. He stands tall, but he will sit out this ball.

"Why must I dance every dance with Dmetri?" Anastasia complains through her teeth so that Mother doesn't hear, although she has no trouble expressing her frustration to us. We try not to upset Mother at times like this. Social situations are terribly stressful for her.

Mother has carefully chosen who will attend this ball and more carefully who will dance with her daughters. But she isn't as outgoing as Papa's mother, the previous tsarina.

Grandmaman Maria is a social butterfly with connections all over Russia. But since Maman has become the tzarina, Grandmaman spends most of her time in Paris. Mother's ties are also, mostly still in Europe. She grew up in Germany, but her German friends are not welcome here. Mother's only real associations in Russia are my father's siblings and a very small number of the otherwise closely-knit Romanov family.

My father's sister Aunt Xenia, her husband Uncle Alexander, their only daughter Irena, and five of their six sons are attending the ball tonight. Little Valisi is six. He will not be here, but our next youngest cousin, nine-year-old Dmetri's name fills Anastasia's dance card, except for the waltz that is saved for Father. We will each have at least one dance with His Imperial Highness the Emperor of Russia.

The guests all stand at attention as Father leads us into the ballroom. Mother takes the arm of our distinguished-looking brother Alexei, and they majestically enter. He must grin and bear the pain. He is not accustomed to putting weight on his injured leg, but he cannot show weakness. My sisters and I follow, in order of age, Olga, me, then Marie and Anastasia.

A few young women, most of whom we have never met, excepting our cousin Irina, wear beautiful dresses and stand waiting in the corners with their dance cards in hand. Maybe twice as many gentlemen in dark, cropped jackets surround the room. Most are soldiers in uniform, students of the Corps des Pages Military Academy here in Petersburg, but Olga turns to me and whispers, "Most of my regiment has been invited." She seems very pleased.

Mother and Father are seated, and the first chords of the first waltz are strung. Alexei's chair is next to Mother's. Normally he would dance the first dance with our sister Anastasia. He leans to me and frowns, "She hates that she has to dance with Dmetri, but at least she won't be stepping on my feet."

"She steps on you on purpose?" Anastasia is known to be an imp, but even I am shocked that she would purposely cause physical pain to our delicate brother. I look at her accusingly. Her mischievous eyes tell me that Alexei speaks the truth, but she has done her duty and is standing next to her dance partner. With her tiara, she is at least a head taller than he, adding to his discomfort, I'm sure. Then unsympathetically, she gives him her hand and with a sly smile lets him lead her to the dance floor.

Before I can do anything about it, Marie swooshes by, beaming as she takes the arm of Prince Igor Konstantinovich wearing a Corps des Pages uniform and looking older than his nineteen years with a full beard. It makes me forget my mission to reprove my sister.

Igor's father and mine are good friends. The Grand Duke Konstantin Konstantinovich is said to be the most artistic of the Imperial house. He and his wife often travel to Rome and Greece, studying art as they surround themselves with culture: museums, the orchestra and ballet. Mother has chosen Igor for Marie? I heave a sigh of relief and turning, I look into a familiar pair of green eyes. I bow and step aside so that Olga can see that her partner has arrived.

I do not notice the look on Stepan's face when he sees Olga. A uniformed man has stepped in front of me. He bows and shows me my name at the top of his dance card. Looking up into Igor's older brother Prince Konstantine's, handsome face I am pleased. They are also both very eligible and considered good suitors for Olga and me. He's not exactly "the soldier" I dream of someday meeting, but at least he isn't immature and arrogant like his younger brother. Konstantine has always treated me like a child and seems to favor Olga, but maybe tonight will be different. I give my mother an appreciative smile as I am escorted on to the dance floor, but the tzarina has her eye on Olga and Stepan. Watching, hoping, for the sparks to fly.

One dance blends into another as the night progresses. Olga explains that she has developed a headache, "probably from an evening of strained conversation," and disappears out on the veranda. I am waiting for my next dance partner to find me when I look up to see Stepan Karenin.

"Your sister has abandoned me," he whispers with a mysterious smile. "I talked to your cousin, Prince Andrie," he takes my dance card out of my hand and points to the next name, "He has agreed to let me have this dance."

Stepan seems unsure as he searches my eyes to see if that is all right with me. "We can just sit this one out, and have some ale." He offers me his arm while I search the room for my mother.

"She is dancing with your father." Stepan reads my mind. He spends so much time with our family, he knows us all well.

"Watching them on the dance floor, I am reminded of the story of how my parents first met at a wedding, when my mother was twelve." I say, mostly to myself.

Stepan invites me to continue. "I don't think I've heard this story."

"I'm surprised. It's my father's favorite to tell. They met at the wedding of my mother's sister Elizabeth, and Father's Uncle Sergei when they were both very young, but he saw her again when she was nearly seventeen. They had kept in touch through the years through post, and had become friends, but my father said that when he saw her again that night he immediately fell in love. He proposed soon after their second meeting. Mother refused his first proposal. Grandmaman Victoria was alive then and would have had something to do with discouraging it. Father never liked Grandmaman Victoria."

I turn to Stepan and he smiles. I'm surprised he's still listening. It seemed for a moment that I was talking to myself, but I go on. "When Maman was eighteen she finally agreed. Grandmaman Victoria could have nothing to say about it then. 'When Alix finally said yes,' my father used to say, 'My dearest dream had come true.'"

"The way he looks at her, I can see it," Stepan steps closer and looks into my eyes, "there is still love there."

"He calls her his 'Sunshine.' One can only dream of finding such love." I breathe.

Stepan's eyes lock onto mine for a moment. I shift my whole body away from him and focus on something in the opposite corner of room. I feel exposed, and Stepan's expression makes me uncomfortable, I don't usually discuss family intimacies with him. I take a step away from him, but he takes hold of my arm and pulls me back, leading me to a quieter part of the ballroom, away from the dancing, and seats me in a chair. Moving to the refreshment table, he picks up two glasses of ale and asks, "Can I get you something to drink?"

"Thank you?" I look at him suspiciously. I'm not sure what it is, but I have the feeling he's hiding something from me. We sit in silence for a moment as we watch dancers swirl around.

"Marie seems to be engaged in a conversation with a man twice her age." I frown. "I wonder how Mother decides on our dance partners." I think out loud. Embarrassed, I turn back to Stepan. His eyes seemed to be focused on me. I feel a flush of blood running to my cheeks and turn back to the ballroom floor so that he doesn't see me blush. As the waltz finishes, my eyes are drawn toward the veranda. I put my gloved hand to my mouth in shock. Olga is standing in the doorway, smiling.

"Her headache is apparently cured," I observe as she walks arm in arm to the dance floor
with a man in uniform I don't recognize.

The music to the next dance starts up again. Stepan stands up, "Who's next on your card?" He asks scanning the floor and standing in front of me.

"Prince Nicholas Volcachec—hey, you're blocking my view."

Make yourself comfortable, I'll be right back." He marches out to the dance floor, finds a man in a waistcoat with a well groomed moustache, and then saunters back to where I'm sitting, sipping my drink.

"I told him you were exhausted and needed to sit awhile."

"Acting brotherly already? Isn't that presumptuous of you? Nicholas is a charming fellow. I…" I start to stand, but Stepan places his hands on my shoulders and firmly keeps me seated.

"All of the effort I go to, to make you make you comfortable and you show no appreciation." His smile is teasing, but his eyes seem to be searching mine for my approval. I can feel Mother looking in our direction.

"I'm not sure the tzarina would approve of your playing host to her extravaganza."

"Your mother could not oppose to you being with me, instead of Nicholas Volcachec."
He explains in a defensive tone.

"Besides… we're creating a distraction." He sits down next to me and places his hands on the sides of my face. My heart races. How much of a distraction does he want to create? But then he turns my face to the dance floor and I see what he wants me to see. Olga is in the arms of a soldier, and judging by his uniform, he is not from the Corps des Pages, more likely a soldier from her regiment.

I am shocked and a little jealous. How dare she? She is the oldest. She must do what is expected of her or she will ruin it for everyone else. It's the oldest daughter's duty to marry well. If she does well enough, it takes the pressure off the rest of the family. If Olga were to choose a man of no standing, she would be disgraced and the responsibility of creating a strong alliance would be passed on to me.

As if reading my mind, Stepan leans in and whispers, "she knows what her duties are, but can't she have just this one dance?"

I loosen the grip on the handkerchief I have taken out of my satchel and twisted until my fingers are white.

"Scandalous," I throw back my head and look wildly into his eyes.

When the next song begins, Stepan offers me his hand and escorts me from my seat. "Who are you going to rid me of this time?" I ask presuming.

He points to his name next on my card. Humbled, I let him lead me to the dance floor.

III

"Did you have a favorite?" Mother asks Marie, starting with the easy questions over Sunday morning tea, after we have taken Mass.

"Are there no young men my age in Petersburg that I'm not related to?" This is the same thing I was wondering when I saw the men Mother had chosen for her.

"Darling, you don't have time to waste with a boy. We must find you a man that has already made his place in the world. You didn't seem to have any trouble relating intellectually to the men you danced with last night."

Olga and I look at each other. It seems that Mother is able to watch three of us carefully now.

"No," Marie places her hands in her lap and looks up at Mother like a student trying to impress her teacher.

"No, you're right. Boys my age are certainly not at my intellectual level."

"Of course you can only assume," I laugh from across the table. "With Feodor tying your braids during mass and Nikita putting frogs in your shoes?" Marie scrunches up her face, irritated by my interruption, and our cousins. They are not the finest examples of clever young men. Feodor is a year older than Marie, and Nikita is just her age. She has grown up with them, but certainly doesn't think of them as on her intellectual level, much less as interesting dance partners.

Marie gives me a pious smirk, and turns back to Mother. "Prince Alexander Baronovich was quite well versed in English literature," she says acting coy.

Mother smiles pleasantly at Marie and then looks sternly at her youngest daughter.

"Anastasia, we need to get you some more dancing lessons. Your Aunt Xeina tells me that poor Dmetri's feet are bruised this morning." Our eyes all turn to our naughty little sister. Her face is angelic as she sweetly turns and offers her apologies.

"Which dance instructor shall we bring in?"

"The Spaniard." We all cry out at once.

Maman stifles a giggle of her own. "The Spaniard it is then, tomorrow, dancing lessons for everyone."

For once, mother has planned an activity that we can all look forward to. Senior Ricardo Rodriguez is not only handsome; he has a style when teaching the waltz that no Russian or German could teach. Also, there are dances from his country that, while Mother would never allow us to perform, are exciting to watch. We must become educated in every aspect of European culture.

"Oh, I hate Sundays, there is nothing to do." Olga flops on her bed and slams the book she's been reading on the dresser. "Nothing to do—no one to see..." She sighs as she looks longingly at the ceiling. In other words, she will not be seeing her regiment today.

But I look on the bright side. "There will be guests," I correct her, "after dinner." Mother and Father are having friends over to play cards in the library. Uncle Alexander and Auntie Xenia are bringing all seven of their children tonight. "We can talk to Irina. Maybe she found someone interesting at the ball last night." Irina, Auntie Xiena's only daughter, is just a few months younger than Olga, and single as well. They can relate to each other's situation.

"Ah, someone interesting," Olga gets a dreamy look in her eyes. My mind goes to Stepan Karenin. Of course he will be here. I will watch him tonight to test and see if he does look at Olga differently, or if I've been wrong about him all along.

Yes, tonight we will have plenty of company. Besides the Alexandroviches, Stepan's parents, The Grand Duke Andrei Karenin and his wife, Helene of Saxe-Altenburg will be there, as well as The Grand Duke George Makhailavich, and his wife, Maria. Maria is my father's first cousin and Mother's closest friend in Russia. She grew up in Greece. I guess she can relate to Mother's feeling that she doesn't belong here. Their daughters, Nina and Xenia are my younger sisters' dearest comrades. Marie and Nina aren't only the same age, they share birthdays in June. They will keep Marie and Anastasia busy tonight.

When the guests arrive, the adults are led into the library, but we, along with the other children, are sent to the den where we are allowed to listen to the radio. A servant adjusts the box until she finds a program we all enjoy, The Sunday French Mystery Theater. The older Alexandrorich boys, Andrei and Feodor, tease their younger brothers. Their banter turns into a wrestling match on the floor. Knowing my mother would be appalled if she were to walk in and see such behavior, Uncle Alexander puts a stop to it.

"Must these gathering be held in the ballroom so you boys will have room to kill each other without tipping over our hostess's tables and finery? Maybe I should take you out to the stables until we are ready to leave?"

The younger boys look tempted, but the older boys, feeling their pride threatened, put their elbows into their brothers' ribs.

"Good then," their father seems satisfied. "Stop this nonsense at once or I will call for our carriage and we will leave."

When the door is closed behind him, the boys still continued to stir, but settle down when blankets are spread out on the floor and popcorn is brought in from the kitchen.

Nina and Marie move to a corner where they can giggle quietly and talk about the men they met at the ball last night. Anastasia and Xenia sit listening intently to the radio program. They shush the

Alexandrich boys and threaten to get their father if the noise gets too loud, but the boys are mostly interested in the program as well. Olga and I sit with Irina on the blanket, but Stepan has chosen to sit at a table near us. Though his company is welcome with the adults, I suppose for the sake of my sister, who, though she commands an army, has not yet been invited in with the adults, has chosen to mingle with the younger people.

"It wouldn't do for a government official to be seated like a child on the ground with popcorn stuck to his trousers." He tells us with a dignified air. We take offence to this and proceed to bombard him with popcorn, but eventually, Olga raises her skirt, stands, and pulls up a chair next to him.

As the program goes on, I have a difficult time paying attention to the French narrator. I'm more interested in the couple at the table. They lean in close to each other, engaged in some serious conversation in a whisper. Occasionally, Olga leans back in peals of laughter. Stepan can be quite entertaining. I refuse to let myself feel left out. I turn to whisper something to Irina, but she seems to be interested in the mystery. Intent on refocusing my attention back on the radio program, I turn my body away from the table, but as I turn, I catch

Stepan's wide green eyes. He smiles as if to let me know, he knows I've been spying on them. Blushing and irritated, I turn my back to the table. Even though I have been fluent in French since I was a child of four years, I cannot seem to translate another word of the radio program.

After supper, my family gathers at the door. The servants bring out our guest's coats and we kiss our friends goodbye. When Stepan leans in to kiss my cheek, he whispers French in my ear, *"Bonne nuit, Unpetit Feminin."*

His reference to me as his "little sister" indicates, I deduce, his intentions toward Olga. I hurry up to my room and close the curtain that separates our beds. I have no idea why I'm upset, but I don't want to see my sister again tonight.

When I wake up the next morning, the bad feelings are gone, I can only think of one thing—thanks to Anastasia—we will all have a dance lesson. My sister's and I are giddy as we gathered around the table for morning tea. We dress in our most colorful dancing dresses with skirts that flare out just above the ankle. Short enough that the instructor can watch our feet. Olga is already in her uniform. Of course she will be excused for the first hour, while she inspects her regiment. Senior Rodriguez will stay long enough to give her a full lesson when she returns.

The time passes quickly while the lessons are underway. Most of the time Marie and Anastasia are partners and because Olga is missing, I get to dance with our instructor, though each of my sisters will get time for some one on one instruction.

The dance studio is at the far end of the palace so the music won't disturb Alexei's medical treatments with his healer Rasputin. His "treatments" are kept very private. Always in a secluded wing of the palace, but my mother never leaves his side. Alexei's other doctors, Dr. Fedorov and Dr. Derevenko, also stay close, in case of an emergency, but even they are not allowed in while Rasputin performs his spiritual healings. For the most part, my sister's and I, bridle out curiosity and try not to wonder what goes on at the end of the hall. Alexei is alive and well. That's all we are to concern ourselves with.

After an hour of unnecessary waltz instruction (Anastasia is really a talented dancer), Senior Rodriguez puts another record on the gramophone. Soon the sound of a guitar accompanied by castanets fills the room. He claps his hands and stomps his feet with the music, and encourages us to follow along. He calls this dance the Fandango. With Mother at the other end of the palace, we take advantage of this free exercise of our independence and we are able to relax and enjoy ourselves. It isn't until our instructor puts away his music that we realize how late it's gotten. Olga has not yet arrived.

She enters the dance studio, just as we are leaving. She's still in her uniform, out of sorts, and begs us not to mention it to Mother. We are all in good spirits so we agree, and try not to give it another thought. But I remember the ball and suspect there is a tantalizing story behind her tardiness. I resolve to get it out of her later. But first there is Geography and Arithmetic lessons and then tea with the tzarina.

We are true to our word and don't mention Olga's absence earlier. Alexei is not present for tea. Mother explains that his healer suggests he lie quietly and undisturbed. Then Mother remembers the earlier lessons.

"Anastasia, I hope there will be no more mishaps with your cousin's feet at the next ball."

She nods and smiles at us, perhaps wishing there was another way to make it seem that she requires more dance lessons, but she knows Mother won't be fooled again.

After tea, it's time for our daily stroll around the palace ground because my father insists that we have an outing every day. The courtyard isn't large, but to the east, it borders an evergreen forest (we are not allowed to go there). A narrow stream flows, refusing to freeze, making a natural barrier that marks the borders of our walkway. To the south are the stables. There are many men that work in the stables and so far, Father has not had too much concern about us spending time there, though he frowns on us interrupting the workers tasks.

Not long after my grandfathers death an eight foot wall was built to surround the courtyard. This stops much if the wind that usually blows the snow, and piles it in the courtyard. Somehow a path (more like a tunnel) is shoveled for us to walk on daily. As if the cold and the snow weren't barriers enough, the yard around the castle is heavily guarded.

Servants bring out armfuls of clothing keep us warm. Our fur lined coats and valenki keep us covered from head to toe. We will stay together until we are out of the view of our Mother's window. Then we will venture off on our own.

Anastasia usually heads to the stables with sugar cubes in her pocket for her horse. His name is Носки—the Russian word for Socks. He is a black Arabian with a mischievous spirit, similar to his owner's, with a white diamond on his nose and white on all four legs, just past his ankles, thus the name. The horse was a gift from Grandmaman Maria, the Dowager Empress, for Anastasia's tenth birthday. Our Grandmother was a fine rider herself and was the first to notice Anastasia's love for the animals, but my sister hasn't been allowed to ride Носки in almost a year. The guard seems to get stricter every season as to where they feel comfortable in keeping us safe from the rebels. Just before spring, Anastasia, who has her own ideas of where it is safe to ride, was denied her limited access to her horse. She was upset of course, but what could she do? Father had spoken. As she steps inside the stables, I notice the stable hand take her fur coat and trade it for a leather apron, probably so she can brush Носки and not get hair on her dress.

Marie always ventures to the garden. I watch her go to a bench and place her mittens on the seat, using them as an insulator against the cold. Then she sits to read the book she has snuck out of the house and hidden in her pocket. She doesn't think we notice that she skips her exercises. Father would certainly rebuke her.

The daily promenade around the palace grounds gets very tiresome, so I like to explore the farthest edge. I always have to run to get back in time when the maid calls us in for dinner. Olga usually dutifully marches the circumference of the court and is ready and waiting when the maid calls. But there is something different about today.

When I reach the north gate, I feel like someone's watching me. The trees in this part of the palace grounds are dense. Pines and firs grow so high they block the sky. Some branches extend over the wall. For the first time, after weeks of wandering the palace grounds under the darkened sky, I'm afraid. Mother's warning about terrorists rings in my ears. I can think of lots of hiding places in the forest, and wonder if the unfamiliar grounds at the Winter Palace are truly safe.

A rustling noise behind me makes me jump, but my scream gets caught in my throat as I turn toward the noise. A uniformed soldier drops from the trees and scurries to a different hiding place. I take cover in the foliage and wonder what to do next. Before my mind can wrap itself around the situation I hear another shuffling sound come my direction. It's Olga. Before I can jump out and warn her, the uniformed soldier reaches out from his hiding place and grabs Olga around the waist. She squeals with delight. It isn't until then that I piece together that the uniform is that of the royal army, Olga's regiment.

My eyes get big. I never would have believed it if I hadn't been squatting there in the brush watching it myself. My conservative sister is sneaking off to be with a man—a soldier. Not from the academy, but a country boy, I imagine, whose father owns a little land, and has sent his son off to make his own fortune. It's so disgracefully romantic. Disgraceful for Olga, the dutiful daughter who is supposed to stay morally spotless, so she can marry well and help our father's political position, but also so gloriously romantic that it almost makes me wish I were in her place.

I sit quietly in my hiding place, listening to the deep rugged voice coo affectionately (I can't hear his words, but from his tone I know he's cooing). I cringe when I hear my sister's silly giggles, and stay hidden and wait until I hear the maid ring the bell. With one last passionate kiss, Olga flees the arms of the soldier, and arrives first at the palace door. I am scolded for my lateness and questioned about the pieces of brush in my hair.

Olga is in good humor with rosy cheeks as Papa enters the dining room and kisses us each on the forehead. Dinner is the first time we have seen him all day. Anastasia talks excitedly as she explains the foreign dance lesson that we participated in earlier. She doesn't tell him every detail of the exciting dance we learned, she doesn't want get Senior Rodriguez in trouble with our vigilant Mother, but she seems to feel free to discuss her enjoyment with our father present. He eases Mother's concerns.

Our brother, Alexei is still resting in the hospital area of the palace. This is unusual. Father likes us all together at dinner. He ardently questions Mother about his therapy.

"Dinner is family time and sitting at the table is good for digestion. The boy can't stay in bed all day. He must play to strengthen his muscles."

The room unexpectedly darkens, as if the sun has gone behind a cloud, but in the winter in Russia at dinnertime, there is no sun. A stale, foul smell fills the air.

"The boy needs to rest." Rasputin's strong Siberian accent cuts through the thick air. Though the smell should have been a warning, the sound causes us all to jump from our chairs as he speaks. Father has a guilty look on his face as if he has been caught—a look that is not befitting the tzar.

"The doctors bother him too much. He needs to rest his muscles before he can strengthen them." The wild eyed man explains in a monotone voice.

"And why have the nurses stopped giving my son his medication?" Father demands.

"Healing starts with the soul." Not a hint of emotion can be detected on his mouth, but his eyes say we must believe everything he tells us. "The medications dull his spirit."

Father would have never let such a man into our home, he is eery and his hygiene does not match his pride. But Rasputin, the mystic, was recommended to Mother in her most desperate hour. When the boy, the heir, my brother Alexei, was finally born, all the hopes for Russia and the royal family were on his tender shoulders. But when we learned of his disease, his hemophilia, when he was still a babe, Mother, the carrier who passed it on to him, felt like his murderess.

Not only the killer of her own son, but the cause of the death of my father's line in the family. She would have done anything to save him and Father would have done anything to ease my mother's pain.

Rasputin, the healer, has been the cause of much contention in the palace. He is a commoner, a peasant by birth, but as I mentioned before, he arrogantly puts himself above the other doctors, as well as most of the court. His behavior is uncouth, like tonight, showing up to the family dinner without being announced and without an invitation, but unbelievably his methods, though unconventional, seem to work, or at least give Mother hope that they will. My sisters and I don't know what to think. He scares us, but no one can deny the miracle we saw just a short time ago in Spala. So, even though Father has been advised to be rid of him, he lets Rasputin treat Alexei secretly.

My sisters and I look at each other around the table in shock. Just when we think we know what to expect from "Our Friend"—the title my mother has given him—he does something unusual like showing up seemingly out of nowhere All eyes, including Father's go to Mother. Rasputin is now standing next to her with his hand next to her's on the table. She pats it gently and looks adoringly up into his straggly face.

Father seems to be biting the inside of his cheeks, but he finally sighs. "We shall see."

Speaking his final word for now, he piles his plate with food, not looking around the table again until it has been cleared. After letting his presence be known, Rasputin leaves as soundlessly as he arrived.

After dinner we go to our suites and prepare for our usual guests that are sure to come this evening. Olga follows me into our room and shuts the door behind us. Her eyes are wide and her cheeks are flushed. She looks as if she will burst any second. Facing me she takes both of my hands in hers. Her eyes are glistening with tears.

"I am told you were on the north end of the grounds during our stroll today." She waits for me to explain. Not knowing where to begin, I remain silent.

"Spying in the bushes? Well," Olga continues, "what did you think?"

"I think what I saw today was appalling," I burst.

Olga stifles a giggle and continues, "I know, it is, isn't it? I don't believe this is happening to me."

"What is happening to you?" I roll my eyes at her silliness and demand an explanation.

"I'm in love, love, love, love!" Still holding my hands, she swings me around in a circle with her.

"How can it be love?" I frown with doubt.

"Because Dmetri told me that it was. He says that we are 'spiritually connected.' He says he knew it the first time we saw each other. I felt it too of course; I just didn't realize that's what it was. I didn't know for sure until we danced at the ball Saturday night. Then he told me, under the moon on that cold, chill night, how he felt about me, and I felt it to—love. Deep, passionate love." Olga shyly sits down on the bed, hiding her culpable smile.

"So let me see if I understand." I ask cynically. "You, a crowned princess, the eldest daughter of the tzar, are 'spiritually connected' to a common boy you see along with dozens of other men every day and have talked to only once or twice. How is this possible?"

"Destiny."

I look into my sister's eyes and can't believe what I'm hearing. This, coming from the girl that always does what she is told, and frowns when anyone else veers from the path of perfection. But looking into my sister's eyes I believe her.

"What about your responsibility to the family, Olga? Have you thought about that? Do you think of nothing but yourself?"

"Zatknis! Hold your tongue Tanya! I prefer not to think on such matters. Can't you just be happy for me?"

I contemplate that idea for a moment, but instantly another thought enters my mind. "What about Stepan Karenin? What of his heart? You will crush it."

"Stepan? Why should it matter to him? He knows all about it. I had to confide in him Saturday evening so he could help me talk to Dmetri without Mother knowing."

Confused, I think back to last night. "He all but confessed his intention of marrying you last night as he was leaving."

"Impossible. You must have misunderstood. Stepan has his sights set on someone else. He won't tell me who, but I can see it in his eyes. He is like a brother to me." Olga stands before our mirror and smoothes her hair.

"And I thought he was going to be my brother all along." I say to myself as I join my sister in the mirror.

"I trust you to keep my secret," she whispers as she straightens and turns toward the door.

I stand and follow, still a bit confused. I feel honored to be trusted with my older sister's weighty secret, but still a bit skeptical. A princess in love with a common soldier? No, I'm sure that Stepan Karenin will still be my brother someday.

IV

After a tedious twenty minutes of watching Stepan and Olga play a pitiful game of chess (they are always too busy chatting to concentrate on where to put their pieces), I check on my brother. He is always expected to be dressed and out of his room when our guest arrive after dinner. Rasputin has gone home for the night.

"We missed you at dinner Brother," I say with a sly smile.

Alexei seems to prepare himself for the teasing he knows to expect from me.

I ruffle his hair, letting him know that my concern is legitimate. "How are you feeling?"

"I'm just fine," he insists as he rolls his eyes. "Well," he seems to do a little self assessment. "I could do with a little more of that baklava we had after dinner."

"Since the Alexandroviches were unable to join us tonight," I suggest, "there should be plenty left over. Should I go see if cook will let us have some leftovers?"

Alexei nods with a smile. I'm always glad when I can do something to serve the young tsarevich.

Despite the extra dessert, I miss the Alexandroviches. Although I don't find Irena to be the most exciting conversationalist, the boys' antics are always entertaining leaving Alexei and I are positively bored. But on my way to the kitchen, I walk by the library where the adults are playing cards, and I overhear an interesting conversation.

"My daughters need more choices." Mother complains to her guests while they sit around the card table in the library. With her brother and sister-in-law not here, she must feel it not improper to voice her dissatisfaction with the pool of male suitors in the Russian court. The Karenins are too open minded to take offence. "I was forced to pair Marie with men twice her age at the ball Saturday."

I silently nod in agreement.

"It's Russian men." Our Grecian cousin, Marie, pipes in, "They seem to age twice as fast as European men. By the time our daughters are old enough for marriage, the men will all be leaning on canes."

"Excuse me, Wife," my uncle interrupts, "I have been as frisky as a puppy since our wedding day."

All of the adults laugh, as our cousin's face turns a bright shade of pink.

"You're right, Maria." My mother goes on once the laughter has died down. "I need to introduce my daughters to some European blood."

The Grecian princess clasps her hands together. "I have a remarkable idea. I can't believe I hadn't thought of this sooner. My brother Konstantine, King of Hellenes," she adds with a wink, "has two dashing sons, and a daughter, Helen; oh your girls would adore her, and a son Anastasia's age. They have had some trouble with the Balkins in the fall, but I think things are more settled now. I'm sure I could persuade them to come and hunt wolves with my husband within the month."

"These boys are the nephews of your cousin George, Dear." Mother turns to my father. "You haven't talk to George in years."

"I think Nikolai and my brother had a falling out." Father's cousin Marie explains.

"We didn't have a falling out, we just haven't spoken recently." Father defends. I
wonder what the story is. Father always spoke fondly of his cousin George yet, I have never met him.

Mother agrees that the arrangements should be made immediately and even offers to
 house them in our palace for the length of their stay.

Within the month? Anxiety wells up in my belly, as I realize how disconcerting it will be to have a strange family stay at our palace, my sisters and I under constant scrutiny, but a European heir to a throne would be irresistible to my English bred mother.

"Oh yes," Stepan's father pipes in, "It should be easy to persuade the Greeks to leave their homes and come here. Most Europeans prefer the snowy forests to the Mediterranean climate this time of year."

The women ignore his sarcasm and continue with their planning, but my Father adds his feelings on the matter.

"Which of our daughters would you be willing to send to Greece?" He's trying to sound like he is joking, but I think the thought makes him sad, which in turn makes me feel a little sad as well, but Mother chooses to not let this remark affect her plans. I quietly continue on to the kitchen with a smirk on my face. I have acquired some inside information and I can't wait until bedtime so that I can share this news with my sisters.

We soon hear that the Greeks have accepted the invitation. Not surprising, my father has had a long history with his cousin, George, and the prospect of hunting the Russian forest would have been an opportunity the men couldn't pass up. Tales of the Russian beauties must have already reached their Grecian ears. That must be what persuaded Helen to come along, so she could see for herself.

Foreign visitors at the palace are something to get excited about, and the whole place is upset as the maids and servants prepare for the arrival of the Grecian guests. The young Princes and Princess are bringing their court; servants, ladies and gentleman in waiting as well as the Prince Paul and Princess Helen's personal servants and tutors.

When the visitors arrive, the party consists of Prince George, heir to the throne. At age twenty-two, he's five years older than Olga. His brother, Prince Alexander is nineteen, and more gregarious than his brother, so far as we can tell. Princess Helen is sixteen, right between Olga and me. She presents herself as quiet, dignified, almost solemn. The youngest, Prince Paul, has a dimple in each cheek, and the shimmer in his eyes advertises a zest for life. He is eleven. Just Anastasia's age and can only be intended for her.

"George is quite handsome," I tease my older sister as we all gather in Olga's and my suite before getting ready for bed. "His clean-shaven face makes him appear young."

"I don't know if I can trust anyone that doesn't have a beard." Lately Marie claims that she likes older Russian men.

"At least he doesn't have a strange, scary mustache like his brother's." Anastasia cringes. We laugh in agreement.

"It's probably fashionable in Greece," Marie indicates, showing she's worldly.

"They all seem quite self-assured," Olga puts it graciously. She doesn't seem to be at all concerned. She must feel secure that our parents are satisfied with her match with Stepan Karenin, and since he understands her feelings toward her soldier she has nothing to worry about. But I don't have anything like that to reassure me. I know that these men are here for my benefit and I am certain I won't like them.

The first outing with the foreigners is to the stables. The men have brought their hunting horses and want to be sure that our facilities are adequate for them. Mother suggests that we know our way around the stables and can show them whatever they want to see. Anastasia leads the way, followed closely by Paul, the youngest Grecian prince. When she approaches the stable, a tall, young, overly-thin stable hand quickly meets her at the door and leads her to Носки. When we arrive at his stall, she pulls a sugar cube out of her pocket and scratches the horse behind his ears.

"I've already taken Носки out for his exercises today, but I'm sure he would enjoy another outing with you if you want me to get his saddle." The stable boy teases her. He knows she is not allowed to ride.

Anastasia wrinkles up her forehead and gives the boy a look, telling him she doesn't appreciate his sarcasm, but still smiles sweetly. "No thank you, Peter. These men," she says indicating to the gentleman standing behind her, "would like to see the accommodations."

"Oh, then please, follow me." Peter says with a bow, "I will give you a tour."

Anastasia turns back to her horse while we follow the stable hand. Although he seems young and slightly built, he proves to be knowledgeable and experienced with the horses.

Not long after the tour is over, we find Anastasia pitching straw into Носки's stable.

"Is this your chore?" Paul questions, but before she has a chance to answer he has another accusation. "You were very friendly with that stable boy."

"I like to make friends with everyone around the palace. You must understand how cut off from the world we are here in Russia, especially in the wintertime. It's not that often that we are graced with the presence of someone like you."

Paul scrunches his face as if he is trying to discern whether or not he should be angered or flattered by this comment. Is Anastasia being sarcastic of flirtatious? I'm not sure I know.

"I know how you feel," Paul tells us sincerely. "Two years ago my family went into exile as part of a military plot to put my father on the throne in place of my Grandfather. It was a very dark, lonely time for my family. My father had been told that his father was going mad, and it was the only way to save our country. We spent the summer at the home of my aunt, and then the winter in a hotel. I was so glad when that year was over."

Listening to Paul talk so candidly softens my heart. I think Anastasia is affected by the boy's openness as well. It's true that there are worse situations than ours. We should be more grateful for the freedoms we have.

We leave the men to inspect the stables and retire to the salon to get acquainted with Helen. She's beautiful with flowing, light brown hair. She wears it long down her back. It makes me think of her as Helen of Troy. When Anastasia brings up the subject of her family's exile she expresses her frustration at the time, but doesn't go into as much detail as her brother. I wonder if, being older at the time, it was even more difficult for her.

Before the men return, we head upstairs to help Helen get settled. Her maids have already unpacked her clothes, and she is satisfied that her personal belongings are arranged like they were at home. After seeing to Helen's comfort, we go back downstairs and meet with George and Alexander for tea.

"Tomorrow, your uncle, The Grand Duke Makhailovich, will be taking out a hunting party," Father announces. "Have you ever hunted wolf in Russia before?"

"No sir," Prince George answers. "We thank you for the privilege."

"But isn't there much bigger game in Russia than wolves?" Prince Alexander interrupts. "I was hoping we'd be hunting boars, or even bear. Russia is known for its big game." Alexander covers his rudeness with a compliment, but George clears his throat and gives his brother a discerning look.

Father chuckles, "Of course there is bigger game," his chest puffs out, "but the wolf hunt is very entertaining. Your horses have to be in good condition and the chase is invigorating. I am only sorry I don't have time to come along." He pauses as if he is checking his schedule in his brain, but finally frowns and turns back to his guests who wait eagerly.

"No," he finally says. "I will not be coming along this time, but you are here a whole month. There will be plenty of time for the big game."

George and Alexander sit tall and smug, pleased to hear the news.

"Will I be coming on the hunt tomorrow?" Paul asks politely turning to my father, "My horse is the fastest of all my brothers."

"Because yours has the lightest rider." Alexander laughs.

"You have lessons tomorrow," George answers, saving my father from having to bare the bad news. Prince Paul's bright face drops and he looks as though he's going to cry, so George goes on reassuringly, "but there will be other hunts. Let your brother and me check out the landscape and you can come on the next wolf hunt. We could use your horse."

"Maybe I can hunt bears too?" Paul asks hopefully.

"We shall see, Λίγος αδελφός, we shall see." George affectionately ruffles his brother's hair. Olga and I look at each other across the table. I raise my eyebrows, and Olga puts her hand on her mouth to disguise a smile. I think both of our hearts are softened by this brotherly exchange.

The den is filled to capacity that evening as the adults join the children there. They seem to be interested in our interaction with each other. The men and boys stay on one side of the room, while we are congregated on the other.

I overhear Stepan enthusiastically describe the hunt to his comrades, while we stand and chatter on the other side of the room. When he has finished his oration, he crosses to the room to see what we are talking about. For several minutes, the other men seem to be engaged in another discussion. They keep looking over their shoulders in our direction. Finally, Prince George, Prince Alexander and our cousin Andrei come over too. I notice the adults nod to each other and smile, disappearing to the library.

The men appear to be pushing my cousin Andrei towards Helen. I'm embarrassed for him. He is he a few months younger than she is, and though he is of noble birth, he doesn't stand a chance with the Grecian Princess.

"What mysterious breeze has blown this Greek Goddess as far as Russia?" Andrei says.

Helen's face blazes red as the whole group erupts in stifled laughter. Out of politeness she pretends that she hasn't just heard such an unoriginal attempt at flattery.

"Actually, mythology is still a very important aspect of our culture." Prince Alexander pushes the young man on. Andrei's arrogance has disguised his intelligence, but the Grecian Prince acts like he is enjoying his sister's discomfort. George shakes his head and escorts Olga and Irena away from the awkward scene, but I'm enjoying the show. Andrei continues to unknowingly make a fool of himself as Alexander eggs him on.

"It's so sad isn't it?"

The voice next to me takes me by surprise, and I jump. When I realize that Stepan has been standing beside me all this time without me knowing, I put one hand on my heart and backhand him in the chest with my other.

"You shouldn't do that to a person. Do you want to cause me a heart attack?" I pretend to fall back as if I'm going to faint.

Stepan puts his thumb to his chin and ponders that for a moment. I swat him again—for good measure.

"I was just saying," he puts his arm out defensively, "that it's sad that beautiful women have to put up with such nonsense."

"Why don't you go save her from my cousin then? My sister seems to be occupied for the moment." She, George and Irena are standing on the other side of the room. They must have come up with something to talk about because they are smiling and laughing.

"Apparently the beautiful women of Greek mythology have been living in Russia all along." Alexander appears out of thin air.

Stepan and I both groan at once. Alexander gets a crooked grin on his face. The expression is unnerving—both vile and attractive at the same time. "Well, the line worked for that oaf." He points at my cousin.

Stepan and I both turn to look. Amazingly, Helen and Andrei seem to be engaged in a conversation of some sort.

"Impressive," Stepan expresses sarcastically and then turns to Alexander. "I was just telling the princess how sorry I was that a beautiful woman had to be put through such condescending behavior, but perhaps I was wrong." Though his words sound apologetic, his eyes glare with disdain.

"It can work, if used correctly. The young man had a good teacher." Alexander scowls back.

I bite my bottom lip and look from one man to the other. Somehow this conversation has become hostile. I excuse myself to relieve Helen from the uncomfortable position she been forced into and leave Alexander and Stepan to growl at one another.

The next morning, I lie in my cot and listen to the sounds of men. Men washing up, men getting dressed, men eating, it's such a strange sound to have in our house. The sounds are so much bigger and louder then we're used to. A cupboard door slams, something crashes to the floor followed by cursing, and then deep hearty laughter. I imagine it was Alexander who cursed. George seems much more reserved. I close my eyes and try to picture them in my head. George is good-looking; dignified, a leader, but I also grin as I picture Alexander and his silly moustache—that sly smile. He must be trying to appear older, I muse. I imagine that there is a rivalry between him and his brother similar to that which exists between Olga and me, friendly, but a rivalry still.

As things quiet downstairs, I ring for my maid to bring me some water. I wash, dress for the day and then go downstairs to join Princess Helen and my sisters. We are all sitting to tea when Paul finally comes sulking down the stairs.

"Did you sleep well, brother?" Helen greets the young prince.

"They're pigs," he complains, "Both of them. They kept me up half the night with their epic stories of bravery, and then they wake me up at four this morning grunting and rooting around like pigs."

Everyone around the table laughs at his accurate description.

"Your tales of bravery will be epic soon enough," my mother attempts to soothe Paul's foul mood. Then she turns from him and addresses us all to explain the day's schedule.

"You will have your lessons together this morning. The tutors have been discussing your education with me and we have agreed that between our tutors and Helen and Paul's they each have a specialty—something new they can share with you all." Mother makes the announcement as we pass around plates filled with sweet biscuits. "Olga will be excused while she inspects her regiment, but she will be back before tea time."

Anastasia coughs and whispers quietly behind her hand, "Don't count on it."

The Empress doesn't hear, but frustrated by the interruption her eyebrows knit together. Anastasia yelps as she gets a boot from under the table. Mother goes on, "Tatiana and Helen, you will have your classes together and when Olga returns, she will join you. Marie and Anastasia, you will go with Paul and his French tutor, Monsieur Bertrand this morning."

Marie frowns her disappointment. We know that she considers herself much farther along
in her French studies then her younger sister. She often compares her wit to Olga's. But she doesn't voice her discontent. Instead she purses her lips together and remains silent.

"After tea, you girls can show our guests around the grounds." The Greeks look
 discouraged as they glance out the snowy window.

"We could take them skating," Anastasia suggests with glee.

"I think we have had quite enough skating outings this winter." The tzarina looks irritated. Anastasia's sly comment seems to have distracted her from her hostess duties. She rubs her temples and frowns.

Everyone, even the Greeks, who don't have an idea of what she's talking about, moan their disappointment.

Paul gets the last biscuit on the plate as we gather up our dresses to go upstairs for our lessons. Olga quickly dresses in her uniform, and with her sash straightened and her plumed helmet on her head, is out the door before the rest of us have had a chance to wash and get ready for class.

The tutors have divided the large school room by placing the desks in two separate sections. Each tutor has a blackboard and podium to stand behind. Helen and I take our seats on the north end. She leans over to me and asks, "What did the little one mean when she suggested that Olga wouldn't return?"

I whisper to my new friend in French, hopefully discouraging any servant that might overhear. *"Olga a une affaire avec un de ses soldats."*

I explain her involvement with the soldier. I probably shouldn't reveal such personal details to Helen so soon after meeting her, but sometimes my mouth moves without my control. Helen puts her hand to her lips and turns pink. When she removes her hand, it reveals an understanding smile. I think Helen and I are going to get along just fine.

On the south side of the room, Marie is acting like she has decided to accept the situation. The French tutor, Monsieur Bertrand, doesn't teach French as it turns out. "You children are well versed in French. You could probably teach me a thing or two." He tells them with his deep French accent and dark European eyes. "I am going to teach you European history, or rather, oversee you teaching each other. Each of your families understands your own history well. I want to hear you explain it to each other."

The Frenchman is young-looking, but speaks with a dignified air. He seems more sure of himself than most young tutors. As the young students pull out their books and begin making outlines for next week's lessons, he goes around to each student and compliments them on their knowledge. He spends extra time with Marie, assuring her that he understands her intellect and admires her creativity.

She's all smiles when we meet downstairs for tea. Olga is already there, changed and waiting. Helen gives me a knowing glance when she sees my sister, waiting, hoping that no one will mention her absence. After a quick break for tea, we change teachers. We study European history with Monsieur Bertrand, while the younger students have a Geometry lesson with their usual Russian tutor. After working with the Frenchman, I understand Marie's renewed interest.

When the lessons are over, we gather in the doorway and get ready to go outside. The Greeks are stunned by the amount of clothing they have to put on to take a stroll around the grounds: first boots, then a sweater buttoned to the chin, followed by fur coats, then mittens and a scarf.

Olga goes missing as soon as we walk out the door. "Let's follow." I suggest to Helen.

"What if we get caught? No, I think I would like to get more familiar with my surroundings before we get into trouble and have to make a run for it." Though I think we have bonded, Helen remains reserved and cautious. Sometime in the next month that they are here, I will get her to loosen up.

Marie looks as if she's waiting for an invitation, but I don't ask her, knowing that she's just waiting to rebuke me. Finally she shrugs her shoulders and heads for her bench in the garden. As she sits to read, I see that it's her history book she's chosen to bring with her today. Helen and I decide to follow Paul and Anastasia to the stables instead. Paul has to skip to keep up with my little sister. It seems that Anastasia is determined to lose him, but he soon falls into pace with her.

We're greeted at the stables by the boy we'd met earlier. Anastasia's eyes light up when she sees him. "How's Носки?" She asks, looking up at the young lad through her eyelashes.

The boy turns red and starts to stutter, but quickly recovers. "Anxious to see you, I'm sure."

She's definitely flirting. I wonder if this is a frequent thing or just for Paul's benefit. Paul doesn't wait to find out. Looking apologetically at Peter, the stable boy, he grabs her arm and pulls her back toward Носки's stall. Anastasia looks shocked, but impressed. The horse neighs a greeting.

"Do you have another sugar cube?" he asks presumptuously.

"Of course," Anastasia shyly reaches into the pocket of her skirt and hands a cube to Paul.

He reaches up, lets the horse nibble the cube out of his hand, and scratches her forelock. The horse rumbles her pleasure and nudges him for more.

"Носки likes you," Anastasia's voice has become tender.

"Of course," Paul agrees, "I'm the best horseman I know."

"How many horsemen do you know?"

Paul ignores her teasing. "Do you have another sugar cube?"

The young princess puts her hand in her pocket, pulls out a few more, and hands some to Paul. Still grabbing Anastasia's mittened hand he leads her past Носки's stall to the part of the stable where the hunting horses are kept. One large bay horse stands alone, a huge, gray, Friesian stallion. Paul helps Anastasia through the fence, and cautiously, she approaches the big animal. He reaches his arm around the bay's neck and pulls its head down so the horse can see into his eyes. "*Αυτός είναι αυτός αγόρι. Πώς ήσαστε;*" The young horseman coos something reassuring in Greek. Though at first, the horse had looked concerned and uneasy; Paul's words seem to put it at ease. He places a cube of sugar to his horse's mouth. "You're gonna like this boy; something sweet on your lips."

"He's beautiful." Anastasia seems overwhelmed by the boy's strange behavior with the animal. "What's his name?"

"Hercules." Paul announces with bravado.

"Of course." Anastasia rolls her eyes.

"I've had him since I was a boy," Paul explains. "But when you see him run, you'll see that the name fits."

"Peter," Paul calls, remembering the name of the stable hand, "What is Hercules' exercise schedule?"

"The horse seemed restless this morning, jumpy, after your brothers left. I decided it was best to wait a day or so, before beginning his daily runs." Peter explains apologetically.

"Hercules would have become anxious after seeing my brothers leave with his brothers. It wasn't fair to leave him out of this trip." I wonder if Paul is only talking about the horse.

"No," he turns his attention back to the stable hand. "You acted correctly, Peter. I must supervise his exercise from now on." He looks questioningly at Anastasia for an idea.

Anastasia turns to me then flashes a smile. "Did I tell you about the skating outing we took last month?"

We're all ready for dinner when we hear a ruckus outside. Uncle Alexander can be heard stomping the snow off at the back entrance near the kitchen.

"Nikolai, my good man," he yells to my father as he removes his boots by the stove. "Sorry we're so late, I had to drop my boys off at home. They are hanging our kills in the barn. I will let George and Alexander tell you all about our hunt, but they are still in the stables getting their horses settled. Those men have some fine Grecian horses."

"So I've heard," Father pats Paul's shoulder.

Moments later the private living area roars with of the sounds of men, as they take off their boots and coats and try to find a place to store their hunting gear. The cooks and the kitchen help scramble to prepare dinner, and before long George, Alexander and Stepan are seated with us around the large table in the dining room. Their ruddy skin and mussed hair will be forgiven for this occasion.

"So tell us what we missed out on," my father insists.

Paul and Alexei are on the edge of their seats while Alexander and Stepan take turns telling the tale. They seem to have forgotten whatever aggression was between them last night.

"Just as I was starting to think we would never find a wolf…" Stepan starts to explain.

Alexander interrupts, "…my brother next to me blows the horn and suddenly the horses and dogs are off. He'd spotted a pack of wolves moving slowly, probably tired after a night of hunting." Alexander turns to George as if checking to see if he is correctly telling the story. George nods, so Alexander goes on. "A whole pack of wolves," he repeats, "and George was on them before they knew what hit them."

"Wolf hunting must be in this man's blood." Stepan points to George. "Having never been on the hunt before, he seemed to know exactly what to do. He overtook the pack's leader and with knife in hand, jumped off his horse, and landed right on the animal."

"The wolf kept running as George held tightly to his fur." Alexander continues, "I thought he would be dragged to death, but then I saw that the knife had already been perfectly placed and the animal dropped to the ground seconds later."

"Your wolf was also quite large," George humbly gives his brother his due credit.

"My wolf was strong. I had to stab him several times before he was taken down," Alexander demonstrates, his whole body acting out the event. "But I never would have been able to catch him, if his leader hadn't already been killed."

"Big, strong wolves," Stepan agrees with Alexander, but his eyes are on me across the table. "George was the hero on this hunt."

Alexander follows Stepan's eyes. He too is looking at me and seems to have gotten distracted. George, the modest hero in this epic, has his eyes locked on Olga, no longer hearing his brother's praise. Apparently our clean, well groomed appearance seems to be a warm, welcome change, after a day of primitive male activities.

The men excuse themselves after dinner to go to their rooms to clean up. We gather in the den and wait for the men while the rest of the guests arrive. Mikhailavich, his wife, and daughters arrive first. He organized and led the hunt, but his wife wants to hear her nephew's impression of Russia.

The tales that were told at dinner are retold, this time from Makhailavich's perspective, but his audience is mostly our parents. The young men find us to be more entertaining for the time being.

"How was your day, Tatiana?" Alexander corners me with a glass in one hand. He has a mischievous look in his eye.

"Not nearly as exciting as yours, I'm afraid. Did you really overtake a wolf with only a knife in hand?" I've played this game before, and I must admit, I'm good at it. I feed a young man's ego until he thinks he has my attention. Then I ignore him until he has to work to get mine, it always works for me.

"The wolves don't worry me," Alexander continues, "but I hear a bear can really put up a fight."

"Please don't tell me you're going to take on a bear." I plead with my eyes looking big and afraid into his.

"Oh, you can't ask me not to, Princess. The hunt is too captivating for a man like me."

"Did I hear you say that you were ready to take on a bear?" Stepan steps in and interrupts.

"Our host did mention that possibility." Alexander looks annoyed, but I'm appreciative. I was already starting to tire of his need to talk himself up.

Anastasia uses the space in the conversation to turn to me, the most resourceful member of the family, and remind me of Paul and Hercules's problem. She tries to pull me away so we can talk privately.

"The security around this place is completely unreasonable." She complains throwing her hands in the air. "Paul's horse must be exercised, but none of the stable crew are able to handle Hercules. He only trusts Paul." Anastasia has her fingers crossed behind her back. Apparently she doesn't believe this is completely true. "I need you to help me come up with a plan to get around the guards."

Though we thought we were alone, it seems that Alexander has been eavesdropping.

"What does your sister think you can do to help?" he asks me.

"My sister has a talent for finding ways around our father's strict security." Anastasia is not too embarrassed to clarify. "Have you ever heard of the Great Ice Skating Caper?" My sister grins in my direction.

"The Great Ice Skating Caper?" Alexander looks as if he is racking his brain, trying to come up with the correct response.

"It wasn't really a caper," I apologetically play it down, but then Stepan steps in. He seems to have overheard the conversation as well, and adds his version of the story.

"The girls wanted to get out of the castle, so Tatiana orchestrated a plan to go ice skating one morning."

"It was just a silly idea…" I play humble.

"The palace guards surrounded the pond with lanterns so the girls could see the ice in the dark," Stepan explains. "It really was breathtaking to see. I almost hesitated before joining them."

"You were with them?" Alexander turns to me with raised eyebrows, asking for my clarification.

"He broke through the guards." Anastasia says dramatically.

"And ruined our outing." I'm starting to feel like I am no longer the hero in this story. Stepan has taken over that role. As he and Alexander continue to discuss who is the bravest, Anastasia pulls me away from the discussion to talk to me more discreetly.

"Just explain the problem to Father," I tell her, "and don't let Mother find out until he has already said yes. That's how I did it before."

"But you already had the plan arranged before you ever went to Papa. I think he admired your resourcefulness. I don't know what kind of landscape lies beyond the trails we take when we stroll around the palace, but if there is a big enough parcel of land within the walls there would be no reason for Papa to say no. You have gone beyond the trails have you not? You know the grounds better than anyone."

"Well, better than almost anyone." I do have an idea, but first, I need to speak to Olga.

The men soon become tiresome. They are no longer entertaining to us, as they attempt to entertain each other. We ask to be excused to our rooms. As we are leaving, they plan another hunt for tomorrow. This time they will hunt snipe. It will be a shorter hunt, and closer to home. The snipe live in the marshland just beyond the palace walls. Paul will be going this time, with Hercules; it will give us another day to make our plans.

Helen, my sisters, and I stay in Olga's and my suite until after the men retire to their rooms. I am the only one, besides Helen, whom I told today, that knows Olga's secret, but everyone needs to be in on the plan. Marie would tell if she were left out, and we need Anastasia to convince Papa.

"What are you scheming about this time?" Olga asks. This isn't the first time we've congregated in our room after bedtime.

"We need to borrow your soldier." I explain bluntly. Olga plays acts like she doesn't understand, but can't pretend for long.

"No, I can't let you put him in danger. If Maman found out it would be the end. I would never see him again," she begs dramatically.

"This is for our foreign guests, in the name of diplomacy. Papa will understand, and once Maman knows why we did it, she'll thank us. They never have to know anyone else was involved. I'll take the blame," I reassure her.

Olga throws back her head. "What then, what is so necessary to diplomacy?"

I push Anastasia forward. Olga has never been able to resist her little sister. "It's for Paul," Anastasia blushes, "Paul's horse, Hercules. He really is a special animal, beautiful, strong; even Paul's brothers said he was the fastest horse."

Olga's heart is softened, either because of her sister's love of animals or because she, being in love herself, senses that the affection isn't only for the horse.

I step forward again. "So here's my idea. The soldier must know the landscape beyond the trails within the palace walls. I know there is an open field just beyond the creek. What I'm unsure of is if there is a safe way to cross the creek and what kind of terrain lies past it. Your man, Dmetri," (Olga blushes on hearing his name), "will have to act as guide until Paul and Hercules can cross safely."

"And also Носки and I." Anastasia adds. "If there is going to be horseback riding, I'm definitely going to be part of it."

Although this complicates the plan I don't argue. Perhaps Anastasia's charms work on me as well.

"Maybe Paul will be able to take Hercules hunting every day," Marie suggests.

"Maybe," I shrug.

"Ahhh," Anastasia stomps her foot. "That would be no fun."

I agree. For fun's sake, this has to work.

V

Everyone is around the table for morning tea—the Russians and the Greeks. Snipe
 hunting doesn't have to begin at dawn like the wolf hunt, but Paul has already been twice down to the stables to be sure Hercules is ready for the trip. When the biscuit plate gets to Olga and me, it's empty. The men smile sheepishly as they wipe the crumbs from their chins.

After morning tea, the princes, led by the Grand Duke Makhailovich, head toward the marshes in search of snipe and we have our lessons. Except Olga, who is hopeful that she will be able to speak to Dmetri about the land east of the creek within the palace walls. Classes began as they did yesterday—Helen and I study physics with our grave Russian tutor while Marie and Anastasia study European History with the enthusiastic new French teacher the Greeks have brought with them. With the absence of Paul, there will be no reason for the girls to teach each other their own history, so the student taught lesson will have to wait. Instead my sisters' take turns giving their presentation to the teacher who looks eager to hear what they have come up with.

The French tutor acts impressed with Anastasia's knowledge of our family's history, starting with Peter the Great, the first Romanov ruler of Russia. But she feels even more passionately about Catherine the Great, and concludes with her dissatisfaction with Catherine's successor, her son Paul I, who issued a ukase during his reign declaring that the succession was to be only through the male line. The tutor looks amused by this and tells her that while he agrees with her for the most part, he thinks she should study more thoroughly the childhood of Paul I. Marie chuckles at this suggestion demonstrating to her tutor that she is familiar with Emperor Paul's turbulent relationship with his mother.

It's evident that Marie has put some time and thought into her project. Not only are her stories entertaining and accurate, she has sketched some drawings to accompany them. Monsieur Bertrand appears outwardly moved by Marie's drawings.

"You have true artistic talent, young lady." He tells her while placing his hand on her shoulder.

Marie looks as though her heart will burst, but she modestly accepts his praise. "You flatter me, sir. My drawings are rudimentary and untrained. I have had very few lessons, but I adore art, especially painting."

"I studied painting a little at the academy I attended in Paris." He continues to look over Marie's drawings, while Anastasia rolls her eyes. "If you like, I could give you some lessons while I'm here."

Marie puts her hands together with glee, but quickly regains her composure. "Oh, I couldn't impose on your time."

The tutor's eyes sparkle. "Time, I have," he laughs. "In this palace surrounded by snow. You tell me the time and the day. I am at your service." He bows.

Marie blushes, and Anastasia watches the scene play out, amused. When the teacher's back is turned, she leaned over and whispers mischievously, "You did say you liked older men."

I meet Olga in our room washing up for tea. She has been with her regiment and her smile tells me she has spoken to Dmetri. I predict good news.

"So your soldier? He will help us?"

Olga can't disguise her pleasure. "The silly boy has accepted the challenge. He says he has been on the other side of the creek. There is a passage near the north gate through the forest that is wide enough for a horse to cross. He says the area is vast with plenty of room for exercising a horse. In fact, he believes that area was originally meant for horses. He thinks the calvary once gathered there for inspection and for practice running drills, when the palace was used during the summertime."

I have a discouraging thought. "The snow must be deep there then."

"No. I asked Dmetri the same question. He said that the trees are all south of the meadow, so there is nothing to block the wind. The snow has been mostly blown off. It's almost dry."

I can't believe our luck, but Olga reads my expression. "There's a rain-washed gully on one end. Dmetri doesn't know how deep it is and it will be hidden. He thinks that the horses are smart enough to sense it and avoid it, but it still might be dangerous."

"It will be too dark in the morning to be safe. I think this might have to be done in the afternoon."

"Yes, Dmetri said the same thing. It will make it more difficult. No?"

"It will be tricky in the afternoon, but I was thinking the best time will be when we're usually outside. Your man will be there anyway." I ignore Olga's embarrassed giggle. "Will he be willing to show Paul the passage?"

"Dmetri said that he can show him today if they are home from the hunt before our stroll."

"Then you take Paul with you this afternoon and I will go with Anastasia to talk to the stable crew."

"And then you will talk to Father?"

"I don't think we need to involve Father for this one. I think he will be more likely to give his blessing after he sees that it works."

We can't focus on our afternoon lessons. The tutors seem glad when the hunting party is heard below and dismiss us early. After taking off their winter gear, the huntsmen quickly go upstairs to clean up, but are hungry and glad when they are called down for tea. Tea at noon is usually a light meal, but the cooks arrange for *piroshok*—a fried bun stuffed with mushrooms, rice, and onions—to be served along with the usual vittles in the dining room. It turns into a noisy, enjoyable event.

Stepan Karenin joins in the meal and sits down next to me. Reaching for a roll, he leans in and quietly asks, "What kind of surprises do the Romanov girls have brewing this time?"

The air from his breath in my ear and on my neck gives me a shiver. I'm unable to disguise my shock that he knows my thoughts. With unexpected pleasure I look into his green eyes. "What on earth are you talking about?" I say a little too loudly.

Stepan smiles and waits for everyone's eyes to turn away, then he leans behind my head, acting like he's trying to get the attention of a servant behind us and whispers softly enough that only I can hear, "Tatiana, I have seen that naughty gleam in your eyes before. I know you're up to something."

"A stroll around the grounds would be interesting." Alexander seems unusually enthusiastic. George agrees, which brings about an unexpected complication. It's imperative that Paul be informed of the plan, but letting him know without his brothers finding out will be tricky.

"May we assist you with your boots?" Alexander and George seem determined to impress Olga and me. I try to disguise my impatience, but Marie catches on and quickly thinks to help us out. As soon as Olga and I are dressed, Marie asks for their assistance and Helen follows her example. They are able to keep the men busy so we can sneak out unnoticed. Paul and Anastasia are already out the door while Marie and Helen hold back George and Alexander.

Stepan catches on that we are trying to separate ourselves from the princes, so he helps stall them. Olga and Prince Paul go to the forest to meet Dmetri, and Anastasia and I head to the stable to talk to Peter.

Anastasia explains the situation to him. "As you know I've so missed riding Носки. Well, it seems that the Grecian prince has offered me a solution to this problem. He stubbornly wishes to exercise his own horse, and I think that if we ride on the palace grounds, in the name of diplomacy, my parents cannot object. However, we don't feel that they will understand our need if we ask, so we have planned a secret exploit of our own."

Peter turns to me, although we have never spoken before. "Ah, like the Great Ice Skating Caper."

I blush, but Anastasia speaks for me. "This is different than the ice skating. We don't have Papa's blessing, nor do we want to bother him to ask. We think that once it has been accomplished, he cannot object, but we must have some willing accomplices.

"Count me in." Peter is one of the many who cannot say no to Anastasia.

The conversation is finished just in time. I hear Stepan's voice around the corner. He's talking loudly, as a warning, I imagine. I excuse myself, but Anastasia stays to fill Peter in on the details.

"What was your hurry?" Alexander asks when he sees me.

"No hurry," I smile and take his arm. "I was just trying to keep up with Anastasia. She's always rushing to bring her horse a treat, and I wanted to make sure she didn't get hasty and slip. The path has gotten icy after the thaw yesterday."

Stepan pipes in. "Yes, a thaw then a freeze. It happens here all winter long."

"Where's Paul?" George seems concerned as he holds more tightly to Marie's arm.

"With Anastasia I'm sure." Marie answers for me. I hope Anastasia doesn't come out of the stable before Paul arrives back with Olga.

Because we have guests, it's a special day and the maid doesn't call us in from our outing, leaving plenty of time for Olga to return and eventually Paul and Anastasia to join us as well. Before our frozen cheeks force us back inside, the plan is finalized and Princes George and Alexander suspect nothing.

Tomorrow will be the real test. There isn't a hunting trip planned for tomorrow.

Mother is determined to keep the Grecian princes amused at the palace. To Marie's dismay, we have been excused from our lessons. Since no hunting trip has been planned, the tzarina has scheduled an entirely different set of activities for the day. Concern for our afternoon exploit sets in over morning tea, but our mood soon changes when Mother announces that the first activity will be dance lessons. Ricardo Rodriguez has been invited back.

"Wait until society sees them at the ball on Saturday. Everyone will be talking about how beautifully our daughters and our guests dance together," she says to Father, who has joined us this morning.

Olga appears worried. I suspect she is concerned that if we have been excused from our lessons, she will be asked to abandon her regiment.

As if reading her mind, Father turns to her and before Mother can object tells her that her men will be expecting her. "I know this is all very distracting to you, Colonel Nikolovna, but you have a responsibility to your soldiers."

"Yes sir," Olga hides her relief.

While upstairs changing into our dancing dresses, we explain to Helen what the excitement is all about. "Señor Rodriguez is an exquisite dancer." Olga says.

"And he's so handsome." Anastasia gets right to the point.

"Bronzed skin, eyes like chocolate, refined…dancing skills," I give her his credentials.

"His knowledge of European dancing is exquisite," Marie sighs.

"But I'm more impressed with his defined back side." Sometimes Anastasia does not behave appropriate to her age.

Helen giggles at my sister's description. "All right, I get it. This should be fun, but
don't expect my brothers to be as enthusiastic. They are not keen on dancing or good-looking Spaniards."

When we meet in the practice room after we have changed we see that Helen was right about her brothers. Alexander, at least, makes an obvious effort to demonstrate his disdain for the Spaniard. He rolls his eyes as Señor Rodriguez takes my hand and kisses it.

"I see I have been replaced as your partner," his exaggerated eyes become sad, and I giggle.

"If I am needed for a demonstration, Señor, I am at your service." I pull my brightly colored skirt back and curtsey.

This time Alexander's eye roll is accompanied by the clearing of his throat, but his tone becomes more positive when he is paired with me. Señor Rodriguez puts George with his sister Helen. Paul gets Anastasia and Marie has the privilege of dancing with our instructor. Alexander seems to enjoy the rest of the lessons as long as I am his partner, which is a credit to the señor. He makes us all, even the men, feel like we are the most elegant dancers he's ever worked with.

George and Paul even relax and seem to enjoy the activity. George and his instructor trade partners depending on the intimacy of the dance. I'm sure everyone notices, though no one mentions, Olga's absence.

After practicing the dances that Mother wants to see at the ball, we join our teacher in a demonstration of the Fandango. Helen joins in, but the men refuse.

"You call that dancing?" Alexander steps forward, "We will teach you what true dancing is."

He starts sliding his feet and clapping his hands with slow and heavy movements. George reluctantly joins in. They seem to be dancing in a line with Alexander as the leader, but with only two people dancing, it's hard to tell. Helen has refused to join her brothers.

I lean into Señor Rodriguez and whisper, "What are they doing?"

"There are many dances in Greece, depending on what area you live in. Most of them are line dances with a leader… improvising." His whisper inadvertently invokes laughter from me and my sisters.

Alexander stops, embarrassed. "It's hard to see without the music."

"No, go ahead. I think you're onto something your highness," Ricardo Rodriguez jumps in. "I'm sure her Excellency, the Empress, would be delighted if you were to give her guests a demonstration."

He skillfully appeases the prince, but my sister's and I are not sure where the señor is going with this.

"But we do need some authentic music, and, if you will pardon me, I think a couple's dance would be more appropriate for the ball." Turning to Helen he asks, "Do you know the Ballaristos?"

The Spanish dance instructor offers his hand to Helen and starts humming a melody. He stands in one place, holding loosely to Helen's hand while she dances around him. She does looks like a Greek goddess, and our Spanish friend has become a Grecian warrior.

"I think I can come up with this music for the orchestra before Saturday. How would you ladies like to perform this at the ball? I could teach you, with the help of these gentlemen." The Spaniard bows as he waves his hand in the Grecian princes' direction. Alexander especially looks as if he has just had the carpet pulled out from under him, but how can he argue? We are pleased and excited to try the dance, and Olga arrives just in time for her lesson. She and George make a handsome couple.

"The Horse Heist," as Anastasia had nicknamed it, is set to happen after noon tea. We sit through it quiet and anxious, Mother must suspect something, but I think she thinks it has something to do with the dance lessons.

"Did you have an enjoyable time with Señor Rodriguez this morning, Helen?"

"Oh yes, Your Excellency," the Grecian Princess blushes. "The señor is quite educated in all aspects of dancing."

Unknowingly George saves us by breaking into the conversation. "You'll have to excuse my sister's bashfulness. She was quite taken by the Spaniard."

"Ah yes," Mother sighs. "I have met the señor. I'm only sorry I couldn't peek in and watch. I was occupied on the other end of the castle."

Alexei's illness is strictly a secret. Though everyone in the palace is aware of Rasputin's presence, and that Mother spends the majority of her time with the prince in the hospital wing, it is not talked about.

"I spoke with Señor Rodriguez just a moment ago. I am so delighted that you have offered to share your culture with our daughters. Your dance will be the highlight of the ball on Saturday."

As soon as tea is over, the Horse Heist will begin. Anastasia and Paul know what to do,
but Olga will be most important in pulling off the scheme. Though she wasn't missed yesterday, her presence is certainly apparent today. Again George and Alexander behave gentlemanly helping us prepare for the cold outing. The youngsters sneak off, barely noticed. By the time the princes, Olga, Helen, Marie and I are dressed in our gear and out the door, hoof beats can be heard in the north end of the forest. I notice a forlorn look in my sister's eye. Olga will miss her soldier today, but only I recognize it.

From George and Alexander's perspective, it seems to be an ordinary stroll around the palace until a group of palace guards, the same ones that had been so useful for our skating escapade ride by, spur their horses past us. Next our Father, along with his brother and a few of his advisors, march out of the palace looking upset about the interruption. The guards have caught Anastasia and Paul and are leading their horses by the reins to him.

We haven't rehearsed this part, so I sneak in closer so I can hear what they are saying while avoiding Father's eyes. If he guesses I had a part in this, we will all be in trouble. But instinctively, Anastasia bows her head and sweetly confesses, "I told Paul it would be alright for him to exercise his horse as long as it was on the palace grounds."

Her humility does the trick. Father's heart goes out to his little one.

"But you must be careful Anastasia. You are not familiar with the grounds." He turns to the head guard, "Are they safe?"

The guard isn't so quick to forgive. He looks harshly at the guilty pair, but answers honestly. "Yes. I believe their highnesses were in no danger."

Anastasia doesn't let on how pleased she is by the guard's revelation. Her eyes fill with repentant tears.

Papa wipes her rosy cheeks and lifts her chin. "Am I to understand that the two of you wish to exercise your own horses from now on?"

Finally now, she is able to express her joy. "Yes Father, oh yes! If the prince and I could ride in the afternoon, I, we would be so grateful."

"Send some guards to oversee the area on the east side of the creek every afternoon until further notice." He orders the men standing around. Olga, Helen, Marie and I hide our eyes. I am proud of my sister for the ease of which she has fooled our father.

After watching for a minute longer, the guards disperse, and Father and his councilmen return to the palace. Anastasia and Paul return their horses to the stable.

"We did it!" Anastasia doesn't hide her smugness, but her celebration isn't with Paul. Instead she goes to Peter to thank him for his hand in the plot. "I couldn't have done it without you."

Paul agrees. He can take no credit for the privilege that has just been won for him. He looks at the princess Anastasia in awe.

VI

"Give me your dance card," Stepan Karenin instructs as my sisters and I step onto the dance floor. It is the first ball we've hosted since our Grecian friends have been here. Mother is excited to show off her foreign guests, and show her friends how perfectly they fit her daughters. The orchestra plays its first chords.

Stunned, I gingerly hand him the square piece of stock paper that Mother has taught us to hold sacred. Stepan, the Grecian princes, and my cousins, Andrei and Feodor, stand in a circle guarding a pile of pink and blue papers. Mother and Father have chosen to dance the first waltz, giving the men time to rearrange the dances. I turn to see Olga standing beside me looking pleased. The soldier, Dmetri stands in the doorway in his uniform; his hopes for the night also hang in these men's hands.

Mother will only be distracted by our father for little while, so it is essential that each of her daughters have a dance partner before she takes her eyes off him. Within seconds Olga is with George, Marie with our cousin Feodor, Anastasia with Paul, and I with Stepan. Helen is with Andrei and there seems to be one odd man out. This time it's Alexander.

"Marie will complain if she spends the night dancing with her cousin," I say, apprehensive that this will work, despite the satisfaction I feel at being Stepan's first choice.

"There are plenty of bearded, Russian men for Marie. She's not who we are concerned with."

I pout unintentionally, thinking once again, it's all about Olga. "Marie prefers moustaches to beards as of late."

"Good, now I don't feel so bad pairing her with Alexander most of the night," Stepan chuckles.

"Ah, but I was sure Maman intended him for me," I say with mock disappointment.

"Yes," Stepan smiles, "Like you were certain that your mother intended Olga for me."

I try to discern whether the tone of his statement is disappointment or teasing. At fifteen, men's intentions are still a mystery to me. Olga beams as she dances with George. Maybe it's for our mother's benefit.

It seems that tonight Marie is not concerned with beards or moustaches. François Bertrand, the Grecian's tutor, has been invited to the ball. He is not dancing, but sits and watches with the other adults, taking in the event as if it were an educational experience. Dance partners in general are only a distraction as she watches him watching us, and reports everything to Nina.

"He knows something about absolutely everything," I overhear her rave. "And he holds my hand so delicately when he shows me how to hold the brush. It's important to make the most precise strokes." Marie is radiant, not only because Nina looks jealous, I think, but because her tutor seems to look at her as if she weren't a silly young girl. "My painting has improved so much. Father has asked me to paint him something to hang in his office. Can you imagine all the dignitaries that will see it?"

"You are so lucky, Marie. I can't imagine having a grown man dote on me so." Nina joins her cousin and best friend in her happiness. "But what will you do when they go back to Greece?"

"I can't imagine it. Therefore, I refuse to think of it."

Marie's first crush is sure to lead to her first heartbreak.

As the night goes on, I'm always surprised with who my partner will be. The rewritten names on the card seem to be only a possibility of whom I will dance with. Anastasia doesn't have to guess who her partner will be. It will be Paul then our cousin Dmetri or Dmetri then Paul. Despite her limited selection, she seems to enjoy the ball much more tonight than usual. She doesn't even try to embarrass our cousin by stepping on his toes. Mother seems to be blissfully unaware that changes have been made to the dance cards, as if all of the time she had spent analyzing our dance partners has been forgotten. Having European choices for her daughters seems to have put her more at ease. Marie does seem to have a lot of dances with Prince Alexander, leaving Stepan and George for me, and plenty of time for Olga to be with her soldier.

"My sister doesn't deserve you. For someone who has taken second chair in the relationship, you have been very kind." I comment as Stepan and I waltz for the fourth or fifth time.

«Je l'aime comme une sœur. »

He tells me that he loves her—like a sister—in French.

"I seem to recall you telling me not so long ago that you considered me a sister," I boldly remind him of the night he whispered in my ear before kissing me goodbye just weeks ago.

« Comme je vous ai aimés. »

My heart stands still as he softly speaks and tells me he loves me too. The tone of his voice is not brotherly. For a moment I feel as if he is confessing his love—trying to make me understand how he truly feels. My knowledge of the French language isn't perfect, but he doesn't specify brotherly love, though we were just discussing that very thing.

He's teasing me again. I tell myself, but his words ring in my ears and I can think of nothing else as his hand holds onto my waist and we circle each other. The waltz ends before I am able to wrap my head around what has just happened. I forget about the time until Alexander takes my hand and leads me away from Stepan to the center of the floor. The orchestra is playing a foreign melody; it is time for the Grecian cultural presentation.

My eyes go to Stepan's face. I can't concentrate on the dance while I'm still thinking about him, but his intense eyes give me no solace. Alexander notes my hesitation and squeezes my hand harder. His gesture reminds me that this is important to him and I try to remember what I am supposed to do next. I watch Helen with her long flowing hair and graceful moves—she is dancing with my cousin, Andrei—and I remember what I am supposed to do, sort of. But once I get the hang of it again, my eyes are magnetically pulled back into the audience and into Stepan's pools of green. He beams. Alexander moves one way and I move the other and we bump into each other. My dance partner groans under his breath and I am reminded again, that this is important. I focus my eyes to the floor and count the steps in my head so I don't get distracted again.

When the dance is over, the first person to approach us and give his congratulations is Monsieur Bertrand. Señor Rodriguez returned for the ball to be Marie's dance partner and of course she danced extraordinarily. Her face is aglow as she accepts his praise. No one says anything to me about my mistake until after the next song has begun. I'm dancing with Alexander when Stepan and Irena come along next to us.

"That was some fine dancing," he says as he saunters by. I note the sarcasm, but I'm not sure if my dance partner will perceive it that way. I became irritated. It seems Stepan is still having fun at my expense and now he has possibly insulted our guest. I feel Alexander's shoulder tense under my hand and I look down at the floor.

Alexander lifts my chin. The look of agitation in his eyes matches mine. I can see that he is aware that Stepan is teasing me. "Our dances are very difficult and can't be learned in a single day." He comforts me.

"Your Russian men have no appreciation for culture."

The last part wasn't directed to me. He said it loud enough that Stepan and any other Russian man in listening distance could hear. Though I am embarrassed at his insult to my country, at this moment I'm inclined to agree with him.

Spring 1914

The arrival of spring is always a wet, messy affair in Russia. The once beautiful, billowing white snow now mixes with mud and becomes slushy and grey. But it turns out that the spring is the perfect time to hunt the Russian brown bear. Finally wakening after their deep sleep, they are disoriented and grouchy. This makes finding them and taking them by surprise both easier and dangerous—prefect for adventure seeking young men. Paul, after proving his hunting skills with the snipes—he killed eight jack snipes, more than his brothers combined—has been invited back on most of the trips. Although he occasionally chooses to stay at home to take lessons and ride with Anastasia, he is usually with his brothers. Of course Paul will be on this hunt.

Anastasia seems solemn as she takes off on her afternoon ride. Our new Grecian friends will soon return to their home. Anastasia and Paul, the fearless young horseman she rides with in the afternoons, seem to be enjoying each other's company, but Father has agreed to allow her to ride Носки alone the afternoons that Paul hunts with his brothers as long as Peter accompanies her on horseback and the guards stand their posts surrounding the meadow. She spends much of her time with the stable boy Peter. He's close to her age, maybe a couple of years older, but his lack of education makes it difficult to judge. The boy is tall and thin, thinner than most thirteen year old boys, with dark curly hair and icy blue eyes. With the arrival of spring and the departure of our guests we will be leaving for The Lividia Palace in Livadiya, Crimea in the southern Ukrain. I think she will miss Peter and the rest of the stable crew here in Petersburg.

The bear hunt will be the grand and final hunt before our new friends return to their home in Greece. Father has arranged his schedule so he can accompany the huntsmen. At dinner, the night before, he explains to our guests how it will work.

"We will be dividing into four groups. Makhailovich, Karenin, and I will each take a young man and a boy. Alexandrovich has decided to bring his oldest five, so his group will have an extra boy."

Upon hearing this news Alexei, who despite his injury feels left out and interrupts.

"Rostislav is going? He'll get you all killed!" Alexei fumes.

"He is ten, Alexei, that's still two years older than you." Father tries to sooth my brother.

"But he is not to be the next Tzar of Russia. How am I to learn to be a soldier, a leader, a man, if I have to be constantly with women?"

Father tries to hide his smile, but soon the memory of our trip to Spala last year brings a sad look to his face.

"You're right, your cousin Rostislav is not to be the next tzar. You are. This means that above all else you must stay alive. What would the future hold for our family—for Russia—if you were to die in an insignificant hunting trip?" He doesn't have to remind him of the accident; it still weighs heavily on all our minds, but my father hates for Alexei to feel that he is different.

With dogs, horses, and the party divided, they will head in four opposite directions. Each group carries a banner that can easily be spotted if someone gets stuck. The bear isn't the only dangerous adversary in the Russian forest. The elements are a danger as well. The deep snow that seems firm on the surface can give way causing a mud slide or a horse to break an ankle. The conditions are unpredictable in March. A seemingly clear sky can turn to clouds and wind resulting in rain, snow, or hail. March always comes in like a lion, but these are the dangers that call the men out into the cold.

Alexei sits and sulks, as I predict he will until my father is home and the hunt is forgotten, but we are happy to remain in the den where there is a warm fire. Our cousins Irina, Nina, Xenia and little Vasili will be spending the day with us, so our regular schedule is cancelled. At first Marie protests, not wanting to miss any of the remaining days she has left with her tutor, but Mother suggests that maybe Monsieur Bertrand will be willing to give us all an art lesson. Marie is excited by this idea because it will allow her cousin, Nina, to see for herself how affectionate our teacher is towards her.

While we older girls are content to sit around the fire, roast chestnuts and gossip with our Aunties and Maman, Anastasia and

Xenia put on their winter clothes and go out to the stables. Always curious, I decide to follow.

Because of the cold sharp wind, Anastasia has chosen not to take Носки out for the day, so Peter acts pleasantly surprised to see us. He's wearing a worn canvas jacket and a long leather apron. I notice that his boots are coming apart on the bottom. I wonder how he hasn't gotten sick in the moist barnyard.

The stable hand trades the girls' coats for aprons and hands them each a brush. He does this without being asked, like it has been done many times before. Носки whinnies her pleasure on seeing my sister and nuzzles her neck as Anastasia puts her arm up around the horse. I'm happy to see the fondness that has developed between her and her animal in the past weeks. It warms my heart.

Xiena proceeds to take out the brush and work a cowlick out of Носки's rump. Anastasia pulls an apple out of her pocket, tosses one to Peter, digs in again, pulls one out for Носки and then reaches into the pocket on the other side of her skirt and finds one to share with Xenia. I am surprised by my sister's behavior toward Peter. It's almost as if she is closer to him then her cousin. I didn't get an apple.

When the horse is fed and brushed and the stall is filled with fresh straw, the noon sun comes into the stable windows indicating it's time for tea. I am astonished again as I watch Peter pick the straw out of Anastasia's hair as he helps her put her coat on. Her eyes stay on him as Xenia leans in and whispers something into her cousin's ear. Anastasia flushes and smiles, but does not take her eyes off Peter who is smiling as if he's heard the secret as well.

Monsieur Bertrand is ready for his students after tea. All of us girls and Alexei have chosen to participate in the art lesson. Marie sits her easel down in front next to her tutor.

«Oui, ma chère, je pourrais utiliser votre aide, merci.»

Bertrand puts his hand under Marie's chin and tells her affectionately in his native language that he needs her help with a demonstration.

Marie looks over her shoulder and flashes Nina a smile, who, in turn, gives her cousin an approving nod.

Before long the French tutor has all of us, including Alexei, laughing as we create our masterpieces. Marie looks as if she has become the most important person in the room as Monsieur Bertrand compliments her and asks her to assist her fellow students. I overhear my aunt and mother hovering in the doorway.

"I haven't seen the girls enjoy themselves like this since we first discovered Ricardo." Mother giggles to Maria. "And the paintings Marie has done since he's been here are exquisite."

"Yes, look at Nina's. I think I would hang that over the mantel."

"And he wasn't hired by your brother to teach Art. He's been teaching French and European history. Your brother is wasting his talents. I think I'm going to steal him away and offer him a job here."

"Good luck getting a handsome European man to move to Russia," Maria chides. Mother laughs in agreement.

"Even Alexei," she goes on. "I've never seen that look of satisfaction on his face before, and painting is something that he can enjoy without doing harm to his body. I must secure this man as a member of my court," she resolves again.

The men are staying the night at a lodge in Vologda. The first day will be spent traveling north and the hunt will begin tomorrow. They hope to successfully kill a bear after it has been stalked and baited, but I think, this early in the year, they will be lucky to find one at all.

My aunts and cousins have made plans to stay the night at the Winter Palace. Alexei and Valisi are the only male members of the family here, but only Alexei seems to mind being with the women. During dinner he turns to me, "Was I as spoiled as Valisi when I was his age?"

"Of course. You are Alexei Nikolaevich, Tsarevich of Russia; we were to give you anything your heart desired," I quickly tease him.

"Yes. I still am and don't you forget it." He appears to think I can't be serious with him, so he turns away, but I surprise him.

"You have always been soft-hearted and kind, little brother. Spoiled, yes, but not a brat like that annoying little Valisi."

The next day we spend reading, painting with Bertrand, and of course Anastasia and Xenia go out to the stables to see Носки and flirt with Peter. This time as she walks out the door, she carries an old pair of Father's hunting boots. She stops cold when she sees me looking at her. Realizing she's been caught, she quickly explains herself. "Father was throwing them away." Then, as if she has already read a response on my face she says, "He would never ask for these. Peter's boots are falling apart. I can't let him walk around the stables letting the muck seep in."

I quickly reassure her. "You are kind, but won't you hurt his pride?"

Anastasia looks at me as though I know nothing. "I would never let him know they were from me. I plan on leaving them in a place where I know he will see them but not until after I am gone."

I know my sister well enough to know that she would do the same for anyone, if she saw a need, but this act reaffirms my suspicions that Olga is not the only member of this family that has developed feelings for a commoner.

Anticipation is rampant in the house. Though the men aren't expected until late, we maintain hope that they will be here sooner. Dinner is eaten in silence while we listen closely for the sound of hoof beats outside, but the sound isn't heard until long after the dishes are cleared and the games have gotten old.

Aunts Maria and Xenia are standing in the foyer trying to decide if they should go home or stay another night when a commotion of horses, dogs and men is heard through the streets of Petersburg. Inside, the palace has awakened, and is almost as noisy as the men outside as the servants rush around preparing food and drinks and make room for the men to undress and change out of their wet clothing.

Father's voice can be heard above the others crying out to his son, "Alexei come see! Come see what your father has brought you from his trip!"

Every member of the household follows Alexei to the back door where the men are taking their horses to the stables and dogs to their kennels. The only men who aren't busy with their animals are Father, George and Paul. They hold a giant brown bear stretched out on display between them. He's already been gutted, but judging by the strained look on their faces, his flesh is still terribly heavy.

"Should we mount his head over our bed, Alix?"

"Or maybe our guests would like a souvenir to take home with them instead?" Mother suggests diplomatically.

My father drops his portion of the weight of the bear on the boys on each side of him while he places his arms on their shoulders and pulls them to him with pride. "I have never hunted with a more skillful horseman or a braver soldier."

The Greeks grin as they bear the weight. Soon the Grand Duke Alexandrovich brings his horse over so the bear can be loaded on and taken to the barn to be skinned, leaving the Tzar and the boys to revel in their accomplishment.

The rest of the hunting party is disappointed. Even with the number of men, horses, and dogs on the hunt, the kill by Father and the Greeks is the only one. Uncle Alexander and Aunt Xenia gather their boys and head home first. Although Makhailovich begs his wife to let him go home, they can't drag their daughter's away from their cousins. Finally he agrees that Nina and Xenia can stay one more night. He will stay for supper too, if after, his wife will take him home and help him to bed.

The young men are not the least bit tired. Stepan wishes to stay longer to re-hear the tales of the hunt, so his father agrees to join them. A light supper of cheese, bread and sausage along with ale and cognac is served and the party sits around the dining room table. Before the Tzar can tell his story, the Grecian Prince, Alexander complains about how he and his Uncle Makhailovich got stuck with the Alexeandrovich boy.

"The boy whined so much, he scared all of the bears away for miles. I was on horseback stalking a bear we had seen traces of earlier. Makhailovich was preparing the bait, and all the while young Alexandrovich was complaining, 'my socks are wet, didn't we bring more food, na na na.' If Makhailovich hadn't been along to protect him, I would have shot him instead."

Everyone laughs. "I would have given you my permission if I had known you were up to it," Makhailovich admits freely.

Alexander is not laughing. He's still irritated.

"Well at least we can say we had more success then you." Grand Duke Karenin brags. "At least we had a bear."

"Or rather the giant brown bear almost had me," Stepan interrupts. "I too was in charge of stalking the bear, only to find out the bait my father had prepared was me." Stepan puts his arms out and pretends he is being eaten by a bear. He does a convincing impression. I feel a sense of evil delight at the thought of Stepan getting eaten by a bear.

"It would have worked, too, if my son wasn't so concerned about his precious vital organs."

Everyone around the table is almost on the floor with laughter at this point. Father has to settle everyone down so that he can proceed with his bragging rights.

"The difference in our case," he said, "was that we didn't take a boy along with us. Instead we had this fine horseman here." Father reaches across the table and ruffles Paul's hair. He doesn't see the heartbroken look on his own son's face next to him.

"Paul, on his fine horse, Hercules was our stalker. That left two men to bait and kill the bear. Our bear was not at all happy with being disturbed in his foraging either and also thought that George and I were the bait, but George stood fearless and I was able to get a clear shot as the bear pounced toward him."

"And I was ready with my rifle in case he missed." Paul adds, "Which of course I was sure would never happen, Your Highness." Paul quickly catches his blunder, and the whole party breaks down in laughter again.

VII

The Greek's departure is very sad. Helen, though quiet and somber, has fit into our family like a sister. The men added an element to the household that we've not experienced before. Although no romantic feelings have developed, I think affection has. Paul and Anastasia especially seem to have developed a brother/sisterly bond. They plan to stay in touch after he leaves, reminiscent of Father and Mother years ago, I'm sure my mother expects that something stronger will develop.

Marie is most miserable and has refused to leave her room until it is time to say goodbye, but Olga and I keep ourselves busy helping Helen prepare for the journey. She will be taking the train with her court, while her brothers have chosen to journey with the servants on horseback. They will be leaving first.

When the arrangements have been made, our family follows George, Alexander and Paul to the stables. The horses are packed and ready to be mounted. First George says his goodbyes. He takes each of us in turn by the hand and gently kisses both cheeks. "I will see you all again, I'm certain." Then he gallantly mounts his horse and awaits his brothers' goodbyes.

Alexander respectfully kisses our mother and father on each cheek, then Anastasia and Marie, but when he comes to me he takes me by the shoulder and plants his lips square on my mouth. Before I can react, he has moved on and does the same to Olga. "Farewell ladies, don't miss me too much," he calls as he leaps astride his stallion.

Everyone's eyes are wide with shock. George shakes his head in disapproval, but can't hide his smile. We almost forget that Paul hasn't said his goodbyes yet. But refusing to give his brother the spotlight, he steps forward firmly taking Alexei's hand in his, he shakes it with vigor. Paul has always demonstrated to us that he isn't afraid of showing emotion. His eyes well up with tears. "Goodbye, my friend," he chokes out.

Then, turning to Anastasia, he cries out loud, and wraps his arms around her in a sweet embrace. "I will always remember you," he says softly. He also hugs my mother and father, but has gotten control of his emotions when he gets to me. I get a quick peck on the cheek, as does Olga. He jumps onto Hercules' back and salutes my father. "Till our next hunt, your majesty."

George turns his horse first, followed by Alexander who spurs his horse ahead of his brother's. Paul lingers just long enough to get emotional again and then catches up with George who reaches out a loving hand to comfort him. Helen has tears streaming down her cheeks as her brothers leave. My sisters and I offer our commiseration and share in her sentiment. Though she will see her brothers soon, we have no guarantee that they will ever be a part of our lives again.

The emotional goodbye is too much for Marie, who hurries up to her room to prepare herself for the one that will soon follow. My father has summoned the imperial train to transport Helen and the remainder of her court, including her tutors.

A carriage arrives to take them to the train. The station is near the capitol. This is the train that transports all foreign dignitaries around Russia. When the carriage pulls up to the front of the palace, we get to go out front to meet it. This in itself is a treat. We rarely get to see the view from the front of the palace.

As the servants load the carriage Marie watches and waits for Monsieur Bertrand's items to be loaded. But as Helen descends the staircase, all of our eyes turn to her. I am overwhelmed by her beauty, and imagine once again that she is the reincarnated Helen of Troy. She is smothered with kisses and hugs as we say our tearful goodbyes. Her maid and the rest of the court have already loaded into the carriage. Marie's face falls when she realizes she didn't see the tutor and missed her goodbye. Helen kisses us all one last time and tearfully begins her journey.

As soon as the horses are out of sight, Marie quickly turns to go to her room. She takes two steps and collides with a tall man in a dark suit. We are all in shock as we watch Marie look up into the face of her beloved teacher. He adjusts his dark glasses and takes her chin in his hands as he wipes her tears with his handkerchief. "I have accepted an offer," he explains, "To teach a family here in Russia."

Marie's bewildered look matches all of ours.

"I'm staying here." He laughs at our confused expressions. "Your mother is a very persuasive woman."

We turn to Mother who is still standing in the doorway. "Yes, it's true." She walks towards us and puts her arms on Anastasia's and my shoulders. "I wanted to surprise you."

Forgetting Monsieur Bertrand for a moment, Marie runs like a little girl to our mother and squeezes her tight. "Yes, Marie. I expected that reaction from you. Now go upstairs and start gathering your things. We are leaving for Livadiya the day after tomorrow."

Anastasia's face drops and Olga's face mirrors her sister's. Mama and Papa don't like to

delay our travels. I am thrilled to be escaping the darkness of the Winter Palace. There is no longer any reason we should stay, but I don't know what this will mean for Olga's regiment. It would be impractical for them to travel with us. Lividia is a vacation. I'm sure the regiment will also take leave while she's gone.

Livida Palace

Livadiya, Crimea—Ukraine

Helen traveled back to Greece on the International Imperial Train, but the trip to Crimea only requires the Russian Imperial Train. Originally built in 1896 and then updated for our larger family in 1902, the train is a technological masterpiece, years ahead of its time. It has ten carriages: a sleeping-car, a salon car, carriages intended for children, the grand dukes, and the Emperor's regime, as well as a kitchen and carriages for railway servicemen, servants, luggage and workshops. Oh, make that eleven carriages, Mother recently insisted that one more be added for use as a chapel.

We spend most of the long journey in the salon carriage, while we read, play cards or board games, converse, and, in some cases argue with and bother each other. The car is luxuriously decorated—walls and furnishings are upholstered, and silk fabrics and leather have been amply used with comfort being the focus—but the trip takes over a week, sometimes longer, depending on the weather. It's long, but worth it.

The Lividia Palace is on the Crimean Peninsula, surrounded by the Black Sea. Black sandy beaches and high cliffs surround the water's edge. The beautiful scenery can be seen from the balconies and patios surrounding the palace. Lividia is everything the Winter Palace isn't—open, airy, surrounded by familiar gardens and a welcoming community. Anticipation is the only reason for my distress on this trip—my sisters have other reasons.

Olga spends most of her time in her compartment of the sleeping car, and when she does come out to the salon, she sits and gazes forlornly out the window. Even though Marie should be blissfully happy, rather than expressing her joy, she timidly sinks into her shell, reverting back to a quiet, studious wallflower. Anastasia is the source of the most contention on the train. With four daughters, my parents have come to expect the mood swings, especially at Anastasia's age. She becomes mischievous, pesky and downright mean to our brother, sending their governess off to her room in frustration more than once.

After one such episode, to save my mother from another migraine, I decide to try to discover the source of Anastasia's agitation and see if there is anything I can do to help her alleviate it.

"Do you want to talk about it, sister?" I ask after she's had time to cool down.

"If I could find someone worth talking to. I'm sick to death of this family. Everyone is so dreary. Marie is afraid to say or do anything that will make her appear to be anything but sophisticated, now that her wonderful art tutor has become part of the court. And Olga acts as if someone has died." Anastasia looks out the window.

"And where does that leave me? I'm not the least bit dreary. Crimea is my favorite spot in the whole world. I can't understand why this family acts as if they are marching towards a death sentence. When will everyone stop being miserable and realize how great it's going to be? Talk about not having anyone to talk to. Who will share in my joy?"

I get Anastasia to crack a smile, so I go ahead and delve into what I think the real problem is. "Do you think Hercules has gotten his master home yet?"

Anastasia doesn't try to hide her concern this time. "We won't even know until weeks after we have made it to our destination."

"And is the stable crew bringing Носки on foot? It must be a dangerous journey." I say without realizing that it could cause her more concern until after I've already said it, but she seems to be more focused on the first part of my question.

"Some of Father's guards are bringing Носки with their party. The stable crew stays at the Winter Palace."

"Oh, I would hate to have to stay at the Winter Palace all year. Yes, I suppose it will be different, maybe even tolerable after the snow melts, but I wouldn't stay there if I wasn't forced to." My mouth keeps moving. I guess I'm the one who has needed someone to talk to.

Anastasia acts like she didn't hear me, and goes on talking to herself. "What if those boots get too small? Who will get him what he needs?"

I no longer have to try to guess who she's thinking about.

When the tedious train ride finally comes to an end, we still have to travel across the small Sea of Azov by steamboat. Father's family was once almost killed in a storm crossing the sea to the peninsula, but today the sea is calm. Sitting on the boat's deck, I realize how different this vacation will be when compared to the days of drudgery spent in Petersburg. It's like the difference between being cooped up in the luxuriously upholstered padded cell—the train—and sitting in the open air, with salty breezes running through my hair and hearing the sounds of the gulls chirping while the waves crash against the shore—freedom versus captivity. As night falls, we are forced to go below deck to sleep in the cabin, but tomorrow we will reach Crimea and the beautiful Lividia Palace.

When our carriage arrives at the palace and the servants start to unload our things, my sisters act like ostriches pulling their heads out of the sand. I'm finally able to hear their laughter and my brother's excitement as my father takes us to a garage and shows us an automobile.

"The French newspapers raved about this car. The same model as the 1912 Monte-Carlo that Andreiy Nagel raced in the St. Petersburg-Tver-Moscow-Orel-Belgorod-Kharkov-Yekaterinoslav-Melitopol-Simferopol-Sevastopol rally" Alexei prattles off.

My sisters and I stand gaping. "Did you memorize the entire official title of that race?" Anastasia finally asks for all of us.

Alexei's prideful beam has been diminished to a pinkish hue. "The race was very important." His jaw firms in a defensive stance.

Father comes to his rescue. "Yes," he agrees, "and the car was not only noted for its speed, but it traveled the farthest of all the vehicles in the rally." He ruffles my brother's head with pride.

"But there aren't enough seats for all of us," Mother complains.

"Perfect for a romantic drive don't you think?" Father raises his eyebrows and Mother blushes.

In the garage, there are also bicycles for everyone in the family, including my brother.

"We discussed this Niki." I overhear my parents talking as we inspect our new toys. Mother's voice is filled with concern. "That bicycle could be the death of him."

"There is no need for concern, darling. I will keep him much too busy to ever ride it. But just having it seems to give him a sense of pride." Father says.

Seemingly to prove him right, my brother's face beams with joy. When my brother is happy, everyone in the family is pleased.

The sun is shining for our arrival today, though it will probably be raining later. About the only thing you can count on about the weather in Crimea if that you can never count on the weather. At least once every day the sun comes out to warm the sand, and at least once every day the rain washes the foot prints away. But even when you are inside the palace, you feel like you are outside. There are floor to ceiling windows in every room, and each room opens to a patio, or, upstairs, to a veranda overlooking the sea

The palace was originally used by my grandfather in the 1860's. He brought my ailing grandmother here. Her health seemed to improve in the Crimean climate. But a couple of years ago, while my parents were in Italy, they fell in love with Italian architecture. Soon after, my father commissioned a famous local architect to redesign Lividia. It was finished just in time for Olga's sixteenth birthday party. Marie, Anastasia, and I will celebrate our birthdays here in June.

Many of my parents' friends follow us to Crimea every year, mostly my cousins. My father's sister's family, with their seven children, has already arrived. Also the Konstantinoviches have returned from Paris and are already here. My father always enjoys the company of his good friend Konstantine; he is liberal, yet opened minded. He is said to be the most artistic of the imperial house. His sons, Konstantine and Igor are on break from the Corpse de Page military academy, so of course they will be here too along with ten-year-old George, my brother's favorite comrade. I have always felt intimidated by Konstantine and Igor, they are much older. Or at least older than Olga, about Stepan's age actually, but they were pleasant when they attended the ball at the palace this winter. Mother chose them to be Marie and I's first dance partners. Maybe we have all grown up.

Uncle George and Aunt Maria will arrive with their daughters soon, along with the Grand Duke and Helen Karenin. I am told Stepan still has business in Petersburg and will be unable to vacation in Crimea this spring. I say hooray to that. We could use a break from Stepan Karenin for a while.

The better part of the day is spent unpacking and making the Lividia Palace our home for the next couple of months. But in the evening, a welcome party comes to dinner. After a refreshing meal of pheasant shot by the Alexandrovich boys and a salad of kale and winter lettuce—green vegetables fresh from the garden—we retire to the Italian patio for dessert. The air is still a little chill, so we snuggle up in our shawls and the men wear their jackets. While chatting with my cousin Irena and looking out at the moon, we are approached by Igor Konstantinovich. "Ah, what beauty you ladies add to the landscape."

Irena and I giggle at his attempt at chivalric charm. He has grown into a tall, handsome man. His hair is dark, but his eyes shine blue. Though charming in appearance, he seems to lack the cleverness I would expect from a man of his linage.

"You flatter us, Igor. To what do we owe the honor of your company?" I return his clichéd remark.

As he steps down the patio toward us he seems to relax and smile. He stretches and takes a seat next to a small table on the deck. "Isn't it great to get away from the snow?"

He seems to be mostly talking to himself but he reflects my sentiments. I look at Irena for permission, and then follow him to the seat next to his. Irena stands behind me.

"I hate Russia in the wintertime. No," I correct myself, "I hate the Winter Palace." After giving it more thought I speak again, "No, I hate Russia in the wintertime." Igor has patiently waited for me to make up my mind, so that I can correctly express my complaint. "Ah, but here it is lovely."

"And as I said earlier, it is made lovelier by the company of a beautiful lady or two."

My sister Olga is stands with Igor's brother Konstantine, motioning for Irena to come to her. Irena gives me a pleading look. I nod and she leaves us.

"Or just one beautiful lady is fine too." Igor pretends to look insulted by Irena's defection, but his expression quickly changes and he smiles as if this is what he wanted all along. We sit in silence for a moment and share the atmosphere of tranquility.

"There aren't a lot of women at the academy," Igor interrupts the quiet. "Well none, really. We are allowed to go out, but with all the studies we do, there isn't a lot of time to meet people. Actually the ball at your place was the first time I'd been around a woman in weeks, so please excuse my awkwardness." He pauses, and just as I think he has said all he wished to, he quickly starts again. "Would you accompany me tomorrow on an outing? We could ride our bicycles down to the shore and look through the shops."

The shocked look on my face must not appear to be an affirming one, because he looks concerned. "Maybe it's too soon? Maybe you would like to spend some time with your family?"

"Oh, I have spent enough time with my family," I burst. "But maybe I should ask my mother first."

"Good, then." Igor looks satisfied. Pulling up the legs of his trousers he stands. "I'll come by your place around noon, and if it's all right with your mother, we'll leave after tea. Good night, Tatiana, and thanks for making me feel at ease." He flashes me a smile that makes my heart flutter and he saunters across the deck.

When he is out of sight I lean back in my chair and raise my arms over my head. I can't believe I'm going to spend the afternoon tomorrow outside the palace away from my sisters. This is certainly not Petersburg.

II

My mother seems as pleased for me as I am to be getting out of the palace. She quickly gives her consent. It seems everyone has made plans last night. Olga and Irena have been invited over to the Konstantinovich home with Alexei. Father plans on taking them in his automobile. That sounds exciting, but riding a bicycle is excitement enough for me. I learned to ride last summer. Papa taught me by holding on to the seat while I pedaled fast and hung on tight. I hope I still remember how to do it. I've never laughed so much while falling and scraping up my legs as I did learning to ride a bicycle. Even Alexei got a lesson, but after Maman saw her daughters bleeding, my Father was never allowed to let go of his seat. She is even more cautious with Alexei when Rasputin is not with the family, but to us it's a nice break to be away from him. Alexei has more time to play when he is not constantly receiving treatments.

I put on a white tea-length dress with a blue sash and bow. It has a white, wide brimmed hat with a bow to match and I wear my dark hair long and down my back, pulling back my bangs with a large ivory barrette. Short white gloves and a white drawstring satchel complete the outfit. It holds a brush and some ruble coins in case I find something I want at the shops on the beach.

Igor arrives promptly at noon; his dark hair is slicked back and his icy blue eyes sparkle mischievously. Mother invites him to join us for tea, as we counted on. When tea is finished, Marie and Anastasia go up to their rooms to prepare for an art lesson, and await the arrival of our cousins, Nina and Xenia. Igor and I walk down to the garage to get my bicycle.

Last year we only had one to learn on, but Father has now purchased us each our own. They are all blue and white (thus complimenting my clothing selection) with shiny chrome handles. Igor rode his to my house. His is identical to mine in every way except for the dirt that has already accumulated on the fenders surrounding the tires. He holds my bike upright for me as I mount it and begin to pedal down the sloped trail. I let out a little squeal as I descend the hill from the garage to the driveway. Igor has to quickly hop on his seat to catch me.

"Are you all right?" He breathes as he pulls up alongside me.

"Yes!" I'm thrilled. "This is so natural, like I've been doing this my whole life."

"And so liberating," he agrees. "In some ways better than anything else I do naturally in life."

"It feels like I'm flying," I add to his sentiments. "Do you know where we're going?"

"We're going to the road down there. We'll have to go uphill for a while. Do you think you're strong enough?"

I'm suddenly concerned. I don't know if I'm strong enough. I've never done this before.

"I'm pretty strong," I say questioningly.

"I know," Igor beams. "I can tell."

That's when the pedaling becomes difficult. I take a few deep breaths, but I no longer have the air to speak. Igor has stood up on his pedals, but doesn't seem to be going much faster than I am. I don't trust my balance yet, so I don't copy him. Just when it seems I can go no farther, my body gives me another burst of energy. The riding seems to become easier or my body is getting used to it. We reach the top of the hill and Igor disappears around a corner.

The road pulls me around as well and we are flying again. "Weeeeee...." I hear ahead of me, Igor seems to be enjoying himself, but I'm concerned. I don't know how I am going to stop this thing.

The road ahead disappears back into a grassy trail. I watch my companion veer off the road. I'm comforted that the trail seems to have slowed his descent and the grass looks a lot softer to land on then the gravel road. Relieved, I let the bike coast until it comes to a stop along- side Igor.

"Well done." He vigorously pats my back. I feel like a boxer after a hard-fought match rather than a lady who has gracefully conquered her first real bicycle ride.

He politely holds on while I swing my leg back over the seat and offers me his handkerchief. Embarrassed, I accept. "I must be a mess," I smooth my hair and wish I'd brought a compact with a mirror.

"Glowing," he grins back.

"Glowing indeed." I blot the beads of perspiration on my forehead with his handkerchief and stuff it in my satchel. "I'll have this washed for you."

Igor chuckles. "The trail is all sand from here. We'll have to walk beside the bicycles and push them a ways, but we're almost to the beach." He points ahead and sure enough, the shore is in view.

As we walk along, he tells me about the academy he attends in Petersburg. "The Corps de Page graduates the most honorable soldiers in Russia," he brags. I can't help but remember what Olga told me about the men that came from the Corps de Page in her regiment. She says they think they are better than everyone else and refuse to do anything they think is too difficult to be dignified. I'm sure they can't all be that way, and Igor seems so proud, I choose not to mention that to him.

The sun has been shining all day, but the sky starts to darken as clouds roll in from the horizon. When we arrive at the shore, we take the bicycles up to a shop at the end of the trail. Igor hands the storekeeper a fifty ruble coin to keep them safe. He gives me his arm and we start walking across the boardwalk, stopping to look into shops that interest us. I'm giddy and interested in everything. The salty air and the warm breeze are constant reminders that I am no longer a prisoner of Petersburg. Being on the arm of a handsome, slender gentleman could have something to do with my glee, but Igor has a strange habit of speaking loudly when it seems inappropriate.

While in a jewelry store, the owner shows me some of his wares. I'm impressed at the handcrafted workmanship, but as the man holds a brooch to the light to show me how it glimmers in the sun, Igor calls out from the other side of the shop, "Why would you want something made out of stone, when you have hundreds of diamonds at home?" I'm appalled at his rudeness, but excuse it, blaming his all-male education.

Later we when we are about to leave for home, a girl selling flowers suggests he purchase one for his "lovely lady." Instead of politely declining, he sharply asks her if she has ever tried to carry flowers while riding a bicycle. Obviously the little girl doesn't have access to a bicycle, and even if I were given flowers and had to abandon them before our journey home, it would have been a sweet gesture.

Our bicycles are waiting for us outside the shop where we left them. The store keeper kept them under the eaves to shelter them from the sprinkling rain. Igor wonders if we should wait till it stops, but Mother is expecting me home for dinner, and the rain feels glorious on my face. I tell him I would enjoy riding in the rain. He purses his lips together trying to hide his smile of agreement, and shakes his head. "Very well, we will get you home to your mother even if it means we get a little wet."

The ride home is much faster than the ride there. Once we are out of the sand and back on the road, there is only a short uphill ride. Most of the rest trip is down. Igor lets me pass him up. The raindrops pelt my face. I look up toward the sky and childishly stick out my tongue and try to catch a drop or two. At the final uphill to the palace, Igor catches up with me. "You look like you needed that," he says as he helps me off the bike. My hair is wet and there are strings plastered to my face. He reaches up and gathers the stray pieces with his finger and tucks them behind my ear. "Maybe I'll see you again tonight," he tells me softly.

Walking up the steps to the palace, my legs feel wobbly. I hold tight to Igor's arm until we get to the door.

"I had fun, Tatiana; maybe we'll do it again sometime." He smiles as he closes the door. I turn and stumble into my mother. She gives me a knowing smile. "It looks like you got caught in the rain," she teases. "Go clean up for dinner."

Father wants a detailed account of our day when we sit down to eat. The table in the dining room is set before a large uncovered window so that we can watch the carriages run up and down the street. Another reminder that we are a part of this town, in contrast to our isolation in Petersburg.

"How are the Konstantinoviches?" Father does not direct the question to anyone in particular, but since Olga spent the day at their house, she assumes it was directed at her.

"Busy as always. Princess Elisebeth is trying to get Sergey Diaghilev to bring the Russian ballet to visit the theater here in Crimea."

"Their family has always been very invested in the theater," Mother explains. "I hear Igor is especially fond of the ballet."

"All men are fond of the ballet," I laugh. "All those women with impossibly perfect bodies."

"I admire the ballet," Alexei interrupts. "Not because of the women. Those male dancers are strong."

Father raises his eyebrows, as if he's not sure how to react to that statement, and then turns his attention to me. "How was your day with Igor?"

My sisters turn their bodies towards me, now completely drawn into the conversation.

"He's very nice," I smile, "but he could use a little refinement."

"Which I'm sure you would be happy to assist him with." Anastasia also has a big mouth and speaks out of turn inappropriately. I, on the other hand, have turned red and cannot speak. My sisters giggle.

"I am told that Konstantine has seen his older brother and sister's happiness in marriage and is now ready to find a wife," Mother says.

"He seems taken with Irena," Olga agrees.

"That's not what his father told me." Father's deep voice interrupts from the other side of the table. "He told me that his sons are very glad that our daughters are here, and that Konstantine favors you, Olga."

Olga giggles slightly, to appease our parents, but when the subject has changed and the focus is no longer on her, she looks concerned. I wonder how much longer she can use Irena to placate him.

Our family has plans to go to the theater tonight with the Konstantinoviches. We arrive by carriage since Father's new automobile doesn't seat us all. Konstantine and Elisabeth are there waiting with their sons. Ten-year-old, George is Alexei's closest friend—the closest to his age amongst our associates, but he and his parents have been in France all winter. The boys can't wait to play. George quickly takes Alexei by the hand and runs off to show him something as soon as we arrive. My mother yells out precautionary warnings at his back. The younger Konstantine offers Olga his arm. She gives me a pleading look that says, "Don't leave me alone with him." But Igor is also standing there, his boyish face looking eager and his bright blue eyes calling me too him. I look over my shoulder at Marie and Anastasia. They can help Olga ward off Konstantine. Although it was a confusing day with Igor, I'm still glad to see him.

The theater in Crimea is much smaller than any of the theaters in Petersburg. Elisabeth Konstantinovishan leads us to a tiny private balcony and both of our families squeeze into it. It seems Olga had nothing to worry about. There will be no aloneness here tonight. Igor puts his hands on the back of a chair, offering me a seat, and then takes the chair next to it. I try to keep my hands in my lap, because when I put my arm on the armrest, Igor's hand brushes against mine. It makes me nervous. I'm not sure if it would be rude to move away quickly, or too forward if I were to let it stay there.

Trying to look like I am anticipating the performance, I look straight ahead and notice that Monsieur Bertrand is seated with the general audience. I point him out to Marie.

"When the performance is over," I suggest. "You should go ask our tutor how he liked it."

Marie frowns. "I would not feel comfortable with that," she says flatly.

"What's wrong? I thought he was Prince Charming?" I tease.

Marie stays serious. "It's different now that he's no longer our guest. Having him here in Crimea makes it seem like he's just…a teacher."

"The mystery is gone?" I continue to have fun at my sister's expense, although I do understand and I think she appreciates that I'm giving her a chance to talk about it.

Marie smiles at my silliness and nods.

"He always did seem fond of you," I go on. "Even if it wasn't in a Prince Charming/Cinderella way. I mean he's older, but maybe you could still have a satisfying professional relationship."

Marie smiles like she thinks I'm being silly again, but I think it will give her some confidence when dealing with him later.

Igor readjusts himself in his seat—I suppose to remind me that he's still there—it works. Feeling like I have helped my sister with her problem, I shift my focus back to my own enjoyment of the evening. The music begins and the lights go out.

III

Our time in Crimea sneaks past us, we lose track of the days as each one flows into the next. For me the days are spent at the beach, shopping in the square, playing croquet or tennis, or riding bicycles with our cousins or the Konstantinoviches. Nights are spent at the theater. Igor loves the theater and my mother has joined his mother in trying to persuade the Russian Ballet to come to Crimea. Alexei has been key in Mother's motivation. He has confided in her, telling her of his admiration for a famous male dancer. Any desire of Alexei's always becomes her number one priority.

    One afternoon, between social events, my mother and I are alone in the salon.

    "You seem to have made a friend." Mother attempts to ask me about my relationship with Igor without sounding like she's prying.

I decide to answer her directly. "Igor is handsome. He makes me feel like I have butterflies fluttering around in my chest, but he can be loud and obnoxious. I'm confused by the way I feel when I'm with him. One minute he makes me angry and the next he makes me swoon."

Mother has been smirking since I started speaking. "I agree with you on both accounts—handsome, yes, obnoxious yes. Some men just take longer to grow up. You're lucky. You're still young. You don't have to decide how you feel yet."

"I don't have to choose until Olga does," I understand.

Mother joins my sympathetic frown for Olga. "I know Konstantine would propose to her today if she showed any interest, but she keeps pushing Irena to him. I think she misses Stepan."

Hearing his name digs up an old hurt that I had let myself forget. "I think she and Stepan are just friends."

Mother is shaking her head. "They may have been once, but she gets a message from him almost every day."

I feel strangely betrayed. Why wouldn't Olga have mentioned this to me? She trusted me enough to tell me all about her soldier… but maybe he wasn't as important to her as she let on.

"Have you noticed how miserable she's been since we left Petersburg? I think she and Stepan didn't realize how deeply they felt for each other until she left."

Mother seems pleased, but I am upset and I don't know why or at whom.

As we hurry to get ready for the theater that evening, I confront my sister with my mother's revelation. "Has your relationship changed with Stepan since we left Petersburg?" I ask as she as she digs through her drawer for her gloves.

Scurrying from her dresser to her closet, she stops and flashes me a questioning look.

"Do you love him now? Has distance made the heart grow fonder?"

Olga throws back her head and laughs. "I have always been fond of Stepan, but do I love him? Well, yes, I would say that I do. Where are these crazy questions coming from, dear?"

I feel like I've had the wind knocked out of me. I know my sister and I haven't talked much since we've been here, but I hadn't realized....

"Mother just mentioned that you get a letter from him every day, I was just wondering…"

Olga gives me a look that makes me feel like she thinks I'm a fool. "Of course, of course," she affirms hurrying along and no longer making eye contact with me. "Yes, Stepan sends me a letter every day."

Mother calls up the stairs to tell us that the carriage is leaving, and Olga swooshes past me without another word. I'm confused and a little angry as I leave the house and take my seat on the carriage. But as we pull up to the front of the theater, a tall, dark-haired man with icy blue eyes is waiting at the door. He winks at me as the driver helps me down from the step and for the first time all evening, a smile threatens to escape my lips. He offers me his arm and I don't hesitate to take it. Tonight, I will focus my attention on Igor and try to forget about Stepan and Olga.

I don't listen to the theater at all tonight. I let my mind wander. I usually try to keep an invisible boundary between Igor and me, but tonight I've continued to hold on to his arm after he escorted me to my seat. With my arm wrapped around his, the invisible wall is already gone. He smells incredible, like a mixture of pipe smoke and cedar—

and something else. I lean in closer, letting my olfactory senses get a better chance to discern—cinnamon, maybe? His body reacts to mine as he leans in as well. When the lights go out, he lays his cheek against my head, and his breath warms the spot just above my ear. Before I realize what has occurred, he has removed the glove from my hand and laced his bare fingers between mine. The current is electric. It leaves me feeling a little afraid, but soon I'm comfortable squeezing his hand and feeling his warm skin against mine.

Igor quickly pulls my glove back on my hand just as the performance ends and the crowd breaks into applause. As everyone is leaving, he grabs me by the wrist and pulls me through the crowd. My heart is racing. I wonder where he is taking me. We slip out through a side door, which apparently few know about, and suddenly we are in the street, in the alley next to the theater. Our new surroundings are unfamiliar. I should be concerned, but the hot blood coursing through my veins makes me ignore my rational thoughts. Without warning, he presses his body up against me and I am trapped between him and the building.

He presses his mouth onto mine again and again, so hard that I feel his teeth through his lips. "Ha," he says as he pulls away, "weeks before your sixteenth birthday, and now I have given you something, your first kiss."

This isn't how I imagined it would be at all, but the excitement ignited is so thick in the air, I thoughtlessly try an experiment. I rise up on my toes to reach him. I want to try it a different way. I place my hands on his cheeks and pull his face to mine. I kiss him softly, and my lips stay on his longer. This time it's much better for me. He acts shocked as I lower down to my normal height. My kiss seems to have set his passion ablaze. He aggressively presses me up against the wall again and imposes his open mouth on mine. His lips move all around my face, down my neck, until I'm afraid he will never stop. But to my relief, he abruptly he pulls away, wipes his mouth on his sleeve, and gives me a sinister smile. Once again he grabs my wrist and pulls me behind him. "We'd better get back, before someone comes looking for us."

Lying in bed that night I wonder what happened—if I should tell anyone. I could talk to

Olga, she would understand, but I think I'm still upset with her. No, I conclude, this will be my secret. Mine and Igor's.

After a restless night's sleep I get up and meet my family for tea. Today is Sunday and we will be heading to the cathedral later for Mass. Igor will be there. I wonder what his face will look like this morning in the daylight—if he looks as guilty as I feel. When my sisters greet me they don't seem suspicious. Apparently the big moment last night took so little time, no one even noticed we were gone. After tea, I hurriedly go up to my suite and choose a gown that looks saintly to hide my shame. The collar goes up to my chin and the sleeves fasten at the wrist.

"You look lovely," Mother comments as I flow down the stairs. "I haven't seen that dress on you in an age."

"I saw it in my closet and thought I would try it on again. I was surprised to find that it was flattering as well."

"That reminds me, you and your sister's birthdays are coming up in a couple of weeks. We have to have a new dresses fitted for you."

The reminder of my birthday brings back unpleasant memories of last night, and worse,
reminds me that we will be leaving Crimea soon after the party. Mother tries to decipher my frown. "The dressmakers here in Crimea

aren't as well known as the ones in Petersburg, but we will find you something fashionable."

"I have complete confidence in you, Mother. I was just reminded that we will be leaving soon after my birthday."

Mother seems to interpret that incorrectly as well. "Igor will be going back to Petersburg. The rest of our vacation will be over by winter and then we will return there, too. Who knows, perhaps Olga will have decided to marry Stepan by then and you can pursue a courtship with more vigor."

Her words leave me with a sick feeling in my stomach that gets worse as the morning goes on. I'm tempted to admit my discomfort and stay in bed while everyone else goes to Mass, but it's too late to feign an illness now that I'm dressed. The cathedral is just down the hill from the palace. We choose to walk the short distance, but our friends arrive in carriages and motor cars. Dinner is always held at our place afterwards. I hide my eyes and try to look pious as I worship today. I don't want to be distracted by a pair of blue eyes that I feel burning through my prayer shawl.

We ascend the hill to the palace in groups. The girls gather in front, walking faster and the boys lag behind us. They are whispering something and laughing obnoxiously. I haven't made eye contact with Igor yet, but I expect him to find me soon. The servants attend Mass as well, so we gather in the garden to wait for the meal to be prepared. I wander away from the group and sit down on a stone bench near the roses. Igor finds me there.

I can't help but blush as he looks into my eyes. He does look different—older maybe—in the daylight. "You were on fire last night," He whispers.

In frustration I turn my head. This isn't the way I think I should be spoken to after what happened. It makes me feel loathsome. Igor sits down and tenderly places his thumb and finger on my chin and turns my face back towards him. "You blush," he tells me as if I didn't know. "You have nothing to be embarrassed about."

I'm confused by this man. One minute I'm drawn to him and the next I am repulsed by him. Right now it's the latter. I excuse myself to go to my sister. As soon as I'm gone, my cousin, Andrei takes my place on the bench and he and Igor chuckle about something behind their hands.

Later at dinner. we are seated across the table from each other. I keep my eyes on my plate most of the time, but occasionally he catches me looking up and flashes me a grin. After dinner, while standing on the patio with Irena, my sister, and Konstantine, fourteen year old Feodor casually saunters over to our group. He makes eye contact with me and smiles. "I hear it was pretty hot at the theater last night."

He acts like he'd like to say more, but erupts in laughter instead. The ladies look to me for an explanation. I'm feeling a little warm right now myself.

All the boys join us after that. Though the ladies seem oblivious to what's going on, I feel like I'm in a pen of tigers. Their sly comments and wicked smiles are all directed at me. Finally I get Igor's attention and get him to follow me back to the house.

"Can't wait to go at it again?" Igor's little boy face lights up and his innocent-looking eyes seem hungry for more. His pouting will not get him what he wants today.

I put my hands on his chest and give him a push. "What are you telling my cousins?" I accuse.

"I may have mentioned our escapade to Andrei. I couldn't help but brag a little, but it was out of my control from there." I give him another shove. Igor takes my hand off his chest, and pulls me toward him with such force that a small sigh escapes my body. Before I can react, he twists my arm behind my back. "You like it rough, I see," he whispers in my ear. At that moment I hear the patio door open and my father's voice. Igor is distracted long enough for me to get away and go outside. When I walk onto the patio my sisters and cousins are looking at me with their jaws dropped. I arrive just in time to hear my cousin Rostislav, who's a year younger then Anastasia, say out loud, "No, he said that she kissed him!" Igor walks up behind me with a big grin on his face. I turn and run up the stairs to my suite.

After punching my pillows a few times, I plop face-down on my bed. Olga opens the door without knocking a few seconds later. She sits down next to me and starts to smooth my hair. Eventually, I turn my blotchy face and look up at her.

"This is not the way this was supposed to happen," I sigh.

"No, it's not," she sympathetically agrees.

I stay in bed the rest of the day, and by morning I feel truly ill. I think maybe I was coming down with something before everything started with Igor and I ignored it. By Monday afternoon, Mother brings in Doctor Bolkin, one of Alexei's doctors. I have a fever. Mother reacts quickly, isolating my bedroom so the germs can't be spread. I'm assigned a nurse and she is the only one who can see me. The doctor prescribes the same medication he gives Alexei for pain, aspirin—the new wonder drug. For me it seems to work. By the next morning I'm feeling much better, but my mother's imposed quarantine will be enforced for the rest of the week. The sun shines through my window calling to me—mocking me—maybe because I brought this sickness on myself.

By Wednesday, my sisters feel sorry for me. Marie sneaks in first and brings me some of her favorite books. Anastasia brings in some ice cream later. Finally, before retiring for the night, Olga comes and sits on the foot of my bed.

"Aren't you afraid of getting sick?" I ask her.

"Are you sick?"

I quickly jump out of bed, demonstrating my fitness.

"I didn't think so," Olga smiles. "A broken heart maybe?"

"Heartbroken?" I consider this. It's not one of the emotions I would have thought of on my own. Disgraced, humiliated, but not heartbroken. "Hmmm…" I think out loud, "I don't think my heart was as invested as it appeared."

Olga adjusts her position so that one leg is on the bed and one is on the floor. "I see. You were just experimenting with him."

I'm not sure I like that term. "Is that what you called it when you were with Dmetri?"

Olga looks as if I have punched her in the stomach. "Heavens," she coughs out as she recovers, "Heavens no! Dmetri is my one true love. How could you think…? I've told you how I feel. I've shared my soul with you, Tanya."

Apparently, Mother was wrong. "But when Mother told me about the messages sent from Stepan…"

Olga's face lights up with understanding. "Ah, I see. You've been talking to Mother. Yes, I've been getting letters sent to me, almost every day. Messages Stepan has forwarded from Dmetri. I've told you Tanya, I have no romantic interests in Stepan." She laughs like it's the funniest thing she's heard in a while.

I laugh too, at my own silliness.

IV

Our stay in Lividia will be over soon. We usually return to Peterhof in May, but my Mother and Elisabeth Konstantinivishan are certain that they have convinced the Russian Ballet to come to Crimea. Also, since Marie, Nina, Anastasia and I all have birthdays in June, Mother has promised us an upscale celebration to match the one they had for Olga here for her sixteenth birthday soon after the palace was remodeled.

My stay in bed has slowed down the preparations. So instead of having us each choose a dress, she and Aunt Maria have decided to choose one dress and clothe the four birthday girls to match. The gowns they have chosen are made from a heavy satin with a raised pattern, giving it an upholstered look. It is mostly cream-colored, but the pattern uses a silvery thread. The neckline is wide with an empire waist and sleeves that are puffed down to the elbow and then fitted down the rest of the arm ending in a point at the wrist. Of course, we will all be wearing diamond studded tiaras with our hair set high.

We stand and look in front of the mirror together. The dresses that were supposed to unite us have instead emphasized our differences. We all love them. Anastasia looks young and beautiful in anything she wears, and Marie's pretty round face is framed by the neckline. Her maturing figure fills out the dress, emphasizing her curves. The silvery undertones bring out Nina's sparkling eyes, but the dress acts as if it were made for me. The high waist and fitted sleeves enhance my tall thin body, and the color contrasts my dark complexion.

The furniture has been moved out of the downstairs sitting rooms to make room for the orchestra and a dance floor. The sliding windows that lead to the patio will be left open so that it can also be used as a dance floor as well. The party tonight will be much more casual then the balls in Petersburg—no dance cards, for one, but my sisters, cousin and I must be announced before we make our entrance and descend the staircase.

Fearing an all-too-possible tumble down the stairs, we practice before we put on our dresses. We take turns announcing each other, but after climbing the stairs numerous times, we become silly with exhaustion.

"Introducing, her imperial highness, the princess of high and mightiness, the one with the highest hair…"

Marie can no longer hold back her laughter, so I jump from behind the railing and yells, "The one who can jump the highest…" We are no longer capable of being clever. That was over about three introductions ago, but I have an elaborate descent planned.

The maid comes around the corner. "You're still here? Your mothers are looking for you upstairs." We realize we have lost track of time and the thought of our mothers waiting sobers us. We head straight to our suites where, sure enough, our mothers are holding up our finished dresses, tapping their toes.

Olga and Xenia also have to look gorgeous tonight. They have selected dresses that have been worn before, but not in Lividia. Olga seems extra quiet, like she's hiding something. It's typical for her to have something special planned for our birthdays. At eight o'clock, my sister goes downstairs to help greet the guests. Mother will stay with Anastasia, Marie, and me until the big moment of our introduction.

Anastasia will be announced first, then Marie and Nina. I will be last because I am the oldest. I stand and watch, teasing the other girls about tripping as they stand at the top of the staircase, until finally I am the only girl left at the top. From where I'm standing all I see is a sea of faces. I can't make any out, but I have to concentrate to keep my mind off the blue eyed boy waiting below. I wonder what I will do when I see him, perhaps my heart will stop beating and all of the practice we did gracefully walking down the stairs will be for нет.

I have done this many times before, possibly sixteen, though I'm sure I was carried into the party before I knew how to walk, but today my heart is pounding. Facing Igor will not make this a happy birthday. I am announced, and as I begin to descend the stairs, all eyes are on me. I see a lot of familiar smiling faces as I acknowledge the crowd of guests. So far I haven't seen the familiar blue eyes, instead another pair I recognize draws my attention. I stop abruptly, holding tightly to the railing, and do a double take. I have to squint to be sure, but his face works its way out of the crowd and his green eyes are smiling. I remember what I'm doing, recompose myself, and finish the last stairs.

When I get to the bottom, Stepan Karenin steps forward and offers me his arm. I slip my hand around it dumbfounded. Olga, is beside him, not holding back her delight. "Remember when I told you that I thought Stepan fancied someone, but he wouldn't tell me who?"

My mind can't wrap itself around what she is saying, partly because my job as an honoree is not finished. The orchestra is playing and I am supposed to pick a dance partner. I see that Marie has already chosen a partner, Monsieur Bertrand. With the relaxed atmosphere at Lividia, no one questions her choice to dance with her teacher. If there wasn't so much going on in my head already, I'd go right up to her and congratulate her. She must have taken my advice.

Then I see Igor. He's making his way toward me through the crowd. "I hate to interrupt this reunion," he says as he looks at Stepan, then back to me, then to Olga, then back to me. He is familiar with Stepan. They associate with the same circle back in Petersburg, but now he's trying to discern what exactly is going on here. "Tatiana hasn't chosen a partner." He gives me a pleading look of humility.

Before I can say anything, Stepan speaks, "Oh, but she has. I have been given the honor of escorting her for her first dance on her birthday." Presumptuously leads me to the dance floor.

I have not gotten over the shock of seeing him here. "How did you....? Why? I thought you had business, and it's such a long treacherous journey?"

Stepan doesn't seem ready to explain yet. "No journey on the Imperial Train can be considered treacherous," he teases as he places his hand on my waist.

Neither of us can take our eyes off of each other. He is dressed in his best suit. The one he wears for formal occasions. The jacket is cropped, but it has a long tailcoat. His string tie is bowed about his neck. I've never seen him looks more handsome, but I'm trying to understand what has just happened. Finally my confused look is too much for him.

"Okay, okay, I missed you. I'll admit it."

"Missed me?" I'm still not convinced that he doesn't love Olga.

"Come on, Tanya," His eyes beg me to understand so he doesn't have to explain. "I told you how I feel. I told you twice. Once in the library at your parents house and once again at the ball before you left."

"You told me you wanted me to be your sister," I frown.

"You, my darling, need to study your French." He lifts my hand off his shoulder and kisses it chivalrously.

I cast down my eyes as the pieces of his explanation come together in my head. He lifts my chin and looks deep into my eyes. "I love you," He finally says in a language I can understand.

His words pierce my heart. I realize all at once that this is the explanation I have been secretly hoping for. It makes me dizzy with joy. My heart sings, while his words ring in my ear.

"I was going crazy missing you while you were here, and when your sister told me about Igor… I wanted to kill him."

Reality hits me all at once. "So you *did* correspond with Olga since we've been here. What did she tell you about Igor?"

"That you and he were together all the time. That you hadn't spent a day without him."

"Any news recently?" I frown deeply.

"Not in the last two weeks." His concerned expression makes me realize that he couldn't have received any news while he traveled.

"Let's just say, I wouldn't mind if you did kill him for me."

"Did he hurt you?"

"He was never close enough to my heart to hurt it," I clarify. "But I would say other things were injured."

"I'll kill him."

"You can do that later," I lean into his arms. "Right now, you have to stay with me. You are my birthday present." I catch Olga's smiling eyes. She's dancing with Konstantine, but doesn't seem concerned about it. We are leaving soon.

Until we return to Petersburg, Stepan will stay with us at the Lividia Palace. It only took seeing his face for me to admit to myself what I had been feeling for Stepan all along. At first my mother is confused about the switch—Stepan loves me, not Olga—but Father claims he has suspected all along. We are reminded that Stepan and I cannot court openly until my sister has chosen a suitor, the oldest daughter must marry first, but I don't think that she will be courting anyone openly anytime soon. Having my sister in love with a soldier is not an ideal situation for Stepan and me.

Stepan has spent a lot of time with Dmetri in the past couple of months, and has grown to respect and admire him. He tries to comfort Olga, letting her know he's been as miserable as she has.

"Dmetri says it's been like living through hell without you. He's tried to come several times, but the closest he has been so far is Kerch. The steamboat is very expensive, and his new sergeant has not been as liberal with his time as his last sergeant."

"I was not liberal with those men. I was very strict. Ask any one of them." Olga gets defensive.

"Yes, Dmetri did tell me you were quite harsh with him." His tone is sarcastic.

I suddenly remember. "I'm sixteen now. Maybe now Father will give me a regiment to charge."

"After what has happened with Olga and Dmetri, I'm not sure I want you to command a regiment." Stepan gets serious.

"Tatiana always said she wanted to marry a soldier and have twenty children," Olga teases.

"Twenty?" Stepan's face turns white.

Olga laughs, "But you're no soldier."

Stepan puffs out his chest. "I'll have you know, I'm a very powerful man."

Stepan never attended a military academy. Instead, his father assembled the brightest tutors in Russia for him. He studied linguistics, politics, international relations, then instead of taking the military route, his father, through my father, got him a possession in the government right out of secondary school. Although he is young, my father works with him frequently. He thinks he is very intelligent and looked to for leadership, even without a full beard.

Both Olga and I laugh, but when I see the distressed look on his face I squeeze his arm and lean in closer. The three of us are seated in the salon all on the same sofa. Stepan's face turns somber. "Times are getting tough in Russia. There have been some heavy discussions going on. The old ways are no longer popular."

"It's been that way for years hasn't it?" Olga asks.

"Yes, but it's getting worse. There is talk of eliminating the church's power completely, thus diminishing your father's claim to the throne."

We have heard similar things before, but coming from Stepan it seems real. "What will happen then?"

"It's not going to happen if I have anything to say about it. I can make people listen." He sounds assured, but I'm afraid that's because that's how he wants me to see him—strong, so that he can protect me.

I give him a tender smile, letting it go for now.

Though mother is already busy making arrangements for our trip back to Russia, after the party she and Elisabeth make it official: the Russian ballet is coming to Crimea and mother is planning a reception to be held in honor of the dancers at the Lividia Palace. This way Alexei can meet his idol in person.

This is all very grand, except that it means our family will be spending a lot of time with the Konstantinoviches. I'm not afraid of Igor, not now that Stepan is here to protect me, but I want to spend as little time with him as possible.

Igor and Konstantine arrive at the palace to escort our family to the ballet in their dress uniforms. Alexei has chosen to wear his full uniform as well. Alexei's military ranking was given to him by birth and Mother has had a new uniform made for him every year since his first birthday. He wears it for special occasions—when he wants to look powerful. My sisters and I are wearing tea dresses. Stepan looks like a businessman in his suit. His red beard is filling out. He looks older than I remember, as if he has aged since we've been gone. I stay close to him, averting his eyes from the ballerinas.

But the ballerinas aren't my only concern. I haven't spoken to Igor since Stepan's arrival and I haven't had a chance to explain.

Apparently, I'm not the only one that thinks Igor deserves an explanation. When the ballet is over and our guests start to arrive at the palace for the reception, Igor takes the first opportunity he finds to talk to me. Olga, Stepan, and I are again sitting on the sofa in the salon. Irena is seated on a stool in the corner. He stands before me and gives me a bow. Ignoring the man seated beside me, he leans in.

"Would you excuse me in asking if I may speak to you in private?"

Before I can open my mouth, Stepan stands up. "Whatever you need to discuss with Tatiana can be discussed in my presence."

Though Stepan's forehead only comes to Igor's chin, and the men are nearly the same age, Igor takes a step back, intimidated, then turns back to me. "I think I deserve a proper goodbye."

Stepan's chest puffs out and his shoulders tense as he takes a step toward Igor. The other conversations in the room have quieted. Our guests and the ballerinas have turned their attention towards the salon. This time Igor stands his ground. "She has been with me every day before you arrived. I thought we had something…. Believe me, she had no problem demonstrating how she felt about me at the theatre."

Stepan turns to look at me. I'm upset. Does Stepan understand what Igor meant by that comment? Would he be angry with me if he knew about the kiss? My eyes fill with tears. Stepan only turns briefly, because he's already decided his next move. He turns and with a mighty blow of his fist, he punches Igor Konstantinovich in the jaw and knocks him on his trousers.

The crowded reception area goes back to their conversations, as if to avoid being witness to what has just occurred. I am frozen in shock; as Igor wipes blood from his face, his cold blue eyes lock onto mine.

Father comes in, offers his hand to help Igor off the ground and hands him a towel.

"You'd better go see to that eye, before it starts to swell." He dismisses him and turns to

Stepan. Stepan rubs his hand, still fuming. Father says nothing to him but pats his shoulder. Stepan takes his place next to me on the sofa. I feel like the room has suddenly emptied and Stepan and I are alone as he wipes a tear from my cheek.

"I will not let that man take advantage of you again," he whispers.

Summer 1913
Peterhof

The train ride back to Petersburg is far from treacherous. This time it's glorious, because Stepan is traveling along with us, as our guest. We do nothing all day but sit in the salon, holding hands, reading. Occasionally, he watches as I do needlework, and we converse or play games with my family, but I feel as if we are floating along the tracks escorted by angels. Discovering that I am in love with Stepan, and that he adores me, is the most blissful experience I could ever imagine. But the weather is exquisite and the journey takes barely a week. The days go by quickly and soon we arrive back in Petersburg, ending the dream.

 The days cannot go by quickly enough for my sister. She won't see her man Dmetri until she meets with her regiment, but Olga will have to wait. We are not to return to the city yet. The next few months will be spent in Peterhov. Peterhov is located on the shoreline a few miles west of the capitol, and it takes days to move into Peterhov Palace. It's more of a villa than a palace. Peter the Great, it's creator, called it Monplaisir (my pleasure) based on his own sketches of a palace that he wanted along the coast.

The location was ideal because when Peter the Great decided to build Petersburg at the eastern end of The Gulf of Finland.discovered that to the west of the shore of Peterhof the sea floor dropped off deep enough for sea vessels. Having an opening to the Atlantic Ocean was essential to Russia's economy, but every available port at that time was either frozen in the wintertime or too shallow for large ships to dock. When he first captured Koltin Island he found that it was clearly visible from the Peterhof site. At Kotlin Island he would build a commercial harbor for Petersburg. The original palace design escalated into what is now Peterhov Palace. It's surrounded by gardens with rows and rows of trees and fountains elaborately decorated and run exclusively by gravity using a staircase of pools.

When we stay in Peterhov, we don't stay in the palace built by Peter the Great. Instead we stay in the lower gardens in a palace in Alexandrine Park, constructed by Grandfather Nicholas. When we get to Peterhov I have to say goodbye to Stepan as well. He must go back to work in the Petersburg, and continue to fight for Russia and defend all that it has stood for, for centuries.

When the household has been settled, we can go back to our normal routine. Olga gingerly dusts off her uniform and excitedly puts up her hair the morning of her first inspection of her regiment. She looks as if she can't wait another minute as she chokes down her tea, and then does her own inspection in front of the mirror. Oddly, my mother doesn't even mention her hurried behavior.

Much to my surprise she returns before she's been gone an hour. She bursts through the door, letting it slam behind her. "Where is Father?" Her voice is commanding and frighteningly erratic.

"He's in his office at the palace" I mumble. "Just as he has been since you left."

Olga takes my hand. "Come with me, he may need your protection." She lifts me out of my chair by my arm, drags me out the door and down the tree lined path to the palace. She pushes past his secretary and bursts open his door without knocking.

"What happened to my regiment?" she asks in a clear, calm voice. Father puts down the document in his hand and sits back in his chair as if he has been expecting this reaction.

"The colonel that took your place while we were gone had some concerns. A certain soldier, Efreitor Dmetri Stepanovich, (I assume this is her Dmetri. I've never heard his surname) has begged him for transfers and vacation since we've been in Lividia. His comrades said he had gone to the Ukraine and had become very fond of you."

"All of my soldiers were fond of me. Ask any of them." Olga blurts out.

"That may be true, but no one else has tried to follow you. We were concerned for your safety. Coronel Alexandrovich questioned the other soldiers, but none of them would confirm or deny any knowledge of his intentions. We thought it best to dismiss him to another regiment and then to put you over another, in case he has loyal friends."

"Do you realize how long it took me to win the trust of those men? Do you realize what I'll have to do to make up for this loss?"

I realize it will be a challenge Coronel, but you did it once before, you can do it again. We are only concerned for your safety."

Olga leaves Father's office as abruptly as she arrived, forgetting I'm still with her she as she marches home.

"This is terrible Olga, what are you going to do?" I have to walk fast to keep up as she marches to our room. The door slams behind her and I am left standing outside, afraid to enter.

Lessons aren't required for my sisters and me during the summer. Instead we read, sew and get as much exercise as we can, walking around the grounds and swimming in the pools. They are functional as well as decorative. But Alexei has lessons all year long. There is much for a young tsesarevich to learn. But even his lessons are more relaxed. He spends much of his time with Monsieur Bertrand. Marie is allowed to sit in on his art lessons. After our stay in Lividia, it seems that her feelings for him have matured, from adolescent infatuation to professional respect. Anyway, he seems to tolerate her.

Anastasia is back to her mischievous tricks, but she stays busy, frequently leaving the palace to be outside. Peterhov is probably the best place we stay for her to ride Носки. There are acres of gardens and unexplored paths. The security surrounding the grounds is incomparable. It has to be, there are so many entrances and so many directions harm can come from, but it still doesn't induce fear for me like the Winter Palace did.

For me the openness of the palace doesn't compare with the freedom I feel in Lividia. Olga once said, "We work in Petersburg, but we live in Lividia." I want to feel like I'm "living" all the time, like I felt on the train ride home from Lividia. The magic I felt being with Stepan is still there, but it's been distilled by reality. He is working, and our courtship can not officially begin until Olga is engaged.

Thoughts of Stepan are always on my mind as I go through the lonely routine of the day. He's what I am thinking about over afternoon tea. Father has dropped by for a moment to speak with my mother.

"Tatiana, Tati. Tanya!" He has to address me three times to get my attention. "My darling, where is your mind today?"

Anastasia giggles. "Where it always is Papa. At the capitol in Petersburg."

Despite his tired look, he smiles a sympathetic smile. "Maybe her thoughts won't be so far away much longer," he happily reveals. Maybe if I wasn't so distracted and Olga wasn't still up in her room pouting, one of us would have noticed the significance of that statement.

He doesn't linger on that topic, but instead gets right to the point. "Tatiana," he starts again, "you are now sixteen, and we have a regiment that needs a commander. Here, at the main palace tomorrow, we will have a ceremony of coronation. We will make you a coronel like your sister. Olga can train you. She will know how best to handle these men. They are her old regiment."

Shocked, I speak out, "What about Dmetri?" I mistakenly speak of him on familiar terms, but Father does not seem to notice.

"Efreitor Stephenovich has been dismissed, dishonorably."

The room is completely silent. If there was any question before of his involvement with Olga, the look on our faces has answered it now. Olga is still up in her room, unaware of what has just taken place.

"Yes, Father," I finally find the words. I go on trying to sound as if the last few moments of shock on my part have not taken place. "I will be there tomorrow. What should I wear?"

Mother speaks from the other side of the room. I'd forgotten she was there. "The seamstress will be here sometime after tea to fit you to your uniform."

Tea ends solemnly. Mother sends me up to my room to put on looser clothing so that the tailor can get my proper measurements. I slowly ascend the staircase, wondering if I should tell Olga about the news we just heard. In our room, as I'm changing, even though she is facing away from me and looks like she is asleep, I tell her what I'm doing.

"I have to change." No response. "I am being fitted for my uniform. There is to be a ceremony tomorrow. I am to be made a coronel." I try to say this in an excited tone, one I would think she would expect coming from me. She is still silent. I guess, in trying to evoke a response from her, I say more than I should.

"You are to train me to command your old regiment."

Olga steadily sits up and swings her legs to the side of the bed.

"It will be your pleasure," she finally speaks in a hushed tone. "They are good men."

Now I'm silent. I don't know what to say. The silence is stifling. In an almost inaudible breath, Olga cuts through it. "He's gone, isn't he?"

"Discharged," I verify, "dishonorably."

"Ha!" Olga bursts out so loudly, I almost fall back. "Dishonor! What is honor anyway? If loving a princess is dishonorable, then Father is the king of dishonor."

That's all I hear on the subject for a while, because as soon as I go back downstairs, the tailor is waiting. The uniform fitting is an uncomfortable task. This is the first time I will be fitted for trousers. The jacket is cropped to my waist, like I've seen the men wear before. Because I am a colonel, I have a sash that must fit snugly across my chest. After the fitting, Mother brings in a tall box that holds my helmet. She carefully removes it from the container and pulls a bright plume from an envelope. She delicately puts it in place in the helmet and places it on my head, so she can adjust the chin strap. I stand in front of a large mirror in the ballroom before the seamstress takes it for some final adjustments. My mother and my sisters "ooo" and "ahhh." I try to be enthusiastic as I look at myself closely. I look older, more masculine. The plume on my helmet makes me feel like I am a foot taller. I suppose that is it's purpose. I don't think the color compliments my skin tone, but the snug fit emphasizes my slender waist. It will do.

After the uniform has been fitted I go up and change for dinner. There are to be more surprises at dinner I am told. The first surprise is for me. Stepan. One look from his tender eyes and I am secured. Everything will be fine, fine and grand, with Stepan to lean on, and lean on him I do. Not just figuratively, but literally. Although we are not yet courting in public, my family knows how I feel about him. Behind the doors of the palace, we are not afraid to show our affection for each other. He's not only here for dinner, but he will stay in the palace tonight. He is invited to the ceremony tomorrow.

The other surprise waits until we have eaten and are lulled into a false sense of peace.

My mother and father stand up together, combining their strength, probably

knowing they are going to need it. "We have an important announcement to make," Mother gets our attention.

"Your Father has received a telegram from King Konstantine of Greece. George has proposed marriage to your sister." Our eyes move to Olga. She is not smiling.

"Of course we will accept the proposal as soon as possible."

Olga's mouth drops open, but no words come out. This has been expected.

After dinner, Olga goes to Stepan for comfort, and I feel like I did a few months ago when I thought I was an outsider, peeking in on their private relationship, but I wait patiently. When my sisters go to bed, I finally get my chance. I stand beside him as we wish my sisters good night, and Olga finally climbs the stairs to our suite. Stepan lets out a relieved breath and wraps his arm around my waist. I fall back into them and look up into his eyes. He smoothes my hair away from my forehead. "You must be feeling neglected," he sighs.

I avert my eyes from his, making it seem worse than he expected. "All the time I spend away from you, with Olga, doesn't mean I love you less."

I try to smile, but he has hit a nerve, the source of my concerns, and he can see it on my face. He starts to explain himself as if his life depended on it. "You know everything I do is for you—for us. Every day I sit in counsel, trying to win back our followers—keep them loyal to your father—to keep you safe, your family safe. It's a full-time job."

He smiles and this time I'm able to genuinely express my affection back to him through my eyes. "Your sister has complicated things. I love her—like a sister."

"Where have I heard that line before?" I tease.

"Like a dear friend," he changes his wording to placate me. "All she would have to do is say yes to that prince and you would be mine."

I like the sound of that but we both know it could never happen that easily. "She's in love," I sigh.

"And she's stubborn."

I nod in agreement. There's no question about that. "I know how she feels," I say looking into Stepan's deep green eyes.

He puts his hand under my chin and smoothes my hair again. "We can certainly empathize with her on that account."

He bends down, bringing my face to his. His soft lips lightly press against mine. Then his mouth parts slightly and the plump part of my lower lip slips between his. I feel his warm breath as he exhales. My heart and my bottom lip quiver causing Stepan to press his lips together squeezing mine as he gently pulls away. The sweetness of the sensation causes me to stumble. The feeling is so different from when Igor kissed me; I choose to consider this my first kiss.

Stepan takes a step back. It seems he has been affected by this kiss as well, as he takes my hand and holds it to his heart. "Tomorrow will be a big day for you Coronel Nikolaevna. You'd better get to bed." He doesn't seem to want me to leave, and I am not ready to go to bed yet. So, like the last time, I stand up on my toes. This time I slowly lay my warm hand against his rough cheek. I can't help myself as I move in for more of his sweetness. At first my lips just take a sample, but soon I am hungry for more. My mouth parts and our lips move together as he willingly lets me experiment until I am satisfied. When I finally go back down to my natural height, Stepan shakes his head as if to clear it. I search his eyes, feeling that I may have overstepped my bounds, but the smile I see there tells me he enjoyed it as well.

I finally turn from him and clumsily make my way up the stairs.

Up in my room, Olga is waiting. She correctly reads the glow on my face, but her smirk soon turns into a smile. "I'm so happy for you, Tanya. Stepan is a lucky man. He will make a wonderful brother for me."

I'm too happy to be irritated at her, and she's had a horrible day. I can't even imagine. I dress in my nightclothes and climb into bed. My heart is still beating furiously as I pull my covers up to my chin. But before we are asleep, we hear a suspicious noise outside our room. Something or someone has landed on our veranda.

A tapping on the glass clarifies that it is someone. I crawl deeper into the covers, but Olga pulls hers back. She is dressed in a robe and slippers and I notice her hair is freshly brushed. She seems to have been expecting this intrusion. She quietly opens the door and falls sobbing and laughing into Dmetri's arms. "How did you do it?"

I've pulled my covers up so that only my eyes are showing, but I am witness to everything that is happening.

"This place is easier to sneak into then the Winter Palace. Well, the security is better here, but I'm not so unpopular. I have friends among your guards."

Stepan! He's is a double agent. Making me think that he is trying to help us by getting Olga engaged while assisting her lover as well.

"There are trees everywhere. Did I ever tell you that I'm good with trees? My father worked on a walnut farm and I helped him. I would climb to the tops to collect the nuts."

"You may have told me that once or twice," my sister giggles.

The things working men tell their woman to impress them.

"Did you hear me land on the veranda? I jumped from that tree." He runs to point out the French door. "I bet you barely heard me land. I'm skilled at being light on my feet."

My sister and I look at each other. She disguises her smile as she wraps her arms around her soldier. "Oh, it's so far," she gasps with concern as she looks out the door. "We must come up with a safer means of seeing one another."

"I would risk life and limb." Dmetri's face is sincere.

"More than that it sounds like. I hear you have been discharged—dishonorably. What will you do now?"

Dmetri smiles. "Is that what he told you?"

He reads the look on Olga's face as an affirmation. "No, no no. Like I said, I'm not so unpopular as your father would like to think I am. My commanding officers think I'm indispensable." He grins.

"As did your previous commanding officer." She gives him another squeeze.

Dmetri explains, "I have been given leave until the current situation is resolved." He puts his hand on Olga's head, indicating I gather, that she is the current situation. "And then I am to continue my duties."

"So how am I to be resolved then?" Olga asks, disgruntled.

"There is only one way I can think of. We have to get married. Once the marriage is consummated, you will be no good for a dumb old prince, and you will be all mine."

My face is hot under the covers. I have heard too much of this private conversation. I can only hope that my sister stays honorable to her station and to our father. Olga must sense my discomfort, because she leads Dmetri out on the landing and shuts the door behind her.

I can't sleep. Thoughts of Olga's intentions keep running through my head, until I realize that I need to look fresh for my ceremony tomorrow. Then I really can't sleep. I must sleep some time in the night, because I don't hear Olga come in, but for hours I hear her and Dmetri's voices floating in my window. I would be surprised if I'm the only one that heard them. They seem too confident in their love to be cautious.

Morning tea is hurried as the whole family needs to dress and get ready for the ceremony at the palace. Father, Alexei, Olga and I will be in uniform. Mother, as well as the two younger girls will dress in formal attire. I barely bump into Stepan after tea. He takes my hand. "You don't look as well rested as I would like to see you. Did you not sleep well?"

"You should know," I accuse as I pull him to me and whisper in his ear. "Did you not send a guest secretly up to our room last night?"

We are interrupted before he can verify or refute his actions, but my look of disdain is undeniable.

The only people in attendance at my inauguration are my family, Stepan, and a few high ranking officials of the royal guard. Rasputin is also there by Mother's invitation. He has been on vacation for the past several months as well, visiting his wife and son in Siberia. Alexei has been relatively healthy since his accident last fall, and has been trusted to the royal doctors care. They are not as strict with him, which father likes better. But Rasputin wouldn't miss something like this. Mother insists that he is part of the family, and he especially likes to concern himself with matters of state. Father allows it, maybe to humor him, but is careful not to let Rasputin think he has any say on important matters.

This tells me that the ceremony is only a formality, but there is a reception afterwards anyway. I'm tired and still a little upset with Stepan. I try to avoid him, but thirty minutes into the reception, he catches me around the waist as I walk by. The warmth of his hand makes resisting him impossible. His whisper in my ear and runs shivers down my spine. "I'm not sure how I feel about other men seeing you in this uniform." As if flattery will make up for ruining my night last night. It's working. He goes on, "Especially because your sister told me it was your dream to marry a soldier, and then after what happened to her… Maybe no man's woman is safe from the draw of the military."

I turn so I'm facing him. I am still tired—irritable—but I will forgive him.

"You are all the soldier I need, you and twenty children." I laugh remembering the look
on his face when Olga mentioned my desire for a large family before.

He puts his hand gently on my forehead and leans back my face so I can look at him as he speaks. "You could be the mother of all Russia. Twenty, thirty children, it doesn't matter to me as long as I am their father."

He leaves me breathless. I avoid his eyes. "I don't think it's appropriate to talk about my being a mother, on the day of my inauguration into the military."

"Unless you really were to become the mother of Russia. Think of it Tanya, you could be the mother of Russia's next ruler."

I still think he's joking with me, but the words have heavy meaning. "And you would be his father?" I wait for his reaction. His eyes remain soft and sincere. "I didn't realize you had such ambitions."

"I am only at your service, m'lady."

II

The men are all in uniform, seated on horses when Olga and I march through the courtyard to meet them. Olga has told me what to do. I am the colonel now, I must lead. I stand before them and call out orders.

"Джентльмен… спешивается."

Following the order the men dismount their horses.

"Падение сIn. Подготавливайте для осмотра."

The men line up, horses at their side, ready for me to inspect them.

"Внимание!"

I march up and down the lines ensuring that their uniforms are pressed and that their pins are on correctly. When I'm finished, I yell another command.

"На легкости"

The soldiers relax their stance and I speak to them. "I am Colonel Tatiana Nikolaevna. I realize that you have experienced a lot of changes in the past months and some of you are probably wondering how these changes can be taken seriously. I assure you that you are highly respected by your commanding officers and that the duties you are charged with are vital to Russia. I hope to earn your trust as we get to know and respect one another."

The soldiers are excused to go about their daily routines.

"So that's it?" I'm surprised it's over so fast.

"Yes, for the first day. Soon you will learn to lead them in drills, that takes longer, and it's more fun. You did very well. I especially enjoyed your speech. It was personal, yet authoritative."

"You were standing behind me. There is no way they won't be comparing me with you all the time."

"It's true. The same way my new regiment will compare me to the man that has been commanding them up until now."

We head home for morning tea. Olga has been able to put off the subject of her engagement, but not for long. Father and Mother are seated at the table when we return.

"Your mother tells me that you are refusing to marry George on the grounds that you desire to be married to a native Russian," Father says firmly.

"I not only desire it, Papa, I demand it. I am the daughter of the tzar. Our people need to see our patriotism." Olga speaks with confidence.

It should seem that Father would be pleased by her strength of loyalty, but he is not deterred by it. "Marriage to someone outside of Russia has never appeared to be unpatriotic, but rather in our nation's best interest. The Grecian rulers have always been our friends. It would be best if we were to keep it that way. You and your mother will compose a telegram this morning accepting the proposal."

Spoons stirring the tea is the loudest noise heard. Olga leaves the table without being excused as soon as her cup is empty and cannot be found the rest of the morning. Thankfully Mother chooses not to overreact to her disappearance, and doesn't mention her absence to Father. No one speaks of her during dinner and I don't see her again until she climbs into the window that night after I've gone to bed.

She doesn't bother to explain herself at first, but hurries to our parents' suite instead. Finally, as she's dressing in her night clothes I ask her.

"Where have you been all day?"

"Here, there." She smiles mysteriously.

"You're terrible." I give up and hide my face in my pillow.

Olga walks softly to my bed and whispers, "Where do you think I have been?"

I shouldn't play her game, but I've been dying to know all day. "With Dmetri?"

Her face lights up in answer to that question. "And in Petersburg with Stepan."

My body fills with fire as I'm unable to control my jealousy. "Stepan?" I try to hide the fury in my voice.

"Yes, Stepan. He is trying to act as liaison between our father and Dmetri and me."

"Is it working?"

"Not really. Father is understanding, but immovable in his decision. I guess I didn't expect anything different."

"Then why do you seem so happy?"

"Are you joking? I just spent the whole day with the man I love. I couldn't ask for anything better." Olga blushes.

"So what are you going to do?" I'm wide awake now, wondering what I would do if I were in Olga's place.

"Sleep," she says as she climbs under the covers.

The next day I inspect my regiment without Olga standing next to me. She has a whole new regiment of her own to deal with. One of Father's lead commanders takes me aside afterward and tells me he is going to teach me the drill the men need to learn.

"I know you understand the importance of your role, Colonel, but I wish to remind you that these men could be marching into battle at anytime. The Germans and the Turks seem to be flexing their military muscles, and Japan is always a threat. Your father, the tzar, wants to avoid confrontation whenever possible, but at some point I fear it will be unavoidable."

It seems for the first time, my eyes are opened to the purpose of these military shows. Though I was young, I remember the war with Japan. Father was away at battle and Mother was a mess with worry. I also remember hearing about soldiers whose lives had been lost, but I think today is the first time I can imagine people I know, even care about, heading out into gunfire and other dangers fighting to keep us safe.

My soldiers and their lives are in the back of my mind as I spend the day drinking tea and walking through the grounds. I'm full of hope that Stepan will be by this evening. He must have something he wishes to discuss with father or Olga, but at Peterhov, in the summertime, the telephone seems to be the best way for my Father to communicate the information he needs to with Stepan.

Olga's engagement has not been forgotten, but for the time being is put off for another time. The maids, who always gossip, have made a discovery.

"It was a love letter. Yes, oozing with affection," I overhear one maid say to another

"The Empress wrote it, but Anna, the one who cleans downstairs, found it by the boys bed. She gave it to Christoff, the head guard," the second maid says.

"His imperial highness should know about it by now."

I don't have to wonder long what they are talking about.

There is a new scandal at the palace. Our beloved Rasputin, my brother's savior, is often the subject of this gossip. Admittedly, he is a strange man. His eyes are compelling. Some say he uses hypnotism. I myself have never seen him use anything like that, but he and Mother spend hours together treating Alexei. He has cured him many times, like magic. Mother is a very spiritual person. She is convinced that he has been sent by God as an instrument, so the Alexei can overcome his ailments and complete his destiny.

But to the Russian people, it must look bad. They know nothing about Alexei's disease, only that Mother spends so much time with the man.

"It was not a love letter. Only a message of gratitude," Mother pleads. She sounds like she's been crying, for herself of Rasputin, I'm not sure.

My sisters and I have been sent upstairs while Father and Mother discuss the situation, and as usual, I have been elected spy.

Apparently, a letter that she had written in gratitude was leaked out to the public. It was filled with her love and devotion to our great healer, but not knowing what Rasputin's purposes are to our family, it looks as if it were a love letter. This simple note has now turned into a full blown love affair between Mother and Our Friend, and it looks like Father willingly allows it.

"If Tzar Nicholas can't rule his own household," they say on the streets, "how is he to rule Russia?"

"We must keep Rasputin away until this scandal has worn itself out," Father determines on the spot.

"But we didn't do anything wrong. How can I ask him to leave?" Mother seems to be having a hard time accepting her responsibility in this.

Father rubs his temples with his index finger and thumb as he paces the floor.

"Maybe *we* can leave then, but we must make it look like we planned it all along. We don't want people to think we are running from the rumor. Where would be a good place to go this time of year that we haven't visited recently?"

"The yacht!" Mother exclaims. We used to always go out on the *Standart* this time of year."

I go back to our suites with good news. "We are taking a vacation aboard the *Standart!*" I tell them. I will explain what happened to Olga later, but I don't think my younger sisters need to know more than that.

As we prepare to leave, Mother is sick with worry, but Rasputin has proven in the past that he can heal Alexei while he is away, like the miracle that happened in Spala last winter. Though we all consider

Rasputin a treasured member of the family, he can still be frightening. There are so many terrible stories. Mother says that they are only stories and cannot be true, but the servants don't trust him. My sisters and I have discovered him lurking around our suites at the most inopportune times, and Stepan has warned me to stay far away from him. Stepan does not like him one bit.

For Olga, this distraction seems like a good thing. Though it means that she and Dmetri will be separated once again, but she hopes it will delay her engagement to George, but Father has other ideas. He insists that the engagement between Olga and George will be made official before the trip begins.

"We will take the yacht and travel to Crimea and finish out the summer with another trip to Lividia, then on to Poland in the fall. When we return to Petersburg, George will join us there and we will make plans for your marriage."

I am certain the task of making sure that doesn't happen will fall upon Stepan, the always loyal friend to my sister.

The vacation comes at a terrible time for me. Just as I'm getting to know my regiment, and the thought of leaving Stepan again for months is unbearable. But I have no say, and the preparations are made in a matter of days. Mother composes an acceptance message to George's proposal and sends it just before we leave.

The night before our departure, our usual company comes to see us off and wish us bon voyage. I'm afraid that once again Olga is going to dominate all of Stepan's time, but with the private announcement of her engagement, she becomes bombarded with well wishers and aunts wanting to give her advice, especially Aunt Maria who couldn't be happier that our families will soon be have a deeper connection. Neither she nor Irena seem to be aware that George is not Olga's first choice.

This leaves Stepan for me and I'm not sure how to react to my good fortune. I become bashful as he pulls me aside into the hallway between the front salon and the den where the children are.

"We have no need to hide from each other tonight," he whispers into my ear. "As far as everyone here knows, you are free to court whomever you choose now."

"And what makes you think that you are my first choice? I have a regiment of my own now," I tease.

Stepan grabs me around the waist and speaks into my neck, "They are all married old men, if my orders were made clear."

"You are far too powerful for your age and experience. What would Russia think if they knew that a boy in his twenties was advising the tzar?"

"Ah, but apparently my power has its limits. Even I can't stop you from leaving me once again. And I know how you Nikolaevna girls flirt with the diadka."

The diadka are young sailors, personnel assigned to each of us and charged with our safety and entertainment. When we were small, they would play games with us or we would play tricks on them. But now that the young men our close to our age, we find pleasure in their company and good looks. I smile despite myself. "Yes, even Olga might forget about her soldier with those charming diadka boys around."

"Excuse me while I go talk to your Father." Stepan marches away like he really would like to have a word with him, but laughing, I grab his arm and pull him back towards me.

"No, don't you see. If Olga forgets about Dmetri, we'll come home from the vacation to a wedding, and you can be the escort of the maid of honor."

"I think that will be Alexander's job."

"Hmmm." I get thoughtful, "I'd forgotten about Alexander." I'm trying to sound like I'm teasing. It must be working because Stepan pulls me into his arms and presses me against his chest. He holds me long enough for the silliness to wear off and reality to sink in. My tears land on his shirtfront.

Kissing the top of my head, he speaks into my hair, "Don't let the diadka make you forget about me."

Drying my eyes I look up into his big green ones. "Will you be able to come to Lividia? Or at the very least, meet us at the hunting lodge in Poland?"

"The Konstantinoviches will not be in Lividia in August. I've already checked, so you will be safe from Igor if I can't make it to Crimea. But I will be in Poland in September. Wild boars couldn't keep me away."

The Alexandravich boys run through and interrupt our precious time together tonight, but I will see Stepan one more time before we leave. He will drive us to the ferry tomorrow. Olga had to say goodbye to Dmetri already. I'm finally able to sympathize with her loneliness.

Marie and Anastasia are blissfully unaware that the trip is anything other than a family vacation. In past years, our greatest family memories have been created aboard the *Standart*. It truly is a vacation for us. Father and Mother are able to set aside their authoritative demeanors and relax from their duties. The crew becomes like family, except for the boys who, like Stepan said, treat us like girls—flirting, teasing, using flattery to get our attention (which always works, of course).

Then, we'll go back to Lividya in the off season. Just in time to celebrate Alexei's ninth birthday. Only our family will be in attendance at the private celebration, but there will be a national celebration orchestrated by Uncle Makhail back in Petersburg in my brother's honor. The social scene isn't as rigid as it is in the spring. We will spend most of our days alone: biking along the beach path, playing tennis on the palace grounds or sailing with Father. The theater will be closed for the season, so nights will also be spent at home.

The problem with having a family as large as ours is that there isn't an automobile built that can hold all seven of us. Our bags have already been loaded on a wagon and sent to the ferry this morning, but after tea, Stepan and Uncle Alexander arrive each driving a model T from America. Mother, Father and Alexei pile into the vehicle Uncle will drive, while Olga, Marie, Anastasia and I chose to ride with Stepan. Riding up front with Stepan makes me think of happier times yet to come when we will be together. I reach across the front seat and tenderly touch his gloved hand on the steering wheel. He can't disguise his pleasure, as he looks down at me with a grin on his face. He seems proud to be driving the Grand Duchesses of Russia.

We have to board quickly when we arrive. Saying goodbye privately isn't an option, but
Stepan gives me a quick kiss in front of my family. My red face gives them added reason to tease me as I am the last family member to board. I watch him wave until I can no longer see him.

The ferry ride across the Finnish Sea only takes a couple of hours. When we reach the dock on Kotlin Island, we board the yacht and wait for our gear to be loaded and the crew to board. As soon as we are aboard, I duck down to the cabin that Olga and I share. I plan on lying there on my cot until we are finally at sea. I'm not there long when the tzar himself comes down the stairs.

"Are you up for a game of shuffleboard? The whole family is waiting, and you hold the championship position."

It's hard to be unhappy when Father gives you his special smile.

"We have weeks to play shuffleboard," I complain, but I'm already putting my shoes back on. "Don't you think we'll get sick of it if we start playing before we even launch?" I follow him up the stairs.

We don't really have time to play a game before afternoon tea. I think Father was using the shuffle board as an excuse to pull me out of the cabin, before I got depressed. Tea is served as we leave the dock. We are waited on by a whole new crop of charming young men.

"I am interested to know who hires these men," Mother comments as the last boy leaves us to go into the galley. "It's as if they were hand-picked, just for our enjoyment."

Of course Mother means her children's enjoyment. The young servers easily make friends with Alexei, but Mother is also taken in by their charm. Father doesn't seem to mind.

"Isn't it beautiful how the sun sparkles off the waves?" Sitting across from Anastasia and me, Marie remarks to Mosier Bertrand as she drinks her morning tea. Her art teacher has easily settled into the family as he, the doctor, and my mother's cook are the only members of the household who aren't immediate that have accompanied us on this voyage

"Not as beautiful as the way your eyes were sparkling under the light of the moon last night." A tall dark diadka in a cropped jacket with tails comments with an Italian accent as he clears the morning dishes from in front of her.

Marie blushes, but pulls out the chair next to her inviting him to sit. "Ah. Antonio, you

dance like an angel."

"Angels don't dance," Anastasia corrects. "He danced like the wind on the waves of the sea."

We all laugh at her imaginative description. If the balls in the great halls of the Russian palaces were anything like the dances we have here on the yacht, my sister's and I would have all fallen in love when we were Anastasia's age, I observe, still thinking back to the previous magical night with nothing but the sky for a ceiling and the stars hanging from it for decoration.

There were no dance cards or prominent figures to impress; only warm bodies to hold on to and the satisfying smell of sea air and freshly laundered suits. We all learned to dance aboard the *Standart*. We may have taken lessons at the palace, but we dance on the yacht. Being in the arms of a stranger speaking loving words in my ear doesn't make me forget Stepan, but it makes the days without him bearable.

The voyage aboard the *Standart* seems to take us back in time. Back to when we didn't worry about war or political matters. Though I don't think such a time ever existed. Now that I am older, I realize that Father has always been concerned, maybe, probably, even before he married Maman. Other concerns are kept snugly in the back of our minds as well; such as will there be a marriage when we return and what does the future hold for the children of the tzar? Will we ever be allowed to find peace and happiness?

Some happiness may be obtained now. Everything we want or need is provided for us by these beautiful young men, and we have each other. We are reminded that family is the most important thing in the world.

When the shores of Crimea come into sight, we must bid farewell to our doting young friends, but we do not have to say goodbye to our happiness. The family is well and there has been no need for the services of Greggori Rasputin. Perhaps when we return home he will no longer be necessary and my parents can be free of the gossip that has come between them.

In Lividya, we are away from the influences of the world, but not completely. Father has telephone meetings with Petersburg daily—something that was impossible while we were at sea. I often wonder if any of the conversation include my Stepan. I don't hear from him at all. While we are in Lividia there is nothing to do but play and enjoy each others' company, but we have been each others' company solely for weeks now.

"Mother!" Marie runs down the stairs from the suite she shares with Anastasia tight-faced with a piece of white fabric in her hand. "Anastasia wore my tennis dress while riding her bicycle. She tore it when it got caught in the spokes. It is too big for her and she never asks!"

Father tells us that with boys it's simpler. When they have a disagreement, they wrestle it out and then get over it, but in our house the bickering never ends. But sometimes it's Alexei that causes the tension. His memory of last winter is short and he thinks it's unfair that he is not being allowed to go hunting with my father in Poland in the fall.

"We will be traveling to Spala by the end of the week. The boars won't wait, and if we delay much longer, the Alexandrich boys will have killed them all." Father thinks he is being funny, but no one else is amused.

"Nikki, how insensitive can you be?" Father gets looks of agitation from every female at the table, but Alexei won't be content with just a look.

"The Alexandrich boys, the Alexandrich boys. Why don't you just adopt one of them and make him your heir?" Alexei stands and pushes his chair back from the table with so much force that Mother goes white with fear and stands to follow him.

Father reaches for her hand to stop her, but she quickly pulls it away from him. "He could hurt himself when he's so angry. He's not careful."

"Let him be a boy for once," Father says, but Mother won't hear him.

"Are you forgetting last winter? Would you have me live through that again?" Her eyes well up and Father quickly puts his arms around her and pulls her to him.

"I will go after the boy. I will see that he doesn't get hurt," he whispers into her graying hair.

As soon as her tears are wiped and she rejoins us at the table, my mind goes back to the conversation. Will the Alexandrich boys be the only ones waiting when we get to Poland?

Apparently I'm not the only one thinking about what is awaiting us when we get home. Olga's solemn face has not looked up from the table all evening.

I wait until we are in our suite and speak softly. "What have you heard from Dmetri?"

"The same as what you have heard from Stepan? Nothing. Father is not permitting any messages to be sent to us. We are more isolated here than we are in the palace at wintertime surrounded by ice and snow." The thought sends a shiver down my spine.

"We will have word soon enough. Stepan promised me he would meet us in Poland. We will be there by week's end."

The following days seem to last forever, especially the train ride to Poland. I close my eyes and try to remember the outline of his jaw, the touch of his hand, his eyes as they pierce through me. The rest of the family's mind must be somewhere else as well. Except for the occasional bumps and the bustle in the kitchen, The Imperial Train travels silently along its tracks.

My face is pressed against the window as we pull into the station. Someone will be there to greet us. I can only hope it will be Stepan, but instead my uncle's outline comes into view. My cousins Andrei and Feodor are standing beside him. My heart drops, almost splitting open as it hits my stomach. I grab my book and needle-point from the shelf beside me and shove them in to my satchel. I can't show my disappointment. My sisters would never let me forget it, so I throw back my shoulders and walk methodically to the exit.

As I step off the train I suddenly feel something like a gust of wind. I look up just slightly at first but the feeling is undeniable. Another step forward and I am sure—his presence penetrates my soul, right down to my heart. My sisters, my satchel, all are forgotten as I trip over whatever is in front of me to get into his arms. With his hand on the small of my back pressing me into him I bury my face in his neck and inhale the sweet scent of my love. It takes minutes before I'm aware that we have an audience of giggling girls behind us.

"Save some for me," Anastasia pushes the others aside and joins me in a hug for Stepan. It seems he is a sight for sore eyes for my whole family.

"We missed you too," Uncle says sarcastically in his gruff voice.

My father takes his hand and pats our uncle vigorously on the back. "It is good to see you, brother, nephews," he acknowledges the young men who have been ordered to gather our gear. The servants will unload our trunks into the luggage cart, but Uncle Alexander makes sure that our hands are not burdened with anything extra. Stepan takes my satchel.

"How could something that looks so dainty be so heavy?" His eyebrows furrow. I laugh
and squeeze him more tightly.

As soon as my mother and father are occupied, Olga takes her turn with Stepan. She only has to look at him and he answers her questioning eyes. "It has all been settled. We will proceed with the plan when you get to Tsarskoe Selo."

I don't understand what he has told her, but my sister's eyes are glistening and her smile is like I have not seen since we left Petersburg.

Dinner at the hunting lodge is a happy time for everyone, save my brother. Mother has my aunts to gossip with; even my Alexandrich cousins seem entertaining. Everything is good when you're reunited with your loved ones after all these weeks away. My mother will soon have to find a way to keep my brother occupied while the men are hunting, which they will do every day while we are here. Sailing is no longer an option for the young tsesarevich and Monsieur Bertrand has been invited on the hunt this year. Alexei will be left completely with the women and the spoiled boy, Valisi, who is no better.

The men are up and gone before we are even awake enough to hear them. After tea, I try to get Olga to confide in me—tell me what was meant by the comment Stepan made at the train station. She is completely mute on the matter, and she and Irena are busy talking about her wedding plans. In the salon, Marie and Nina, and Anastasia and Xenia are putting together a puzzle. I find my brother sulking in the corner and invite him to go for a walk with me outside.

At first mother objects, but when I promise I will watch over him as if I were his nurse, she gives in. She knows I like to explore and doesn't trust me, but my eyes must tell her that I love my brother and would never allow any harm to come to him.

"It must be a lot of pressure on a boy your age—being the only heir. I can't imagine being expected to rule Russia someday." Alexei and I are dressed from head to toe in fur. Late fall in Poland is almost like winter. Hopefully a hunter won't mistake us for a bear come out of hibernation for a stroll.

Alexei squints at me. He doesn't trust me either. My sisters and I are rarely serious with the boy. Being genetically predestined to the station he was born into, my sisters and I feel it's our duty to make sure he remains humble. But this time I think he senses that I am serious.

"It's hard being me," he starts out lightly. "Father understands the pressures of being born to rule a country, but he doesn't understand the pressures of having to stay alive. Sometimes, I wish I had died last winter. I could have avoided the pain I endure now and am sure to experience in the future—the agony of watching Mother suffer."

"I for one am glad you didn't die last winter." A sincere smile pokes through Alexei's scarf covered face. "Then I wouldn't have a perfectly easy target to hit with snowballs."

"No!" Alexei tries to get out of my way, but he's stuck. He has stood in one place long enough that the melted snow around his boots has turned to ice, and he can't move. I let a few fly, whizzing just past his ears, but missing on purpose. A hard snowball would probably inflict quite a lot of pain on the small young man. The reality that Alexei probably won't live long enough to rule Russia hits me harder than it ever has before, and I am reminded of the comment Stepan made earlier about me being the mother of Russia's next ruler. If Olga does not marry George and Alexei (bless his heart) doesn't survive long enough, that leaves me, my sons, to follow in my father's footsteps. The thought is overwhelming and I push it to the back of my mind as I wrap my arms around my brother's fur-covered body and try to dislodge his boots from the ice so that we can go in where it's warm.

Endless stories about wild boars have begun to bore me. My sisters and I and the majority of the women in the household choose to separate ourselves from the men as soon as dinner is over each night. My Stepan is usually one of the first to come looking for us. Although I am filled with joy as he takes me in his arms, it only lasts briefly. I have to share him with Olga, who, by dinner time is tired of discussing a make-believe wedding with Irena. Olga has confided that part of the "plan" she and Stepan have discussed is getting the wedding postponed—preferably permanently. I feel that I will have to learn to share him always.

We are surrounded by friends, family, and loved ones on the journey home. The silent train ride a week ago is forgotten as its compartments fill with noise; children playing, singing, laughing, all the sounds of happiness. The train ride is the only thing that lies between the blissful summer spent with my family and what new trials await us at home.

Winter 1913
Tsarskoe Selo

"A New Years wedding then," Mother repeats again perhaps hoping that if she says it again, we will become as excited as she. Prince George of Greece's arrival has been detained, but mother's enthusiasm has not.

"The weather will make travel for a wedding party difficult in January," my diplomat, Stepan reasons. No one else in the household, not even Father, has dared to dispute her.

Mother sits back with her thumb on her chin and thinks. She slowly nods, finally agreeing with Stepan. "I see," she continues to nod, "yes, I see your point." Olga takes in a deep breath, relieved that the wedding will now be pushed back to spring at least.

"Have you heard from him?" Olga jumps, realizing she's being addressed. "Have you heard from your fiancé? He must be as anxious as we to get this marriage solemnized. I am so glad you were able to spend some time with him last year and that affection has developed." Mother tells herself this, probably to pacify her guilt.

What mother doesn't know is that Dmetri is already here. He and Olga have been in constant contact through Stepan since the day we arrived in Petersburg. Anastasia has also been reunited with an old friend. During her first escapade to the stables to check on Носки, she finds that the stable crew at the Winter Palace has been transferred to Tsarskoe Selo.

"I didn't realize what a smarty pants he was last year," she tells me when I confront her about Peter. "He told me that my lack of skill could be dangerous for Носки in these conditions and refused to discuss the possibility of me exercising him myself."

"Maybe he's right. He cares about that horse as much as you do," I explain. "I don't think he would have told you that if it wasn't true."

My little sister fumes, and goes on like she didn't hear me. "It wasn't what he said, it was the way he said it, like I was a child. Just because he has grown a foot taller doesn't mean he's any smarter than I am."

"He's grown a foot?" I remember the boots that Anastasia so artfully bestowed on him. "Does he have any clothes that fit?"

"I think he has made friends with a seamstress in town," she scowls. I try my best not to smile at the clearly invidious look on her face.

We could all be happy here—I have Stepan, Olga has Dmetri, and the relationship between Marie and Monsieur Bertram has surprised us all. One minute they are laughing and playing like a brother and sister and the next they are discussing art or politics like two old men at university. Sometimes it seems that they look at each other with such desire that I think the buttons will pop off their clothes. Fortunately for Marie, I don't think Mother or Father have noticed, either that or they refuse to. But we cannot be happy while Father is so troubled.

"Your father must listen to reason," Stepan complains to me one evening. "The world is looking to him. Russia is the most powerful force in the world and our ally forces need him to make a move. Most of the Dumas doesn't know him as I know him—a soft, good man. But Japan has left him without confidence and I'm afraid he is listening to the devil Rasputin."

"How can you call Rasputin a devil after all he has done for my family," I'm shocked.

"He is a charlatan, Tanya. He uses trickery, dishonesty, hypnosis. That is not of God, it's of the devil." I allow Stepan to quietly express his opinion, but I am undecided. Mother loves him and Father still accepts him, even after all of the trouble that happened this summer. But he frightens me, so I remain neutral.

Things are getting back into a routine. Every morning, after tea, Olga and I inspect our regiments, though neither of us have been asked to run drills with the soldiers. That is done in the afternoon by either Colonels Yogot or Koudasheva. Though we have always considered ourselves to be legitimately commanding our men, we are told now that the army is no longer a show. These men need to be prepared to be called into battle at anytime. They seem anxious, and though rumors of war are rampant, I am unable to calm their nerves. I know no more than they do. I would know nothing if it weren't for Stepan needing to vent his frustrations once in a while.

But for days it seems that Stepan has spent every moment he is here whispering with Olga. Sometimes I wonder if Mother and Father think that if they wait, Stepan will go back to Olga—their original choice for a match for their oldest daughter. Sometimes I wonder too, but Dmetri is outside the window of our suite every night, and I think that the next part of their plan is about to unfold.

Olga's eighteenth birthday is November 15. I tease her that she will officially be an old maid at that point. Mother is not laughing. She can see now that the wedding cannot take place in the winter, but she expects that George will come for her birthday so that the Russian people can see that the engagement is official. Mother plans a birthday/engagement party fit for an Imperial Princess.

Olga's birthday officially begins the Christmas season. For our family, devout Russian Orthodox followers, the season is a sacred time. The first forty days are spent in fasting. But during the twelve days prior to Christmas (celebrated in Russia on January seventh) the celebrating really begins. A feast is set every-day as we honor each of the Lord's twelve apostles.

"What am I to expect from my sister in the weeks before her birthday?" I inquire of Stepan as we are seated in the parlor awaiting our usual guests for the evening. "Should I plan on attending an engagement party? Acting as the maid of honor?"

"Certainly," he states matter of factly. "Your mother is planning an engagement party, and so we will have one."

I look over my shoulder to see if anyone is standing behind me, but for now we are completely alone. The questioning look on my face, must be begging for an explanation. Stepan throws up his hands. "Tanya, I don't know what your sister is doing anymore. The situation is out of my hands. Her passion is so strong she won't listen to me, I'm much too reasonable for her."

I'm still not sure I believe him. Confusing people into thinking he knows nothing seems to be one of his greatest tactics. I have seen him use it on my father. But the plans for the party continue, and I fulfill my assigned tasks as sister of the bride with all the enthusiasm I can muster. George will arrive on the evening of the fourteenth. Although this is not the wedding, my mother has developed the notion that he is not to see his future bride until she is announced at her birthday party. It is my task to make sure that's the way it happens. Stepan has offered to let George stay at the Karenin palace, and we, together, will spend the hours before the ball entertaining him.

Stephan and I are there to meet George at the train when he arrives. When I first see him come off the train he stands tall—as handsome as ever, despite the tired lines around his eyes when he smiles. I didn't realize how much I'd missed George's calming smile. I can't wait to ask him about his family. Stepan must notice my enthusiasm because he stays close to me, always with his hand on my back.

"I'm not surprised to see you two together, Karenin," George notes after he greets us both with a kiss, "waiting for this marriage so that you can go public with your feelings for Princess Tatiana." The prince smiles knowingly. "Alexander always thought you were his biggest competition."

"Alexander knew more than I did, then," I admit. "I thought Stepan was competition for you." The men turn and laugh like they have a joke they aren't sharing.

"Well, those rivalries are forgotten now that I expect us to be brothers." George reaches out a hand to Stepan and I blush at George's presumptiveness, but I suppose he speaks the truth. By June, I hope to be in Olga's place, celebrating my seventeenth birthday and my engagement to Stepan. But I'm also worried about George. Should we tell him about Olga's soldier? I know that my saintly sister will be faithful once she and George are wed, but I also can't imagine that she will give up Dmetri without a fight. I look to Stepan, but he seems unconcerned.

After greeting George and exchanging word of our families, Stepan calls for the carriage to take me home. When I arrive home I find Olga in our suite. She is sitting in front of the mirror, brushing her hair, and unconsciously humming a tune. I sit down on the cot behind her. "George is glowing. I think he's happy to be here."

My sister goes on humming like she didn't hear me. "Olga, I have to know what's going to happen to him. Will you publicly break his heart?" The sharpness of my words finally get her attention.

"George's heart should not be your concern." The cold expression on her face makes me close my mouth. I dress for bed, resolving not to speak another word on the matter. At some point in the night, Olga has a visitor at the window. I am used to it by now, so I roll over and I'm back to sleep before I can give it a thought.

Olga seems bright eyed and rested when we meet downstairs for morning tea. Her day will be busy getting her dress fitted, her hair done—making herself beautiful for a birthday ball to be held in her honor. She looks stunningly radiant this morning. I'm looking forward to the day ahead too. Of course some of it will be spent making me look beautiful as well, but I will spend most of my day with Stepan and George.

After tea, I put on my hostess dress. Something flattering, that will get me some attention, but nothing like the dress I have chosen for tonight. When I get downstairs a carriage waits to take me to the Karenin estate. I'm ecstatic about spending the day, or at least some of it, away from the palace, and with Stepan, of course. He has made plans that include games such as darts and billiards, and a tour of Petersburg by sleigh.

"Darts? Billiards?" I groan while I have a moment in the arms of my love. "Men's games are so dull."

"Tsk, tsk." He shakes his head, frowning at me. "You forget how long I've known you, my little coquette. The game for us is darts and billiards, but for you it is to see who will try the hardest to impress you."

I lower my chin and look flirtatiously up at him through my lashes. He grabs me around my waist and pulls me to his side. "It will be me," he professes. "I'll do whatever it takes to keep your eyes off the Greek."

Heavy booted footsteps come down the stairs, "Did I hear someone say something about the Greek?" George's voice is gruff but his eyes show that he is in good humor.

I instantly take on the role of hostess, as if all of the arrangements made for his entertainment have been done by me, and swiftly lead the men to the den. "Prince George, would you like a drink or something to eat? Some ale or cognac?"

"I think I am quite satisfied for now." George gives me a look that he knows will agitate Stepan. It looks like the games have begun already.

Cheese and meat are served with the tea and cakes at noon, but the men have not given up their friendly banter.

"Your friend owes me another game darts after we eat. It was not a fair match with you standing so close to me, Mademoiselle." Even with Stepan sitting next to me it's hard not to swoon as George bats his ultra long eyelashes and looks at me with his warm brown eyes. "Your perfume is so distracting."

"I'm not wearing any perfume," I lie. "You threw your darts masterfully, Monsieur." George and I have been using French titles for each other all morning. I continue, "I'm afraid there will be no time for a rematch. We are scheduled to take the sleigh for a tour around Petersburg after lunch and I need to get home soon after, so I may bathe before the dance tonight."

"And wash off that alluring odor? No, you don't need to bathe. Stay here and let me continue to impress you with my skills."

Stepan has heard enough. "The only odor you are going to smell tonight is that of your bride-to-be. Tanya will be covered in my stench if you ever get down wind of her again." He presses his body to my side and nervously runs his fingers up my arm. The teasing is friendly, and not too different than the usual tricks I use to amuse myself when men are around, but this time I have a man that feels like he is more invested, and that's a good feeling. He will always come out on top.

The sleigh ride is the thrill of the day for me. While it was meant to be informative for a man who will soon find himself an integrated part of this family—this society—it is very romantic for me and Stepan. We snuggle under the furs spread across our laps, probably leaving George feeling uncomfortable. Stepan and I take advantage of this time together away from the palace. We forget our role as host and selfishly indulge in each other. When the carriage drops me off at Tsarskoye Selo I leave Stepan red-faced and wanting more. The way he must remain until springtime when Olga is happily wedded and bedded and our engagement can be made official.

The palace, Tsarskoe Selo, also has a set of staircases that must be descended tonight, but this time I will be waiting with the crowd at the bottom while my sister is on display. I scan the ballroom and the surrounding hallways just to make sure, but there is no sign of Dmetri anywhere inside the palace.

My sister radiates youth and beauty, but stands with the grace of an elegant lady. Her light blue gown is elegant and will stand out against the sea of off white dresses the other girls are wearing, including me. Mine is off-white satin with a full lacy skirt. Olga's is more modern. Her sleeves and bodice are fitted. Even the skirt hugs her legs slightly. Dancing will be a difficult task for her tonight, but I assume that mother has mostly chosen couples dances for this particular affair.

I notice that she shimmers with jewels. Diamonds can be seen circling her neck through her open neckline and cascade down from her ears. She wears diamond bracelets up her gloved wrist, and a ring on nearly every finger. She is wearing more jewels than I have ever seen her wear at one time. Her face glows with happiness. George stands near me at the base of the stairs in a grey waistcoat with flowing tails. His freshly cleaned hair shines almost as much as his eyes, and they are fixed on Olga. To the unknowing bystander it looks as if the two of them have just seen their destiny, and have fallen in love at first sight. Even I, who should know better, am convinced that this was a match made in heaven.

After the couple has found each other and the dance floor, Stepan takes my hand and kisses it. "They make a handsome couple," he observes out loud, and then reveals in my ear, "She is an outstanding actress."

I don't dare look in his eyes for confirmation. I want to believe, if only for tonight, that the fairy tale has come true. That my sister has forgotten her affair with the soldier and has fallen in love with George, securing a happy ending for me and Stepan. For me, it lasts the rest of the night. I find security and comfort in Stepan's arms and all other worries of our future together are forgotten. Tonight, he is mine, and soon our love for each other will be known to the rest of Russia.

I go to bed quickly after the ball, as soon as our guests have gone home. I want to continue the dream in my mind as I sleep. My sister seems much too anxious to go to sleep. The last thing I see when my head hits the pillow is her sitting at the dressing table. She is still dressed and in her jewels.

I wake early the next morning, and turn to my sister's bed. We didn't get to talk at all yesterday, and I'm ready to hear her true feelings. But she is not in her cot. In fact, her blanket is still folded neatly at the end, just as it always is, just as it was last night before she went to bed. I'm frightened and let out a scream. She was wearing her jewels when I saw her last, someone must have come in through the window and kidnapped… It's possible, Dmetri does it all the time….

I cover my mouth to stop the scream. Another scenario has played out in my head, and this one is more likely. I don't know what to do, but I don't have to wonder long. My short scream has alerted the household. First, a maid pulls back the curtain surrounding our beds, my mother standing behind her gasps with concern. It doesn't take them long to figure out what the problem is. Mother's face tells me that her mind has played out the same scenario mine just did, but she acts anyway. "Alert the guards," she commands. "My daughter has been kidnapped."

My father and mother, the head of the palace guards, and Stepan and I circle around in the salon in the early morning.

"Yes, yes, George must be notified, but otherwise, we need to keep this quiet," Stepan advises. "If she has been kidnapped for her jewels she will be easy to follow. No one can pawn off the crown jewels without someone noticing. But if she has run off, which I think we can agree is more likely, we don't want word to leak out. The last thing Your Highness needs is another scandal pertaining to your household. No, if she has run off, she is sure to come home safely in time."

"You didn't see or hear anything?" Father turns to me and begs.

I shake my head vigorously. I wish I could remember something.

"Do you think Stepanovich knew how to get up to you room?"

This time I slowly nod admitting my guilt in this. "He's been here before."

My father turns his head, but he doesn't hide his disappointed scowl. It breaks my already aching heart.

"What do we tell George?" Mother frowns with concern for him.

"I don't think we should tell George about Stepanovich. I think he has suspected an affair all along. Let him make his own conclusions, but I think we should keep him busy, helping us look for Olga. We need to make him think that we believe she's been kidnapped." Stepan steps into the role of Father's advisor.

He has so many different roles; the loyal friend that I see when he is with my sister, the love-struck boy I see when he is with me, and the influential, albeit manipulative and a bit dishonest, diplomat he is when he is at work. I'm not sure who he is when I see them all mixed together like I have today.

"We'll organize search parties using only family. Mikhail, Alexander and I can each lead a small group of trusted men. We'll work undercover, taking turns, so that the routine of governing the country doesn't seem interrupted and the princess's disappearance can remain a secret." Father takes the lead, pulling himself together so that a search can begin immediately. All the men in my family, except Alexei of course, have been asked to help investigate. Stepan and George will look too, though I suspect that Stepan knows exactly where she is.

At first, George seems the most concerned. He's angry that the police have not been notified and that a nationwide alert hasn't been established. He has been told that the forty-day fast is a sacred time and we mustn't interrupt the worship time. So far, he remains patient, allowing my father to lead the search as he sees fit.

After several days of searching, he and Stepan arrive together at the palace, looking tired and frustrated after another lead has been followed unsuccessfully. After a week of silently searching, he finally lets out some aggravation.

"This all seems very strange to me. What's wrong with everyone? In my country, the disappearance of a princess would alert an entire army, or a national emergency would be declared at the very least. Is there something you're not telling me? Does the princess not want to be found?"

When Stepan doesn't immediately rebuke the assumption, George's forehead wrinkles in frustration. As he studies the events of the past week in his mind, and, after a moment of contemplation, he seems to put two and two together. With hurt and embarrassment in his eyes, he sighs, "this engagement was all a hoax. Olga does not want to marry me." The realization that he has been deceived has hit him hard. He hits his forehead with the heel in his hand and then throws up his arms in disbelief. He looks from Stepan's face to mine one last time, and sees our apologetic eyes. Angry, disgraced, he turns without another word and leaves the room. In the days that follow he refuses to join the family for meals or tea, and then quietly returns home.

When I hear the news that George has gone home, I grab my coat and pull Stepan out onto the patio so we can talk privately. "Did

George speak with you before he left?" My heart also aches for him. His betrayed expression is etched in my memory.

The creases deepen in Stepan's forehead as he looks down at me with tender eyes. "I had to let him go. He'd served his purpose and was no longer needed. I felt sorry for the man. This will probably put quite a strain on your father's relationship with is cousin, but hopefully the blood lines will still stay fixed.

I could care less about the political ramifications. "You know where Olga is." I'm appalled that he can seem so unfeeling. "Is she safe? Is she happy? Will she come back to us?"

Stepan perceives the look of distress on my face, and as if he has finally realized the pain I am going through, he pulls me close to him and runs his gloved thumb across my cheekbone. "Olga and Dmetri are legally married and blissfully happy, like she's never been before."

I'm hit with a surprising jolt of jealousy.

"But she will come back," he answers the uncertainly on my face, "when she's ready." He leans down and gently kisses my frozen lips. "Soon."

In Olga's absence I have been inspecting both of our regiments. The men have been told she's ill. Our family knows how to keep a secret well. George too, though he left humiliated, has kept our confidence. Mother and Alexei's secret has been kept quiet for over nine years now. But the soldiers in our regiment suspect something. They know Dmetri. They know him and they like him. I've heard some say that he is a "trusted leader." But if they suspect that something has occurred, they don't let on—probably fearing for his life if he is caught. Olga's return home will have to be orchestrated well if she is to keep her new husband out of prison and away from the firing squad. I'm sure my Stepan will have a role in their safe return.

For now, Father has other matters to deal with. Germany and Prussia seem only to be watching our borders, lying in wait for our armies to make a move while our allies in Europe impatiently expect him to do something soon. Only Rasputin seems to be holding him back. Father's advisors, including Stepan, are encouraging him to declare war now, but Rasputin, through my mother, is acting as his spiritual advisor and claims that if there is war, he will be punished for the lives that are lost and the blood that is shed.

I miss my sister. With the bigger half of the "Big Pair" gone, I turn to my younger sisters for comfort. I soon realize that adolescent Anastasia has concerns of her own. Every day she goes to the stable to see her horse and every day she has to face Peter.

"Peter hates our family," Anastasia confides in me after a lot of coaxing. "He hates our father. He says that there is no God, only wicked men that use God as an excuse to rule over us."

I put my hand over my mouth to hide the shock. It sounds as if our stable boy is listening to the Marxists. I hear my soldiers talk about Marxists philosophies when they think I cannot hear them. Or maybe they do know and want me to hear. I often wonder if they are testing me to see if I will punish them. But it is only talk. I don't think there is anything I can do about it.

Anastasia continues, "He said that there is nothing special about me. Except for the way I dress and flaunt my riches, I'm no better than any other girl in Russia."

I have almost heard enough. I'm about to let Mother know that Peter is a threat and should be dismissed.

"Well..." Anastasia stops me, "at first he actually said that there shouldn't be anything special about me, but then he admitted that that there is."

Anastasia's pink cheeks tell me that the story she is telling me has a bit of a different ending than I first suspected. "He said that I'm sweet and generous and that he has never known another girl like me, and if I'm so different maybe there is something to our royal claim."

I can't wipe the smile off my face, but my dear sister doesn't seem to understand its significance.

"Peter loves you Ani, he loves you and he's afraid to admit it, so he argues with you."

"Well, I hate him. He can't talk about Father that way."

"A lot of people talk about Father that way. Father knows and understands this. Grandpapa Alexander used to say that the only way to lead people was to understand them, and in order to understand them you have to be able to see things from their perspective. Peter's just investigating what's always been out there."

"I have to come up with a better argument for the next time I see him." She shuffles away not letting herself hear my words.

Olga has been gone almost a month. Mother has made herself sick with worry. She has kept herself locked up in her room since the Christmas fast began. She prays constantly. Though the servants have dutifully put up decorations for Christmas, it seems that Mother has completely forgotten about it. Monsieur Bertram, who is far away from his family this year, comes to the rescue.

"I have never celebrated the holidays in Russia," he admits. "I know you have your traditions, but tonight is la Fete de Lumieres. In Lyon, where I grew up, we would pay homage to the Virgin Mary by placing candles in the windows and lighting up the town. We couldn't light up all of Petersburg, but if there were enough candles, the windows in this palace would light a large section of it. Besides, maybe we could light a beacon that will bring your sister home."

This suggestion sends Marie, Anastasia, Alexei and me on an errand, looking in cupboards and begging the maids to help us find candles. By the time Father is home for dinner the whole east side of the palace is lit.

The questioning look on his face brings tears and laughter as we explain our teacher's idea. "It's for the Virgin Mary," Marie chokes.

"So she can lead Olga home," Alexei finishes for her.

Father shakes his head at first, but the lights raise his spirits.

"Has your mother seen this?" He climbs the stairs to her suite and, ignoring her protests, he carries her down the stairs to show her what we've done.

"It was the Monsieur's idea Maman," Marie explains. "To help Olga find her way home."

The next day Mother sends out an order for candles. Hundreds of them, and every day we put them in the windows and light them.

"The Mother Mary will bring her home to us," Mother assures as the twelve days of feasting begin. Along with our celebrations, Mother organizes charities, and every day the palace is filled with people who want to help make and deliver quilts, clothes, shoes, and food as well as toys, and candy for the poor children.

After about a week of hoping, I ask the only person I know, who knows for sure. "Will she come home Stepan? Has she seen the candles?"

"She has and she will. She misses you terribly. She says it will not be a happy Christmas until she is home. But negotiations must be made with your father."

"Negotiations? My father wants her back as we do."

"Yes, but Dmetri is a wanted man, even if he isn't arrested for kidnapping Olga, he has the crown jewels in his possession. He is a thief according to the law. Either of these offences could be punishable by death."

Now I understand. She may never return.

The candles and the charity all keep our mind off of our missing sister temporarily, but as Christmas day arrives our solemn attitudes return. There is no joy the eve before Christmas in the Tsarskoe Selo Palace. The day is spent at church and an evening meal is planned for the family. The feast consists of cabbage and beets as well as Christmas treats and cookies. No meat is allowed on Christmas Eve. After the meal, we will go back to the church for midnight worship. Stepan has chosen to spend the evening with his family. Before we leave to go to church, we light la Fete de Lumieres one last time, our hopes failing, but there is still a chance for one last prayer.

When our sleigh pulls up to the palace, well after midnight, we can see that there is someone waiting at our door. Father rushes to meet the person as the servants help us unload the sleigh. It is a man, slightly built, wearing a hat, coat and scarf. He meets my father in the doorway under the light. There are two more figures still waiting in the dark. Father has a discussion with the man in the hat in hushed tones. When the light hits the man's face, I see that it is my Stepan. One of the figures steps into the light and embraces my father. At that point we all pile out of the sleigh and rush to them. Stepan has brought back our sister. Olga goes to Mother but the other figure in the darkened doorway waits until she returns to him and, with tears in her eyes she escorts her husband, wearing his military uniform, through the front door.

Suddenly, the house is joyful again as we collect our visitor's coats, scarves and boots. Dmetri is invited to sit with Stepan in the salon as Marie pours him a cup of warm ale and I peel Olga away from him. I take her up to our suite to find her a proper dress. I frown as I pull off her worn, dirty smock and let her wash, but she cannot wash the smile off her face.

"Where did you find this?" I hold up the rags she came in.

"It was in a donation box for the poor. I couldn't wear my birthday gown hiding on the streets of Petersburg."

"You were here in Petersburg all this time? I'd wondered if you'd gone out of the country, to Europe maybe."

"Do you know how much it costs to go to Europe? No, we were quite happy here, most of the time." My sister falls into my arms. I understand her completely.

"We missed you, too," I laugh as I pull myself from her to find her an appropriate dress and shoes to match.

Dmetri and Stepan stand as we enter the room. "I was starting to understand how you felt when Olga dominated all my time," Stepan teases.

Dmetri pulls Olga down on his lap. I remember that they are newlyweds and wonder how Mother and Father are going to react to this open affection. Mother is so delighted to be reunited with her daughter that I'm sure Father will say nothing—for now.

But as we get ready for bed, my mother explains the decided sleeping arrangements. Olga will sleep in her own suite with me and Dmetri will sleep in a guest room. Olga's eyes stay on the floor, refusing to look at Mother or Father.

My biggest concern at the moment is that Stepan is grabbing for his hat and scarf and
stepping out in the chill night air. I follow him to the door, begging him to stay.

"You can't go out this late. It's freezing out there. Please stay."

"I'm sorry, m'lady. If I were under the same roof with you all night, I would not sleep at all."

"But maybe Father Christmas will bring you a present in the middle of the night," I snicker.

"Now I know that staying here would be too much of a temptation. No, I will come tomorrow and bring my parents."

I hang on him as long as I can. I don't know how to thank him for the gift he has given my family this night.

I dreamily climb the stairs to my room and find Olga fuming.

"Oh, don't be angry, sister." I'm afraid that if she gets angry she'll leave again.

"It seems that my fear that our parents will never accept my marriage to Dmetri has been confirmed," she scowls.

"Just give them some time. It seems strange to all of us that you are sleeping in the same bed with a man. Heaven knows, it hasn't stopped you from sneaking down to him before."

Olga smirks, but for now she seems to have listened to me and relaxes.

There is no more discussion about Olga and her new husband on Christmas day. It's a day of joy and all contention is avoided. All of our family and friends are here, including the Karenins and their son. We feast on goose and suckling pig. Monsieur Bertrand plays the piano while we sing Christmas carols loud enough that the men working in the stables can hear. Anastasia takes a basket with meat and wine and all kinds of treats out and hides it in her usual spot—somewhere obvious enough that the men won't be able to avoid it.

Stepan gives me a gift, but won't let me open it until he leaves. The sleeping arrangements aren't discussed tonight, so at bedtime Olga and Dmetri happily retire to the guest suite together with not a word of dispute from my parents. I think that this is the happiest day of my life as I enter my suite alone. Sitting on my cot, I carefully tear open Stepan's gift. On the top there is a note:

"My Dearest Tanya, I know I could never give

you diamonds or jewels that

would compare to what you already have, but I can give you the most

valuable thing I possess: my heart filled with love for you."

Under the note is a heart-shaped locket. It's silver with a gold design. I open it and find a tiny picture of Stepan—his green eyes smiling. I touch his tiny face as if it were real and a sigh escapes my lips. Maybe the engagement can be sooner and we can be married in June. I could have my first child before I am Olga's age. I have to get a head start if I'm going to have twenty. I laugh to myself as I fasten the locket around my neck. I press it to my heart as I slide between the sheets.

I'm awoken early by a commotion downstairs. I hear Stepan's voice and Father's and Mother's; Olga is sobbing and someone else is downstairs too. I quickly dress and hurry down the staircase. I find Olga standing in her robe, surrounded by men: Father, Stepan, and Coronel Dolopov Yogot. Dmetri is dressed in his uniform, still tucking in his shirt.

"The train leaves for Allenstein this morning." Father speaks in the tone he uses when he address his men on official business.

Dmetri nods and Stepan turns to Olga to comfort her. "You should be proud that General Samsonov wants him to serve with him as a member of the second army. As far as I can tell he has the best leadership and most experience. No harm will come to him under that man."

Olga turns her blotchy face towards him and nods, conceding to her fate.

Mother notices I'm here. She puts her arm on my shoulder and escorts me to the dining room. "Your sisters didn't wake up did they?" She sounds like she's hoping there are no more witnesses to whatever atrocity took place this morning. As she leads me away, my head is turned toward Stepan, wondering if he will be following and if he can answer my question.

Thirty minutes later, all of us, Olga, Mother and the younger children are present for morning tea. All of us except our father.

"Dmetri was asked to join the army in Allenstein. He had to leave this morning." Mother answers the puzzled look on my sisters' faces. All heads turn to Olga who is pressing her lips together until they are white. Everyone at the table understands what has happened to him.

"Stepan said that his army is in the best hands." I try to act positive, comforting, but time while tell if this is true or not.

We realize that this new arrangement is for the safety of our family. For our safety as well as Dmetri's, the fact that he and my sister are now wed is to be kept completely silent. We all understand, but that doesn't mean that Olga likes it and she takes it out on our parents, blaming them.

I'm curious as to what has happened to George. There has been no word from him or his family since he left as we would expect, but during our afternoon stroll, I find out that Anastasia has been in touch with Paul.

"George told no one of Olga's disappearance, just that the engagement was off. Paul said he was saddened by it—mostly because our families can never be friends again."

"You seem to have stayed friends with Paul," I observe.

"Only friends," Anastasia states clearly, so as not to be misunderstood.

"You're still very young; a lot could change before you are old enough to worry about such things."

"I don't think I will ever fall in love. It's not worth it. It's caused so many problems for Olga, which in turn has caused problems for you. How are you and Stepan ever supposed to be married now that Olga and Dmetri's marriage is a family secret?"

I sigh and frown. She is saying exactly what I've been thinking.

"Don't worry, Tanya," my sister tries to comfort me. "Stepan will think of something. He always does."

"I'm going crazy." Olga complains as we ready for bed. I understand. It's early February
and palace walls have become reinforced with snow and ice. "He's been gone a month and I have received no word. Either Father is preventing his messages from getting to me or the mail isn't making it through."

"Stepan wouldn't let a message get intercepted by Father before it reaches you. He says that Allenstein has been isolated. Our armies have captured it so recently the general suspects there are still spies in the city. No mail is allowed in or out, but our men are safe."

"I have to do something to keep my mind occupied," she goes on like she didn't hear me at all. Olga has become quite arrogant since she has experienced life outside the palace. "I have always considered learning to be a nurse."

"Becoming a nurse is a noble undertaking," I indulge her fancies. "But you already have a job. You are her imperial highness, daughter of the tzar, and you are a colonel in the Imperial Army."

"Funny, isn't it?" she finally pays me some attention. "I outrank my husband."

We both laugh at that, and for a brief moment it feels like things could be back to normal, but that's my fancy.

"I could use my regiment as an excuse though, to get out of here. Then I could change my dress and use my married name. No one would recognize me. I could volunteer. Maybe some of the wounded have come in contact with Dmetri while in Allenstein…"

"I just told you, there are no wounded in Allenstein." Maybe she really is going mad.

My father is so occupied with Russia on the brink of war, and Mother is so occupied with Father that it is almost as if my sisters and I are unseen at Tsarskoe Selo. We have our daily routine: morning tea and then Olga and I go out to the field to inspect our regiments. Then it's back to the palace for me. I must meet with my tutor, but after this year my education will be complete and then I will be left to keep myself busy like Olga.

Marie has always seemed content to stay inside with her studies, and now that she and Monsieur Bertrand have developed a friendship, she seems almost happy despite the constant strain our family is under.

There won't even be a ball this winter. How could we explain my older sister's disinterest in dancing? And how could my mother expect me to hide my affection for Stepan Karenin?

But he too is occupied with the affairs of Russia. When he is not sitting in on meetings with my father he is studying: philosophy, sociology, trying to understand the dynamic political views of Russia's different classes, reading booklets, pamphlets, and propaganda.

"There are so many opinions on how Russia should be run. There are the Marxist, Socialists, Mensheviks, and more every day. Their views, while all of good intent, vary only slightly, and almost all could be deadly to your father." Stepan and I have gone to the salon where we can sit away from our guests. He pulls me into his chest as my hand goes to my mouth in shock.

"There, there, Little One. I didn't mean to scare you."

But I don't believe him. I think he wants me to be afraid, maybe to prepare me for what may yet come.

"I just need to understand these men, so that I can persuade them that our old ways are God's ways and He will bless us if we succumb to his will."

"Are you a politician or a theologian? Do you really believe that, Stepan?" As I await his answer I think that I might be disappointed if the answer is in the affirmative. The old ways don't feel right anymore. I can't explain.

"I don't know what's right exactly. I only know that I must do whatever is in my power to keep you and your family safe."

Olga doesn't seem to care anything for her own safety. I'm not sure when she stopped coming home after inspections. Lucky for her it seems that everyone in our house is more concerned with their own affairs, including my baby sister.

"He has begun to bring me things to read," Anastasia confides when I inquire about her equestrian pursuits. "He wants to convince me that what he's learned is right."

"Does he still think there is something special about you?" I tease. Anastasia's crimson face answers that question for me. I'm not worried that my sister will be swayed. I think the adolescent hormones in the stables will prevent her friend from getting too invested in his Marxism lessons.

All of the newspapers, at least the ones we are allowed to see, tell us that sociological debates are still going on in Petersburg, but my father's concerns have turned toward his allies. Conflict seems to be brewing all over Eastern Europe.

Once our armies had captured Allenstein from the Prussian Empire, he began posting troops all along it's borders. This was meant to be an offensive display of Russia's power. But Allenstein is an up and coming city with a modern railway still connecting it with Germany. There is not, however, a reliable railway connecting Russia to Allenstein. The armies must march through rough, boggy terrain to reach their camps. When they finally arrive they are cold and sick, and their gear is in need of repair or ruined completely. These things must weigh heavy on my father's mind.

In a letter of counsel to my father, Rasputin writes:

"War isn't a good thing, but Christians seem to gravitate towards it. We Russians should avoid war and build a monument. A real monument, I say, to those who work out peace."

Rasputin's admonishments are always frightening, perhaps even for father. So for now he heeds his spiritual advisor, and holds off making a move to join the efforts of France and the United Kingdom a little longer.

My sister's devices seem to have worked so far. She comes home late and sneaks in wearing dresses made from rags found in donation barrels left in the streets. She is disguised as, or maybe has become, Olga Dmetrinova while she volunteers at the hospital and trains to be a nurse. She tells me that there people openly complain about our father's governing leadership. Maybe she is in agreement with them, because at home her disdain for him is also obvious. Although her dissatisfaction isn't uttered aloud, her silent treatment is cold and unjustified in my opinion.

"Why do you act like you hate Father? You must know how much it hurts him. He only did what he thought best for our family and for you and Dmetri. If Dmetri had been given the opportunity on his own, you know he would be there now anyway. Besides, Stepan insists that he is safe." I've had enough of my sister's hostility for our father.

"Stepan lies. I have seen the soldiers, the one that are too sick and diseased to move onward. They are the ones that haven't had to travel so far that it's too late to come back. They tell me they are the lucky ones."

I ponder this observation. Why would Stepan say that he was safe if this is the case?

Plans to spend the spring in Livida are under way. I am both ecstatic to get out of Petersburg and discouraged that my hopes for a seventeenth birthday/engagement party will not be possible. In fact, Stepan may not even be able to travel to Livida this year. He has no need to be concerned about Igor. Both he and his brother Konstentine have joined their regiments and are marching to Allenstein to be part of the first army, under the command of General Pavel von Rennenkampf. Stepan questions the general's leadership and fears for the boy's safety.

The luxurious train ride to the Sea of Azov would be quite lonesome if it weren't for our dear friend and teacher, Monsieur François Bertram. He has become like a family member and has turned my sister and brother into exquisite artists. He entertains the rest of the family with art lessons as well. Also he is very talented musically. The piano in the salon has never been used so excessively.

"I didn't realize how incredibly brilliant I was when I stole that man away from our Grecian friends," Mother brags while she and Father listen to us put on a performance.

"I hope the Greeks are still our friends," Father touches the subject lightly.

Taking his comment in jest Mother says, "I don't think they will hold us in contempt for taking François. I don't believe they knew his value when he was in their service."

Father's face goes dark. "François is not all we have taken from them."

Mother's smile melts from her face. This is the last time I ever hear her refer to the Greeks as "our friends."

The Frenchman and Marie, continue to engage in a relationship that is baffling. Marie has not confided in Olga or I, nor Anastasia that I know of. Their actions are completely professional, which may be only for my parents' benefit because the look in Marie's eyes tells me she's completely smitten. And unless I'm mistaken, which I frequently am, our teacher's eyes tell a similar story when he is with Marie.

Watching them together makes me completely miserable. Though I am pleased to see my sister's happiness, and there is security in seeing some normalcy in the household, I can't bear to be reminded of what I am missing. We've only been away from Petersburg a couple of days, and already the hole on my heart has taken over the rest of my body. I can't sleep, I can't eat. My only solace to this predicament is that maybe Stepan is as miserable as I am. I can finally empathize with my sister.

"How soon will you have word from Dmetri?" Olga gazes longingly out the window of our carriage and I decide to join her in her pain.

"If I ever hear from him again… If only I could have stayed at the hospital. There at least we could have found each other. I could have received word if…."

I won't allow my sister to think of it. "Maybe he'll get a fever and they will send him back before the fighting begins."

Olga shakes her head. "No. My Dmetri is strong. He's been cold and hungry before. He never complains. He won't allow himself to get sick; he would never leave his post alive. If only I could have conceived a child. Then Father would have to either accept our marriage or disinherit me. Either way we would be together right now instead of hundreds of miles apart, with him cold, wet and starving."

My heart goes out to her. I can't even imagine what she must be going through. Thus far, Stepan is still mostly out of harm's way in his office in Petersburg.

When the steamship docks in Crimea it's raining.

"It's good that we can get the rain over early," Mother looks on the bright side. "We'll have sun all afternoon."

But it seems that my sister and I have brought our cloudy dispositions with us to Crimea and it is affecting the weather. After our things are unloaded and arranged in the palace, the servants build a fire in the sitting room. Admittedly it is nice to have the family together sitting around the hearth. Mother and Father tell us stories about their travels in Europe, which leads Mother into stories about her childhood and our Great Grandmother Victoria who, although she was a woman, ruled England on her own at the age of eighteen. Father had always talked of her as a hard-headed, controlling woman, but Mother's stories allow us to imagine her when she was young—brave, independent, and a loving mother of nine children.

"See?" I tell my sister who has chastised me in the past. "My desire for a large family is inherited."

"I just don't want you girls getting any ideas," Alexei interrupts. He has been quietly listening, but now speaks out. "Russia is to be ruled by a man." He puffs out his chest and stretches himself to his full height. His illness has been in control since his accident almost two years ago and his body has decided it is time to grow. He won't get a lot of height directly from Father, though his Romanov brothers were taller. There is some height on mother's side of the family. My brother will probably be taller than Father. He pats Alexei on the back and we all laugh.

Mother credits Alexei's health with the miracle that was brought about by her friend Rasputin. She is fearful when we are away from him, but before we left he comforted her saying that he needed a vacation too. His family lives in Siberia and though it is rumored that he is not welcome there, he says he must visit his wife and son.

The rain continues the first week of our stay in the Lividia Palace. The palace stays warm and comfortable as we watch the storm from the inside. I receive my first message from Stepan on Friday.

> *My Dearest Tanya,*
> *Though my heart is broken, I must go on pretending in court that your absence if not affecting me. It was almost impossible at first, but there is much work to be done here. Now that our*

troops have made it safely (be sure to tell Olga that I have been assured that Dmetri has arrived safely and is in good standing with his officers) to our new compound in Allenstein, our allies are pressuring us to devise a strategy. In your father's absence, all that can be done is more arguing. As always I will fight on his behalf for the lives of those I love—you being at the top of that list. I am told it is raining in Crimea, like it is raining here and all over the country. The sky cries tears for us, Tanya, until you are back in my arms.

Your love,
Stepan

I for one certainly hope it doesn't keep raining until then. The very first time the sun comes out, my sisters and I hurry to the garage to get our bikes. I am the first up the hill. I ride fast, ignoring the occasional droplets that assure us that the rain isn't gone completely. No one else is around so we abandon our cruisers and walk to the shoreline. Gazing into the turbulent waters, I see the gaping space separating me from my love. The unsettled waters reflect unsettled times. I fear a storm is building.

Large heavy droplets are now dotting our dresses and a rush of wind causes us all to scream at once and run back to the bicycles. The sudden cloud burst that follows reminds me of the time that Igor and I got caught in the rain. Not even Igor deserves the fate that awaits him. We arrive back at the palace shivering, and wet. Freshly laundered towel and a message for Father await us. He is needed back in Petersburg.

"Georges Clemenceau, Prime Minister of France, and David Llyod George of the United Kingdom?" Father laughs wholeheartedly. "No one of consequence. You may stay here if you wish; I will be back for the birthday party."

"The Prime Ministers of France and England?" Mother looks almost surprised as if she didn't know my father was such a powerful man. "I said I would never let you leave me again, don't you remember? And with this rain, we might as well all be back in Petersburg."

Mother's plans for the biggest birthday party Livadia Palace has ever seen are crushed by the news, but she insists that we brave the weather tonight and go to the theater. It will be her last and only chance to mingle with the Konstantinoviches, her dear friend Elisabeth, and the other nobility of Crimea before we leave. My brother will once again miss out on the time he usually spends with George Konstantinovich, evidently, the only boy his age in Russia.

The clean, damp air make the night refreshing, and the stars have come out to wish us farewell. This has been our shortest, most miserable trip to the Livida Palace, and while I'm not looking forward to the train ride back, I'm not entirely disappointed either.

June 1914
Petersburg, Russia

Stepan meets us at the train station, and for once greets me before talking to Father. This time Father comes to him and he speaks to him with me draped around his neck while he talks through my hair. "The arrangements have all been made, your highness, and the Prime Ministers will be here within the week. Your timing is impeccable. I was concerned that the weather would slow down your travels."

"It was slow all right," I say loud enough for Father to hear. He gets the hint and leaves us alone.

"So much has happened since you've been gone, I wanted to tell you—share it with you." Stepan's face is aglow through his beard.

"Political matters." I stick out my tongue.

"No, that's not it." He takes my hand and places it on his heart. "This is where the change has been. While you were away I realized what I want more than anything."

Looking up into his eyes I feel his tone getting more serious. There is a lump in my throat and I have goose bumps on my arms.

"I want you," he confesses. "More than I ever thought I did before. You will be seventeen soon. Your sister has made her choice. Your parents must see that by now. I'm going to ask that your father forget that Olga appears to be unwed and ask for your hand—if, of course, you will have me?"

It still feels like I'm on the moving train and the world is streaking by while I casually gaze out the window. "Is this a proposal?" I look down at my traveling clothes and put my hand up to my messy hair. This is not the way I pictured it happening.

"Well, the first one, I guess." Stepan looks down at his feet. "But not the last. There will be a formal proposal with an engagement ring of course, but I will ask you to be my wife every day after this until you say you will."

I clasp the locket he gave me at Christmastime in my right hand and wonder if there was ever any question that we would be married. "I will." I look him straight in the eyes and say it again. "I will."

Stepan lifts me off my feet and swings me around hooting and hollering his joy. It's then that I realize that we are not alone, and though I think our conversation was private, the entire train station is now looking at us, laughing under their breath. Olga smiles for a moment, but then her face turns sad. I would like to comfort her, but I don't want anything to diminish my joy at this moment.

Our embrace doesn't last long as Father and his men scoop up Stepan and take him off to another meeting.

Stepan is true to his word and asks me to marry him every time I see him, and although I answer in the affirmative every time, nothing resembling a formal proposal has happened yet, but the spring rains have stopped and summer is quickly approaching. The birthday party Mother was planning has been moved to Tsarskoe Selo. Although it will only be for my sister's and sister's and I—Nina and her mother and sister are still in Crimea—it's my seventeenth birthday, and it must be grand.

"What do you think Mother would say if I asked if Peter could be invited to my birthday

party?" Anastasia asks as we are having our dresses fitted. This year they will all be different. Anastasia has always worn pastels to compliment her golden hair, but this year she will wear a sharp white princess style gown with her hair in a chigan. Marie's is a muted pink—simple but elegant with a high waist and fitted sleeves. Mine is the most colorful this time. My dress is made from a new fabric called rayon. It flows like silk, but is not as delicate. The dress is slim at the hips and elongates into a train that will follow me down the stairs. The train connects to my glove, so it will be out of the way for dancing. I will stand out tonight, because rather than choosing a subdued tone, like my sisters, I have chosen to have mine made out of a deep plum fabric.

Marie answers Anastasia's question with a frown, "I can't imagine that Peter would be allowed. The hired help has never been invited to a royal event. Even Françoise was only included as a spectator at the first ball he was invited too."

"Françoise," Anastasia emphasizes, proving that she too feels familiar enough with their teacher to use his first name, "was your dance partner at our last birthday. He, though a commoner, has become part of the family."

Marie turns red with rage. "Never use the term 'commoner' when speaking of him again."

"And what makes him any different then Peter, or you and me, for that matter? Did not God create us all in His image?"

It seems that at least some of Peter's lessons have been absorbed.

"All you can do is ask," I advise. "You never know what the outcome will be, but I'm sure that if Mother says yes, Stepan will have a suit he could borrow for the occasion."

"You will have Stepan, Marie will have her precious Françoise," Anastasia scowls, "I don't want to dance with my cousin this year."

"Mother could send for Paul," Marie suggests.

Anastasia shrugs. "I don't think that's a possibility. The Greeks are not as friendly as they used to be….Paul will always be my friend, but I don't think his family would send him alone."

I wonder what my younger sister has brewing. Although I am sure she's being truthful when she says that she doesn't want to dance with her cousin, her words hint that she has another agenda.

To her dismay, it seems that the stable crew is not welcome at the ball. It's a shame, because now I think Peter's political opinions will be strengthened in Anastasia eyes.

"You can choose any young man from the Corps des Pages." Mother explains to my disappointed sister, as we try our dresses on for her that afternoon. "They are all close to your age now and your father thinks it would show our family's support for our soldiers."

Anastasia doesn't show her disappointment. Instead she looks at herself in the mirror and smoothes her new sparkling white dress. She smiles mischievously, and I can see that something is brewing behind her sapphire eyes.

The evening before the birthday ball, Stepan requests an audience with my father. I find him standing in the entry, pacing the floor. He appears to be afraid to knock on the door.

"What's wrong, darling?" I ask, hiding a knowing smile. "Don't you meet with my father, as well as other world dignitaries, on a regular basis?"

Stepan smiles at my teasing and scoops me into his arms. "This may be the most important meeting of my life." He looks at me mischievously. "I might need some encouragement." Before I know what's happened he's grabbed my arm and dragged me through the office door.

My forehead wrinkles. This is not how I expected this to happen either, but Father has already invited us in and is standing in front of us with his eyebrows arched in a questioning glare.

"What is this?" Father acts as surprised as I am that Stepan has decided to include me in this discussion.

"Well," Stepan addresses the bewildered look on Father's face. "It is no secret that I love your daughter." His eyes are on me now. "I beg her to be mine every day, and now I would like her to witness my pleading with her father to let me take her hand in marriage." He then takes my hands, in his and turns to my father in supplication.

"As you know, I am well aware of the predicament your highness is in. Olga and I have been friends since we were small, and while Tatiana and I have waited patiently for her to become engaged so we could make our courtship public, now it seems that nothing about Olga's relationship will ever be known outside these palace walls. I think we have waited long enough. I wish to make our engagement official and marry Tanya as soon as is humanly possible."

His last line draws a smile from the tzar. No wonder Stepan is so highly respected in the Dumas. He showed no sign of the apprehension he seemed to be experiencing just moments ago. I feel warm. I'm glad that Stepan asked me to witness this. But my father still hasn't given his consent.

"These are troubling times," he finally speaks. "We are not only on the verge of war, it seems like we are at risk of losing all we hold dear to changing times. The traditions of our fathers are laughed at and called 'outdated', and yet they are the very fibers that have held this country together for all of these decades. I need to be an example of stability in winds of change. Despite that, I see your desire, Stepan and Tanya, and as your father I wish to give you everything your heart desires, so I give you my permission to make it official, but ask that you to please keep it quiet, just a little longer, until the troops return, so we can decide what to do about your sister's husband."

As Stepan and I leave my father's office, I'm confused, but he seems unconcerned, like this was exactly what he'd expected—hoped for. With a squeeze of his hand, he lets me go get ready for the ball.

Nervously I stand at the top of the stairs and look down at the people below waiting for me to make my descent. My fear this year is not that I will stumble; it's that people will be disappointed in what they see. I am a woman now, a Romanov woman. Will I give off the aura of an Imperial Princess? Will my face show that I am strong and capable of leading them? As I descend the stairs, I breathe a sigh of relief as Stepan's sustaining grin comes into view. All will be well as long as he is near me.

The orchestra rings out the notes of the birthday dance. I do not waver in my choice for a partner. Stepan is a dutiful subject and bows deeply as I approach him and offers me his arm. Marie is already dancing with François. While a row of students from the Corps des Pages are lined up for Anastasia's inspection, she chooses to dance with her cousin, Dmetri. Father's eyes are wide as he looks at mother, but mother's twinkle with the knowledge that this act of protest is just Anastasia's way of saying that at age thirteen, she's old enough to choose for herself.

Stepan and I have no fear of dancing every dance together tonight. Olga looks on as a spectator rather than a participant. If anyone wonders about the arrangement, no one voices their concerns—or I cannot hear them. We frequently step out on the veranda to be alone and the moon shines down its approval of our love. I wish the night would never end. But gradually our guests return to their homes and the once-crowded ballroom becomes more intimate. Mother excuses the servants to their chambers after the food is put away and the chairs and tables are neatly stacked in the corners. Finally even the orchestra decides that the party has gone on long enough. But Stepan and I still hear music. We continue to hum and swirl, staying in each other's arms until we are the only two left in the room. It has cleared without my even being aware. When Stepan takes me out on the veranda, the moon is our only witness.

He rubs the cold out of my arms and holds me in front of him. "You, my dear are the most beautiful woman in the world. It would be my honor," he abruptly drops to his knees, which draws a surprised giggle from me. I was not expecting this. "It would make me the happiest man on earth," Stepan's grin widens. He realizes he's caught me off guard and he is pleased, "if you would be my wife."

He pulls out an ancient-looking box and explains, as my eyes are drawn to it. "As I've told you before I could never give you more than what you already have." My hand naturally goes to the heart-shaped locket around my neck. "But this is special." He opens the box to reveal a ring circled with three strands of diamonds. "It was your grandmother's. Your father wanted me to use it."

"Then that discussion in his office today?"

"A formality. We've discussed this before. But the part about not making this public—that was new. I don't want to keep it quiet though, I want to shout it from the rooftops. In fact, I think I will."

Before I can stop him he yells. "I love you Tatiana Nikolaevna. I love you. I will love you forever."

Through my laughter I'm able to restrain him long enough to quiet him with a kiss, and he stays quiet for long while.

Naturally, I'm the last one downstairs for morning tea. I have chosen not to wash, as the vestige from last night still lingers on my skin, and my hair remains uncombed. The ring that Stepan so gallantly bestowed upon me yesterday is stored safely in a drawer, but when my sisters see me they beg me to show them. Apparently, I was the only one surprised by Stepan's proposal. One by one they each hug me and wish me happiness. I'm overwhelmed by their warmth, but feel a twinge of guilt when I realize that this should have been Olga's moment.

After a while the subject of discussion at the table becomes the ball in general.

"I was told there was a protest," Olga turns her eyes towards Anastasia's, "outside the palace—mostly young men, some from the palace, that study Marxism, protesting the class system."

Mother's eyes confirm the rumor. Afraid to give away our sister's guilt we look away from her and down at our tea.

After dinner as I cuddle in the salon alone with my new fiancé, I decide to discuss what I think Anastasia is guilty of with him. "It wouldn't surprise me if my little sister knew more about the demonstration by the Marxists last night then she will admit to. I wouldn't even be surprised if she encouraged it."

"You girls are always trying to get your parents' attention. It's as if you want to them to see you as naughty." Stepan laughs at himself. He thinks he knows us all so well and it amuses him. I wrinkle my forehead. I wonder where he gets ideas like that. I'm about to rebuke him when he goes on, somewhat changing the subject.

"The Marxists are not a big concern right now. Our world allies are ready to wage war on Prussia and Germany. They have discussed it at length with your father, but he is still dragging his feet. He's still talking about it not being Christian, but it sounds like Rasputin to me."

"You're right," I confide "'Our Friend' did say something about war not being Christian recently, but aren't all spiritual leaders against war?"

"Yes," Stepan becomes grave, "but not all spiritual leaders have such a strong influence over your father. That rat Rasputin wants more than just peace, he wants power. He wants control."

Stepan's words are biting. Although Rasputin does seem crudely bizarre, I have never seen him do anything that would show that he wants our power. I try to change the subject. I don't want to argue with my fiancé. I want him to hold me.

"I think Anastasia is in love." I reveal in a whisper.

Stepan frowns. "With that Marxist stable boy?"

I don't think I'm getting anywhere romantically with him tonight. I'm relieved when
Olga walks in.

"Good evening, sister." Stepan addresses her with a grin. He and I look at each other and smile. It is good that he will officially be a part of the family soon.

"Your Dmetri is a lucky man."

Olga sits down with a pleased smile. Pleased because we are talking about her husband and pleased because she thinks Stepan has given her a compliment, but the look fades when he speaks again. "He is going to be right where the action is."

Immediately concerned, Olga asks him to clarify. "You told me he was safe. Not that he was going to be 'where the action is.'"

"Oh no. I told you he was under good leadership as a member of the second army. General Samsonov's tactics are clever. I have to say, it would be very exciting to be a part of that group of men."

I interrupt, attempting to lighten the mood and save Stepan from my sister. "You silly boy," I accuse, "always wanting to play war and be where the action is."

But it's too late. Olga interrupts. "You talk of action and war tactics when my loves life is in danger? You yourself have never been in a battle before and you envy those who are?"

"Have some pride, Olga. Your husband and your father are showing the world how powerful Russia can be. It's about patriotism. It's about pride."

"You may be swallowing your pride, brother," she spits in disdain, "when someone you love does not come back."

Olga leaves the room and Stepan and I are alone again. I shake my head. He must learn, if he is going to be a part of this family, how to communicate with women. He ignores my frown as he takes both of my hands and leads me to the bench by the window.

"If we do enter this war, which I certainly hope we do, you cannot keep me from joining the forces. They will need leadership. And your father also, must show that guidance and direct his men. Please tell me you will not cry if I go, but wait for me until I return with honor as your sister's husband is sure to do."

I want to cry already when I see the determined look in his eyes. How can he be so naïve?

"If our country goes to war," I tell him flatly, "and you choose to join the troops, I will cry, and I will beg you not to go. But if you must go, if you go anyway, I will be waiting with my sister when you return home."

Just a week after my birthday celebration, on June 28, 1914, we receive a news bulletin.

The Archduke Ferdinand, Royal Prince of Hungary and heir to the Austro-Hungarian throne, and his wife are assassinated in Sarajevo.

Austro-Hungary has declared war on Serbia. We are Serbia's allies. Immediately a special session of the Dumas is called and Stepan and my father are in meetings all night. Before the night is over, the decision has been made to mobilize troops into Serbia.

In the morning Stepan comes in with Father to make sure he gets some sleep, before returning to his own home.

"Your father was brilliant," Stepan acts almost giddy. "He told the men, 'Serbia is our little Slavic brother. We must protect all Slavic and Eastern Orthodox peoples.' He has united those who didn't want war because of their religious views and those, like me, who think Russia should show its power. I think he's even convinced himself that this is the right thing."

"I for one have another reason to be against this war. It will take those I love away from me and put them in death's path," I tell Stepan. As he holds me tightly for a moment, I think maybe my words have swayed him to my side, but when he finally faces me, the gleam in his eye tells another story. "Go home and get some sleep," I tell him in frustration. "You have a lot of work to do."

But hardly before he has a chance to get home, a messenger arrives with the news that Germany, Austro-Hungarian's ally, has declared war on us.

"Dmetri and the first army are waiting in Allenstein, just on the Prussia's border. They will all be killed," Olga cries when Father and Stepan make the announcement, but Stepan comforts her.

"This declaration of war will soon start a chain reaction. All of our allies are prepared for just such a declaration, that's why the Prime Ministers of France and England were here earlier. The first battles have already been orchestrated and our army alone has four times as many men as Germany's. We are prepared for this war and soon your father and I will lead our men to victory."

But Father doesn't have the same glimmer of confidence in his eye. He is older and he remembers the war with Japan when we were much younger. It has always ended in heartbreak for him.

We don't see much of Father or Stepan in the days that follow. There isn't much the woman of the household can say or do, so Mother and Olga pace the floor and the rest of the household are beset with worry. It is during this time of tension that we receive a telegram from Siberia. It comes with more bad news. The very day that the archduke and his wife were assassinated in Serbia, Our Friend Rasputin, was stabbed several times by an angry ex-lover, so we are told, but mother refuses to believe the stories that her "friend" is a promiscuous scoundrel. Now mother spends the days wringing her hands and praying, asking God to heal her friend and protect her family.

Days after receiving the telegram, Mother receives a note from Rasputin. He says that the Lord had heard her prayers and that he will be healed and back to us soon, and he has seen a vision. He asks that this message be given to my father.

"A terrible storm cloud lies over Russia. Disaster, grief, naked darkness, no light. An ocean of tears, no counting them, and so much blood. The disaster is great, the misery infinite."

My father receives Rasputin's prophecy. It doesn't change anything. Without seeing his face I know his heart must have been torn out of his chest when he read it.

Battle plans keep my father and my fiancé very busy for the next weeks, but my brother's tenth birthday is quickly approaching. My mother insists that my father take time away from the war and celebrate with his family.

"Yes," my insightful Stepan agrees, "The timing couldn't be more perfect."

Father seems to be following his reasoning. "This is the first year in a long time we've been in Petersburg for the occasion, and Alexei is as fit as ever."

"He could lead a parade to the city center wearing his uniform, and give a speech in support of our men." Stepan exclaims. "Showing that our future is strong, and that the Empire will live on."

"I will talk to Bertrand. He and Alexei can start working on his speech right away," Father agrees.

Alexei is glowing, it's sure to be his best birthday ever.

Olga and I sulk in the salon after dinner. We've already had enough of this.

"Why do you have to drag Alexei into your war games?" I insist. "He's just a boy. We don't want you turning him into a war monger too."

Stepan puts his finger under my chin and looks down on me like I'm the one that's being naive. "Don't you see he's already a part of it? It's his birthright, just like it was for your father."

"He could at least enjoy peace on his birthday, instead of turning it into a military campaign," I say more to myself than to Stepan. I'm sure he has stopped listening to reason as soon as this thing got started.

"This birthday celebration will unite our people and give them something worth fighting for. They will see that our future is in good hands. It will ignite patriotism like we have never seen before. And your brother wants to do it. See?"

Alexei marches around and waves his hands in the air like he is commanding an army. Mother leans on Father; their faces full of pride. I can't help but smile to see him strong and well, but I'm concerned about the boy. He is bound to get his hopes up only to have them crushed again as soon as the reality of war hits this family.

The birthday celebration is a welcome distraction from the war. Even Olga seems to put her concerns aside as we get ready to join the parade. New dresses are bought for the occasion and the streets are strewn with banners and flags. Three automobiles are commissioned to take us through the city: one for Anastasia and Marie, driven by a handsome young man in a starched uniform. They follow Olga and me in a Monte Carlo, driven by Stepan. (I must admit, he is irresistibly handsome in his new uniform.) Mother and Father are in front with Alexei seated high in the back seat, looking dapper, waving to the crowd. As we reach the city center, a makeshift stage has been built with seats for each member of the family with a podium in the middle.

We climb the stairs to the platform as the citizens of Petersburg cheer. Most are waving tiny flags. Anastasia lets out a small gasp. I stop to see what has surprised her so, and I see Peter, the stable boy, dressed in a worn suit, proudly waving the Russian flag. The sight takes me so off guard. I almost trip on the next step. Maybe Stepan is right. Maybe this is exactly what we need to unify our people. We are greeted by roaring applause as Stepan walks up to the podium to introduce my brother—the birthday boy.

My heart jumps when Stepan turns from the podium and looks right into my eyes. I'm sure the whole audience can see my face redden as he turns back to face the people and stands next to my chair, but the crowd is focused on the words my brother is shouting.

"Good people of Petersburg. We are fortunate enough to live at a glorious time. A time when our nation is strong..."

Monsieur Bertrand coaches him unseen from the audience. He has taught him well. Alexei seems to know when to pause and when to pump his arm to emphasize his words. The crowd hollers their agreement and he continues.

"We will show the world, our enemies as well as our allies, what it means to be Russian. We will conquer this enemy and everyone will know that we have the power."

When he is finished, he makes a snappy turn and salutes my Father. The tzar is caught off guard by this gesture and has to quickly wipe his eye before he stands to address the group.

"My son is wise for his age." My father chuckles and the crowd erupts in laughter. It seems they are ready to get behind anything they are told. Our people are united in this cause. This is good for my father and my country, though maybe a bit too optimistic.

The Russian people roar their approval as father finishes his speech and we, as a family, walk slowly back to the vehicles we arrived in. Several giant birthday cakes are brought out to serve the citizens. We arrive at the palace to a dining hall filled with dignitaries. Stepan and my feelings toward each other must be held in reserve tonight, but his smile speaks volumes when he catches my eye. Due to the war, the length of our engagement is yet undetermined and our love must remain a secret.

The people of Russia have joined my father and the country is on a patriotic high. As the plans for the first battles were underway, Stepan seems to find great joy in rehearsing them to me. I know that we have armies stationed in Allenstein on Prussia's eastern border, but Stepan tells me that our allies France and England are ready to attack Germany from the west.

"While the Germans are fighting off France and England, our first and second armies will take over Prussia. By the time Germany gets to our side to aid their Prussian allies, they will be weak. We have enough men to field ten complete armies, more than Germany has on both fronts together. We will overpower them in a matter of weeks— months at the most."

"Ten armies? But why then was Dmetri put in the second? Isn't that essentially the front line? Some of our men at least will be killed. Won't they be the first?" I can't help but suspect this was

Father's plan all along. Maybe this was his solution for solving the problem Olga presented him with. Maybe he is as the people have called him before, "Bloody Nicholas."

"Perhaps." Stepan waits until he's sure that I am listening. "Perhaps in some circumstances, yes, but the first and second armies are commanded by your father's most powerful generals. The commander of the second army, General Alexander Samsonov, has served under your father since the war with Japan. No one is more experienced than him." He puts a comforting arm around my waist.

"But didn't we lose the war in Japan?" Stepan looks down at me and touches my nose as if to say I am a silly girl.

He breathes out an exasperated sigh. "This I shouldn't tell you, but if it will give you some peace, you should know that Samsonov has a clever plan. The second army will not be heading into the battle first, they are to go around the Masurian Lakes and attack from behind. Tell Olga her father has put her husband out of harm's way."

I will not give Olga such false hopes. My fiancé forgets that this is war, and in war we are never far from harm.

August 23, 1914, we finally get word that the battle has begun. Father and Stepan stay close to the communication hub (the radio, telephone, and telegraph are all at their disposal) for current information. But in our isolated quarters of the palace, we would get no information what-so-ever if it wasn't for the fact that through the years we have become highly skilled listeners. We have learned to make do with keeping our ears open to the whispering that is being exchanged around us.

Apparently, things are not going as smoothly as first planned. It seems that the two greatest generals in the Russian army are not the greatest friends. It's even rumored that a brawl broke out at a rail station when General Samsonov, commander of the second army, made a contemptuous remark about General Rennenkampf's behavior at the Battle of Mukdin. He was so offended, Rennenkampf swore that if Samsonov ever needed him he would not be there to offer his support. Still confident that the services of the first army wouldn't be needed, General Samsonov sent his men out, only to find out quickly that they were not as well equipped as they thought they were, and will have to make do with limited supplies—but we are assured that Russia still has the upper hand.

Mother tries to make it seem like life is going on as usual. She keeps us occupied with our studies, hoping that our limited time spent outdoors won't be missed. Olga is an adult now and her time cannot be scheduled out the way ours is. She manages to sneak out of the house daily to visit the hospital. She says it's the only way she can keep her mind off of Dmetri, and the only way she can help at all. Mother pretends not to notice her absence, or perhaps she understands what Olga is going through. She has sent Father out to battle numerous times.

Unfortunately, it seems that I wasn't the only one who knew more than I should about the battle strategy. Our armies soon run out of secure telegraph landlines and are forced to send messages, non-encrypted, over lines that can easily be intercepted by the Germans.

"I don't know why we didn't plan for this." Stepan and father have been waiting in Father's office for news but now that the news has arrived, Father has gone alone to the strategy room to confer with his Generals. Stepan is left to pace the floor of our salon, with only me to be his sounding board. "All of our strategic battle plans will be of no use if the Germans know them as soon as our men do."

"The men will fight hard, and we still outnumber them ten-to-one. We will learn from our mistakes and the next battle will be better," I repeat back to him the words of assurance he has given me. He looks so pale I go to him to give him comfort, but he pushes me away.

"No. Our count was wrong. Germany has decided to consolidate their troops. They are no longer concerned about their western border. They have a railway that connects directly with Allenstein. In a matter of days, all of their armies will be there. We can't move the rest of our troops fast enough across the bogs to help them. It took us months to get them there to begin with and there may not be another chance for these men. I promised Olga…"

Now I understand. He and father have sent Dmetri to the front lines after all. He may not return alive. I drop my hands and take a step back from him. My poor sister. I wonder how much she knows.

When Olga doesn't come home from the hospital that night, I realize that she knows everything. The hospital is part of the communication hub as well. She must have stayed close to the radio when they heard the bad news there. The next morning at tea Mother makes a decision.

"Today, we will all go to the hospital. Our Russian soldiers are suffering in Poland. The least we can do is show our support to their families as they await word at the hospital." I realize then that Mother knows. I don't know for how long, but she knows that Olga has been at the hospital.

When we arrive, the hospital is almost silent except for the occasional cough or cry of a child. Families fill the halls, waiting for word. None of the wounded have been brought here yet. It is a long treacherous journey to cross the bog separating Allenstein and the Russian railway.

As Mother approaches Olga in her second-hand dress, she collapses in her arms. No one seems to notice that the tzarina seems to be on strangely familiar terms with this nurse dressed in rags. Everyone is lost in their own thoughts—praying, hoping. Even the telegraph is silent. Once it was discovered that the Germans were intercepting our commands, the messages have been kept to dire emergencies only. I pray that we continue to hear nothing. Olga lays her head in Mother's lap as she whispers soothing words.

The sun gets higher in the sky and Mother sends Olga home to change. She must transform herself from Olga Dmetrinova, a volunteer nurse, back into the tzar's oldest daughter.

"Change your dress, darling," Mother whispers so only we can hear. "We must show our support to your father."

Once Olga has stepped into a carriage to return home, Marie remarks, "She will not come back, or at least she shouldn't." Marie seems to end her speaking, but then adds, "If I were her, I would not wish to show support to our father." Mother and I look at her in disbelief. Not only because she has shown disrespect, but also because this is the first time Marie has spoken in such a way. She has voiced the same opinion I share. She must also suspect that Father strategically placed Dmetri in this dangerous position.

Mother surprises us by putting her arm on Marie's shoulder and pulling her to her. "It's a terrible time for all of us," she assures. She casts her arm around the room. "These people have much to lose also. We are no different because of who we are or where we were born." Warm smiles from the bereaved faces of the women at the hospital tell me that her diplomacy has worked and they are touched by her sentiments. I have much to learn from my mother.

After spending hours consoling the families at the hospital, we arrive back at the palace to find that the somber mood has come with us. In our suite as I change for dinner, I find my distraught sister finally asleep on her bed. I decide not to wake her.

Father and Stepan come in later. Father doesn't stay with the family. He goes alone to his office, leaving Stepan to reveal the bad news.

"When the second army's plan for a surprise attack was discovered, the Germans had a surprise waiting for them. Because of our men's lack of preparation and supplies, when the Germans caught up with them, they didn't stand a chance. They were nearly annihilated."

Dmetri's name isn't mentioned—yet.

"News of the attack on Samsonov's army didn't reach the first army in time. They were ready to fight, but were almost entirely out numbered. They took a beating, but more survived than were lost." Stepan's emotions get to him for a moment, but he quickly gets them under control. "May God be with the families of those men."

We all sense her at the same time and turn toward the staircase to see Olga standing in her peasant's dress, leaning over the rail. "Dmetri?"

"He's gone." Stepan lowers his head.

"I know. I've known for some time." She doesn't break down and cry; instead she turns and slowly walks back up the stairs to our room.

My heart is breaking for her, but I'm frightened as well. I've never seen her like this. I don't know how to comfort her.

It seems none of us can bring ourselves to leave the room. Stepan stays as well, but seated in the chair across from me. The ache is in every nerve of my body; even his touch, I fear, could cause me more pain.

Towards midnight Father finally enters. His face is expressionless and his eyes are dull. Mother speaks to him first, softly, calmly. "There will be a funeral of course to honor the young man…"

"No," Father interrupts sharply. "It's too dangerous, and would require too many needed men to transfer the bodies. They will be disposed of in Poland."

Bloody Nicholas has returned.

When I finally decided to climb the staircase to my room, I find my sister sitting by the window.

"How did you know, Olga?" There's an eerie feeling in the room. I don't know what else to say.

"Hmmmm?" My widowed sister turns to me as if my words have woken her from a dream.

"How did you know?" I ask more forcibly this time. "You said you knew Dmetri was gone."

"Oh." Her eyes are far away and she seems to go back into her dream, but then she turns back to me. "He came to me. I was trying to sleep, trying to forget the pain. It hurt so much. Just as I was about to give up trying, his spirit came to me. He told me he was in Heaven and that it was a beautiful place filled with so much love I couldn't even imagine. He said we would be together there soon."

Seemingly unconcerned Olga turns back to the window. He was here, I feel it now. I believe her. But what did he mean they would be together soon? I can't fight the darkness as my mind shuts down and sleep takes over. It is not a comforting sleep. There was a ghost in this room.

The losses suffered by our forces cause them to turn back. Prussia again takes control of Allenstein, and the soldiers that survived are sent to Serbia. The wounded go back to Petersburg to heal and then be reassigned.

The hospital is in need of nurses trained at all different levels, and the tzarina signs herself and her daughters up to help. Olga cannot bear to see the soldiers in pain. It's too strong a reminder of what her Dmetri may have suffered. Instead, she works tirelessly in the reception area and gives her support to the families. It is better there anyway because no one in the reception area knows her as Madame Dmetrinova, wife of a fallen soldier. Now she must remain Olga Nikolaevna, daughter of the tzar.

Mother's prayers still ask for the return of her friend daily

Though my brother seems in good health, no one knows better than she that he could be cut or bruised at any moment. Rasputin has written that his recovery is slow and that the pain is almost unbearable, but he knows her needs and will come as soon as he can.

"Do you believe in angels?" Stepan and I have found a moment alone and I wish to speak to him about Olga's vision.

"I'm in the presence of an angel every day." He tenderly touches my lip.

I softly press my lips against his fingertips, in appreciation of his sentiments, and then press his hand to my heart, so he understands that I'm trying to be serious. I go on as if he didn't interrupt and clarify, "I mean ghosts, spirits. Olga told me that Dmetri came to her and told her everything was going to be all right—that they would be together in Heaven. I don't think she could be functioning as normally as she has been if she didn't have faith that it's true. Do you believe there is a heaven?"

Stepan drops into the seat next to me, ready for an earnest discussion. "As you know, I stand firmly by my Christian faith. Of course there is a heaven, just as surely as there is a God."

"Who will be allowed there? I mean, how will Olga be able to be in Heaven with Dmetri if our family has been chosen by God and Dmetri has not?"

"You and your father's throne will be on the right side of God's of course, but the rest of us will be allowed to worship you." He's teasing me, but gets serious again. "I believe we are all equal in God's eyes. No one will be labeled 'commoners' in Heaven."

"So Peter could be there with Anastasia? If everyone is equal in God's eyes, then why can't we be equal here on earth?"

Stepan takes a bit longer to answer this time—choosing his words carefully. "God has chosen some to be the leaders. If there were no one to lead, then no one would know how they must behave in order to be worthy of Heaven."

Satisfied, I smile. "Then because you were not born a Romanov, God's chosen, I will teach you how you must behave so that you may be worthy to be with me in Heaven." The thought warms my heart. Heaven would not be heaven without Stepan there with me.

As the summer turns to fall and the nights get longer, the air starts to bite in the evening,

but the war wages on. Father and Stepan are anxious to join their men. Mother will not allow him to leave until the spring, and Stepan always stays by Father. Our soldier's supplies have become so limited that the allies step in and help fund our efforts. It's humiliating to Father, but he has been assured that our manpower is needed. The cold air has cooled the fighting, and by wintertime it almost stops.

For Olga's twentieth birthday she doesn't want to celebrate with a ball. Instead she asks to have an outdoor feast, so she can invite all of the people of Petersburg. Mother and Father call her idea inspired and pursue the preparations with gusto. It will also be the beginning of the Christmas fast. Rasputin sends word to my mother that he will arrive back in Petersburg in time for the seasonal observance.

The mood at the palace brightens considerably as preparations are under way. "Maybe, while everyone is so happy, it would be a good time to approach your father and ask him if we can publicly announce our engagement. Then when I return from battle we can be married."

Stepan's suggestion is the best gift anyone could give me, and Christmas is still a month away. Stepan chooses to discuss the matter with my father privately, but returns from the meeting with good news. "I hope you still have the ring I gave you on your birthday." That night seems so long ago, so much has happened, but of course I still have it, I put it on every day and sometimes I wear it to bed.

"Your father says you may begin wearing it publicly at Christmas time, but says that we must wait until after your sister's party. We can't take the attention away from her on her birthday."

The realization strikes me. Her birthday is also the anniversary of the day she married Dmetri, just a year ago. It would be cruel of us to dig up that memory at her birthday party. I'm glad Father has reminded me that it will be a sensitive time for Olga.

No new dresses are bought for Olga's birthday celebration this year. It is better we think, to blend in and not appear to be extravagant. Besides it is cool outside and our coats would cover them anyway.

When the feast begins, we fill our plates along with hundreds of other Russian citizens and sit at large banquet tables. Father sits at the head with my mother on his right side and my lovely sister on his left. The image of her standing at the top of the stairs in her extravagant ball gown with George waiting at the bottom flashes before my eyes. She looks older, wiser now—even more beautiful, as if she's a jewel refined by fire—because of the hardship she has endured. The strain has made her even more stunning, but I know the pain continues to seethe.

The rest of us sit wherever we wish. Marie has joined Bertrand and some of his scholarly friends. They are all old, bearded men. I laugh at the irony. She's attentive to their conversation, but looks a bit like a child longing for some attention.

Anastasia, of course, has joined the group that has come from the stables. They form a bubble around her, as if she were a porcelain doll and the boys have been told they can look, but not touch. She doesn't seem to notice their cautious poses, as she laughs and entertains her captive audience. Peter especially leans in on her every word and swoons when she flashes him a smile. The night couldn't be more perfect, except that we all know that Olga's smile is a good façade and that Dmetri is the only one that could make her birthday happy.

Father stands with his glass held high and the loud chatter that has been constant since dinner was served turns to a low hum. "I'd like to make a toast to my eldest daughter Olga, and thank her for suggesting this celebration. May God bring our soldiers back safely and may we all live together in peace and unity under Him."

"Here, here's," are heard all around the tables. Even Peter's Marxist friends have their glasses raised. But above the joyous echo of brotherhood, another voice is heard. A very vocal figure comes out of the trees and into the sunlight. Rasputin has returned.

Mother reaches for Father's hand, but the agreeable cheer that was heard earlier is replaced by grumbles and groans. Greggori Rasputin looks worse than I have seen him before. His hair hangs gray and coarse in dirty tangles from his bandaged head. The clothes he wears are threadbare and blood stained.

Mother reaches for his hand. "Oh dear. My Friend, your hands are so cold."

Rasputin laughs a devilish chortle. "Maybe you would allow me to place them between your breasts, so I may warm them." He keeps his voice low, but everyone sees Mother blush and must suspect he has said something of the like. Her expression is shocked confusion. She looks at him questioningly like she's not sure she has understood him correctly, but still rips her hands away quickly.

My father stands up abruptly. He looks ready to squeeze the life out of the man, but wisely regains his composure. "You appear to be drunk," he says pointedly. "We will gladly welcome your return when you have had a chance to sleep it off." He sits down and appears to relax. The advisors at his table, their faces still white in disbelief, also relax their postures, albeit warily.

"…and take a bath," Uncle Makhail adds, drawing nervous laugh from the table.

I turn to look at Stepan. He lets out a sigh of relief, but he's still white like he's seen a ghost. "Your father handled that well, I don't know if I could control my temper the way he did under those circumstances."

Honestly, I'm shocked! I have never seen Our Friend in such a bad state, or heard him talk to Mother with such disrespect.

Rasputin comes to the palace the next morning clean and sober in a repentant tone.

"Please forgive my rudeness. The pain is nearly unbearable," he explains. "Alcohol is the only thing that makes it livable, but occasionally I have to become completely intoxicated before the pain is dulled." Mother readily forgives him, but it will take more than an apology before I will ever respect him again and I think Father will consider him a threat from now on.

Christmas is a solemn time this year. Though there is no fighting, the soldiers are away from their families on Christmas. We don't feel like celebrating when they cannot. We continue with François' tradition of putting candles in the window and say they are for the soldiers. No one is ready to explain to Olga why the tradition got started. We don't want to give her too many reminders of what she has lost, especially at Christmas, when her mind is sure to be continually on Dmetri.

Towards the end of the fast, Mother busies herself making feast boxes to send to the soldiers for the twelve days of Christmas. Of course all of our family, as well as many members of the community come to help. Thinking we're helping the soldiers makes it seem like a happier time.

Stepan often comes to visit after supper. One night as he nuzzles into my arms I say, "You're awfully affectionate. What are you thinking about?"

He twists the ring on my finger and lays his head on my shoulder. "I'm just so happy to be marrying the most wonderful girl in Petersburg…in all of Russia…in all the world!"

I can't help but laugh at his silliness. "When we are married, I'm sure there will be a lot of girls in Petersburg who will be sobbing their eyes out."

"Oh, the girls have been crying for a while now," he admits. "You stole my heart long ago." His smile changes to a more somber expression and the flames from the fire dance in his eyes. "Christmastime," he goes on, "is just six days from now. We will make it official, and then everyone in Petersburg will know that you are mine and mine alone."

I wonder if this is an official declaration—if he has spoken to my father about it, or if he has just made the decision now as we are sitting here, but I don't ask him.

The Christmas feast is a welcome treat after a forty-day fast and a day without meat. Though it is too cold to have our meal outside like we did for Olga's birthday, the servants' door to the kitchen remains open and the people of Petersburg have been invited into the kitchen to share our feast. After the meal is over Anastasia is excused to have dessert in the kitchen with Peter and her friends from the stable. I wonder if my parents are being naive about her friendship with Peter; if they know that her stable friends were once preaching against my father.

Stepan and I haven't talked about it since he hinted that our engagement would be made public today. My family and others that are close to me have seen the ring, and though they know what it symbolizes, no one has said anything. Perhaps someone else has told them about the situation, or perhaps they are still waiting to see what will happen with Olga. Our family keeps a secret very well and most of the kingdom probably thinks Olga will end up a spinster. I am sorry for that, but Stepan and I have waited long enough.

 As Christmas day starts to come to a close, only the most intimate circle of family is left.

If the announcement was to be made for all of Petersburg, it is too late. It doesn't matter, because the pleasantness of the evening has made me forget. We are gathered around the piano with Bertrand, singing Christmas carols, when there is a ruckus by the kitchen entrance. Uncle Makhail comes marching into the foyer with fire in his eyes. "I was afraid this would happen. When you open your home and are generous, some people don't know how to be grateful." The interruption causes the party to come to a halt. The singing is deferred for the time being. The men are trying to pretend like nothing is happening—maybe if they don't talk about it we won't notice—but Stepan's forced silence makes me afraid

He and I are standing close to Father when my uncle comes to explain. "Rasputin again. This is the second time he has made a scene in front of your subjects."

Father whispers something inaudible, and then his brother answers him. "He told me that your wife told him he was a welcome member of the household and that I couldn't keep him from seeing her at Christmas."

Father's back is turned, but I can read my uncle's lips even when he is completely silent. "Yes, completely drunk. Something is going to have to be done about this before he becomes a real problem."

Stepan has been overhearing the conversation as well, but finally pulls me away, which is fine. I've heard enough. I think he wants to talk, but I'm wrong. He pulls me into the den and presses his body up to mine, against the bookshelf. I feel helpless, unable to escape. It reminds me a little of Igor, but I like it when Stepan does it. I trust him. His breath is hot on my neck and the hairs stand up on my arms. He presses his lips against mine and moves his mouth all around my face and neck. My heart beats hard in my chest. Just as he starts to straighten and back away, I grab his wrist and pull him to me, but not soon enough. He retreats. Out of breath, he leans against the bookshelf next to me.

"I thought tonight would be the night, Tanya, but your father said no."

"He can't say no, we've waited so long." I straighten to my full height and start moving towards the door to find my father. Stepan pulls me back to him.

"There will be a better time. We don't want to hurt Olga."

My face turns red and I press my lips together. Olga—again it's always about Olga. But I take in a breath of air to clear my head and make myself remember what she has been through and what she has lost. Resting my head on Stepan's shoulder, I sigh. "As long as it's soon. But if I must, I will wait forever."

He runs his finger across my cheek. "I'm glad to hear you say that, because I'm afraid we will have to wait until this war is over." He laces his fingers through the fingers on my left hand, raises them to his lips and kisses our ring. "Just never take this off, and if someone asks you why you're wearing it tell them it's for me. We will be married when this is all over."

"It's funny. Last year at this time, as I was getting ready for bed with you, I vowed that I would never share a room with you again." Olga calls from her bed as I change into my nightgown in our suite. My sister probably needs to talk if she's bringing it up, but I feel a surge of guilt in blaming her for my frustration, and go to bed without a word.

The fighting resumes soon after the Christmas season is over and nothing will keep my father home. But when he leaves the country, he will be take along my Uncle Alexander, Stepan and most of his wisest advisors. This will leave Mother and his brother Mikhail in charge. Uncle Makhail is usually too busy with his personal life to concern himself about matters of state, so the task of ruling Russia will be left to my mother. There is much my father must do to prepare her to govern the country in his absence.

Olga is to take over the household, but the household basically runs itself. Monsieur Bertram is in charge of Alexei's activities, and my sisters and I spend most of our day at the hospital. I will soon be trained in every aspect of nursing—except maybe midwifing. There has not been a need for that at this hospital.

Spring 1915

Finally, in March around the time that we usually leave for the Lividia Palace, Father and Stepan are ready to join the eastern forces. Patriotism in Russia is strong. Father is more popular than he has ever been, but with hundreds of men killed and injured every day, the mood of the country is grave.

Although Stepan made me promise him I wouldn't cry, or maybe because he did, I sob like my heart is breaking as we say our last goodbyes. I want him to know what he is doing to me and what it will do to me if he doesn't return. Father shows complete confidence in my mother as he boards the train to Serbia. Her eyes are dry, when he says good bye, but when the train is out of sight the tears start to flow.

It doesn't take long for Mother to start to feel overwhelmed by her responsibilities, and though he has not been around the palace since Christmas, her spiritual advisor seems to know she is in need of support.

"I have almost stopped medicating myself with alcohol completely. It dulls my spirit. I am grateful that my spirit was on the alert to your needs at this time. I am in your service"

Soon after Stepan and Father leave, Rasputin begins working at the palace again. But instead of busying himself in the hospital wing, he spends time in Father's office, hearing reports as they come in on the radio, and listening in on Mother's phone calls. Mother seems grateful that Our Friend has returned, and indeed, she is more at ease, but Rasputin's reputation is badly blemished, and I'm afraid that she will lose the support of her subjects if they know that he is advising her.

I receive a letter from Stepan within a week after he leaves.

> Tanya,
>
> My darling, I have only been here a couple of days and already I know that I have gone to hell. I am not as close to the danger as some, but I have already witnessed a man

blown to pieces. The stench of death is everywhere. There is not enough food or clothing for our men, and in some places there are only enough guns for two men to share. I fear that we will have to impart some of the hardships on the people of Russia and ask them for more money. Raising taxes is never a popular request. Stand by your mother as she breaks the news to our people, but I cannot bear to see the boys who are fighting with us go without food and protection.

If I were to do it again, I would have listened to you instead of engaging in boyhood fantasies. When I feel sad or alone, I imagine your face and the sound of your heartbeat in my ears. It's all the time. I pray for the day when I can feel you, smell you again.

*Your love,
Stepan*

I appreciate that Stepan doesn't hold back or disguise his grief in order to shelter me from

the hardships he's experiencing. Though I'm grateful that he trusts me enough to share his heart, as well as his pain, his letter is a mixed blessing. The loving words are like a balm to my broken heart, but it also hurts me to hear his concerns and makes me sick with worry.

Tea in the morning has become a quiet time. Mother leaves for the capitol early to address the needs of the Dumas. Alexei and his tutor break their fast in his suite. My sister's and I usually hurry to the hospital in the morning, but today I feel discontented and decide to air it.

"It's utterly frustrating," I say out loud to anyone that is listening. "Stepan and I have waited so long. Now all I can do is hope and pray that he will return to me, and even then I don't know if Father will let us get married."

"Do you think you are the only girl in Russia who feels as you do?" Olga answers, deciding I need some perspective.

"I don't mean to blame you, Olga. You know more than anyone how I feel." I'm filled with guilt in expressing my woes when she has lost so much.

"Tanya, you and Olga are not the only girls in our family who are frustrated in love." Marie unexpectedly interrupts my thoughts as she voices her feelings on the matter. "Olga, you had to hide your feelings for a man that Father and Mother would never approve of. Tatiana, you have a man that our parents think is perfect, yet because of your birth order you've been made to wait and then wait some more. But how do you think I feel? I am almost sixteen, and I am capable of loving a man just as deeply and as passionately as you, but I must not only hide my feelings from our parents, I must be careful not to step beyond social boundaries with François. I may never know if he feels the same for me. Our relationship may never go beyond student/teacher admiration. And our mother will never start looking for another suitor for me until you are both wed."

My sisters and I look at each other in surprise, and then back at Marie. Anastasia shrugs and we sense her dissatisfaction as well. We all begin laughing—it's too painful to cry—I guess I am not alone in my romantic frustrations. Perhaps every royal princess feels as we do.

François Bertrand steps into the dining hall at just that moment. He stands behind Marie and affectionately squeezes her shoulders. "What is so funny? As one of the only remaining men left in this household, I feel like I get left out of a lot."

This ignites us into another stream of laughter. I had almost forgotten that Marie is old enough to experience the heartbreak that Olga and I have suffered. Maybe Anastasia too, but when the war is over, she will have plenty of time to fall in love again.

Mother has been left with the heavy burden of raising taxes on an already impoverished
 people. She seeks counsel from the men in the Dumas, but eventually goes to Rasputin for spiritual strength. I constantly listen in on the gossip at the hospital and find, understandably that the Russian people resent the fact that Rasputin, though a peasant by birth, and presumably a drunk, womanizing rat, seems to have been placed in such high power. Mother insists that he has no power; he only offers her the spiritual strength to rule in her husband's absence. The people are suffering, starving. They are not satisfied with this explanation. They think that he has some sort of power over her. They might be right.

    As the summer moves in, Rasputin becomes increasingly troublesome. His drunkenness alone has caused problems, fights with lovers or lovers' husbands are commonplace and Mother has asked that a police task force be assigned to protect him, or maybe, to protect others from him.

    I have become a skilled nurse. I know how to clean, stitch up, or cauterize almost any wound. I've assisted in surgeries and have witnessed amputations. Currently, I supervise a wing of the hospital. Marie is usually my assistant and Anastasia mostly cleans up after us. It is a humbling job. The emotional toll it takes on my heart would be excruciating, if I haven't taught myself not to feel. I avoid brooding on what has been lost, or what can be lost. I even have a hard time picturing Stepan's face anymore, because when I close my eyes, I see the wounded instead—open wounds, infection, diseases.

"Sometimes I forget he's dead and think he may be out there still," Olga and I sit looking on the streets in front of the hospital, eating what is left of our noon meal. "It's not a comforting thought. It makes me worry all over again."

Having a loved one fighting a war is stressful on everyone, but the common people are not only concerned for their loved ones, they are starving. There is no money. There was no money in the spring to plant the fields or their gardens and I fear that come winter there will be nothing stored to eat through the cold months. We share our lunch with women and children pacing the street in search of something to eat whenever we can.

"Why can't we just open up our storages and give them the food that they need?" Anastasia complains to Mother. "Why do we have so much when others have nothing?"

"God provides for his leaders. We have enough to keep us strong, and still save some for the next generations. If your grandfathers hadn't done this we would be suffering now along with everyone else. But in times of war, in times of need, the nation's leaders must remain healthy and strong. Just like He blessed us with our Alexei and sent Rasputin to help heal him, so he can lead the next generation. God has provided for our future."

Mother makes an interesting argument, but Anastasia isn't convinced. She continually sneaks food out to the peasants, with help from her friends in the stable.

Mother relies on Rasputin more and more each day. It seems that she would rather get

advice from him then the Dumas.

Dear Tanya,

Something must be done about Rasputin's influence over your mother. The Dumas is so upset, they have sent a representative to speak to your father at the Emperor's

> *headquarters. What is he to do? He told them to go back to Petersburg and carry on working. We're fighting a war. Men's lives are in his hands. I'm afraid that if the Dumas gets too discouraged they will give up their talks and we will not have a government to come home to.*
>
> *I know I shouldn't put this burden on you, my darling, but there is no one else I know who has influence over your mother. Maybe you could talk to her and convince her that the man is only out to hurt us. I am concerned, but I cannot trouble your father with it. Do you know the hardship he sees every day?*

I wonder if Stepan knows the hardship we see every day. The debris the war has left behind; the forgotten wounded, a home front on the verge of disaster.

> *My thoughts and prayers are always with you, my love. May this war be over quickly and may God bless and keep you until you can be in my arms again.*
>
> *With all my heart,*
> *Stepan*

I sometimes feel resentful when I read letters like this. What he is forgetting is that we hear almost all communications at the hospital. I don't need him to repeat Russia's troubles to me. We are in the thick of it. I know all about the representative the Dumas sent to Father, I also know that since receiving Stepan's letter, Father has sent them away with no more discussion, and the Dumas has now ended their session in frustration, making no plans to convene again. It is a hopeless situation.

Mother will not let go of her faith in Rasputin. She reminds us again and again about the miracles and his prophecies that have proven to be true, but if Stepan is right and Rasputin is of the devil, then his prophecies are curses and we are all doomed.

Winter 1915

Petersburg

Although its wintertime, the streets are always crowded with people, standing in the cold, waiting in line for food. The Dumas has decided that the food must be rationed, there is so little left. And with no hope that more food will be coming soon, they have only their boiling blood to keep them warm. The months have passed with nothing for me to report to Stepan but death, hunger and despair outside of the walls of the palace. His letters to me echo the same on war front.

Because the peasants are so angry with the government, as a precaution, my sisters and I must be lead by the police to the hospital every day. The sky is dark with clouds and smoke. Peasants build little fires out of the garbage they find on the streets to ward off the cold, and the air is filled with the putrid smell of burning rubbish. The bread is gone and the fires go out before the food line dies down and most go home cold and hungry. We must return home before dark. That is when the angriest of Petersburg's citizens come out. Eventually the cold air slows down the fighting and my sisters and I are no longer needed at the hospital. The palace at Tsarskoe Selo becomes a fortress, keeping Russia out and the Romanovs in.

Anastasia's friends have advised her to keep her food. Her charity only makes the people
angrier. "Peter tells me that because he works at the palace, even he is in danger. They hate us because of our wealth, because of the war we have brought on them, and because of Rasputin."

Olga's twenty-first birthday is celebrated indoors this year, quietly with just the family. A letter from father is the best part. He doesn't have good news to send—only his love. As we begin the Christmas fast, it is filled with prayers for our father and his troops, and the people of Russia. Our usual charities are discouraged also. We are told the people think we are mocking them. The only joy in the season is the lighting of the candles with Monsieur Bertram. The candles have lit the way in the past, and we need the help of the Blessed Mother to bring our men home.

Christmas day, I receive a letter from Stepan. I haven't heard from him in so long, and he's not current about our new situation, but his letter is very sweet.

> *My Precious Tatiana,*
>
> > *I have been told that you and your sisters have become the*
>
> *saviors on the home front, nursing our soldiers back to health so they can be reunited with their families. Ah, Tanya my darling, you are my savior as well. My days are filled with fear and nighttime can be terrifying. When I feel afraid, all I have to do is picture your beautiful face, your loving eyes, and my fears are calmed. The courage you show every day, saving men's lives gives me the strength to make it through another day. I no longer care if we win this war or what the world thinks of Russia, I just want*
> *it to be over so we can be together.*
>
> > *With all the love I possess,*
> > *Stepan*

I'm relieved that he has not given me any more instructions about what I should do regarding my mother and Rasputin. Maybe he no longer hears what is going on here, but the Russian people are getting more and more frustrated. They have to have someone to blame. They choose to blame Mother because she seems to only listen to her healer.

The tension from the streets has entered our home. When Mother is there she is always on edge, even around the family, but she's hardly ever at home. Even dinner at the palace is a rare occurrence. One such evening, we are together as a family at dinnertime. We are grateful to finally have a moment to ourselves, when a maid comes in to tell Mother she has a telephone call.

"Who would disturb us during dinner?" Mother asks coldly.

"It's the general, General Rennenkampf. He says it's urgent."

The eating stops. There is no more clanging of silverware or tinkling of crystal. The
room is silent. An urgent call at dinnertime from the general could possibly mean…

Finally Mother pushes back her chair and stands to go into the office to take the call. The silence continues as we keep our ears peeled for any hint of sound in the nearby room. But the volume of Mother's voice soon makes the walls disappear and she can be heard easily.

"He only wants to pray for the men… Yes, so the battle can be a success….No! No, he is only a dear friend, my spiritual advisor. I see …yes."

All eyes are big in the room as Mother returns. She is obviously agitated while she spreads her napkin in her lap. As if she just noticed the silence, she looks around the room at each of our stark white faces. "Your father is fine." She looks back at her lap until she remembers me, "Stepan is fine too. The general had another concern entirely—so rude of him to call during dinner."

We continue the meal in silence at first, but then Anastasia speaks. "The Russian people think he's a spy."

We all know to whom she is referring, but only Anastasia would be bold enough to say it. Mother puts down her fork and takes in a deep calming breath. She looks directly at Anastasia. Her mouth is smiling, but her eyes say something different.

"That's ridiculous. He is a man of God. We all know that." Her eyes move to Alexei who has his head bowed, his eyes looking down. "He wanted to see the battle plans, so he could pray for the men specifically."

"You didn't, Mother." Olga speaks out this time. Her frustration makes her bold as well. "That could be considered treason."

Mother no longer pretends to smile. "You have no idea how hard it is to run this country during a war. I am not properly trained to be in this position. Our Friend is willing to listen and support me through these times. I need his guidance."

She stands, her body shaking for a moment, then gathers herself together and excuses herself from the table. She climbs the stair to her suite, leaving us in shock, with no more discussion on the matter.

Soon after this event, I receive the most unnerving letter from Stepan yet.

> *My Dearest Tanya,*
>
> *I fear the war will soon be pushed back into Russia. The last thing your father and I want is for this war to end up back home where you and your family could be in any danger, but our men are starving and we are not equipped to fight this war. It seems all we can do now is come home and protect what is ours. I can only hope that we will return to the home that we once knew and that it has not been destroyed by that devil Rasputin.*

*Your Uncle Makhail has been
placed in charge of his demise.
Your mother would never forgive your
father if she knew he had a hand in this,
but we all agree it has to happen.
Makhail knows a man, a distant cousin
of yours who is willing to try and gain
Rasputin's trust. He has knowledge of
poisons. This will be the means by which
Rasputin will be disposed of once and
for all.*

*I have told you much more than you
should know, and it pains
me to have to lay such a heavy burden
at your sweet feet, but you are the only
one I trust in Petersburg with such
information. The one good that I can see
that may come from the misfortune of
this war is that I may see you sooner
than I thought. I am soothed by this and
think often of laying my tired head in
your loving lap, and holding your sweet
tiny hands between mine.*

*Till that day you will always be in
my dreams.*

*Your love,
Stepan*

*PS: Destroy this letter as soon as you
read it. We cannot let your mother know
of our plans.*

I rip the letter in half and then turn it and rip it again and throw it in the fireplace. It would kill my mother if she were to hear that there is a plot to kill her friend. I am completely shocked. I don't believe that Rasputin is a man of God. His drunken promiscuity proves that, but I also can't explain the miracles that have saved my brother, and even Rasputin is a man created by God. Does any man deserve death by poisoning? Is it our choice, or should God choose who lives or dies in this world? Stepan claims to be a Christian, but he is certainly willing to be the judge in this case. And what if Rasputin does have a sixth sense, would he already know of the plan?

We shall soon see. At dinner, for a change, Mother is in an unusually good mood. "It seems that your father's entire family hasn't shunned Our Friend. He has been invited by your father's cousin, Yusipov, for cigars and billiards this weekend. He seems pleased by the invitation."

"Pleased?" I question. "Was he honestly pleased Maman?" I try to cover my shock. It's happening sooner than I had expected.

"Yes." She studies my face, trying to determine the reason for my surprise. "He didn't stop smiling the whole afternoon."

A shudder is felt around the table as each of us imagine Rasputin's sinister smile.

Spring 1916

The winter is long and bleak, but the arrival of spring provisionally brings new hope to everyone—including the Germans. Just as the days get longer and the sun starts to shine, my sister's and I are asked again to work in the hospital. It's agonizing to see the pain, and hear the horrible stories the men come back with. The soldiers usually receive first aid on the front. Then after the bleeding has stopped, the wounded soldiers are dragged across dusty roads and bacteria-ridden swamp lands. Our patients have overcome death, but we have to deal with the infections, the amputations, and the reality of the long lasting effects this war will have.

Farmers stand in line for seeds, but even if they had money to buy them with, there are very few available to purchase. The harsh winter has left the railroad in poor repair and there are not enough healthy, experienced men around to fix it. It has become impossible for food and supplies to be transported across Russia. Lines get longer as more and more of our people grow hungry.

In June, Mother throws a little birthday party in our honor. I'm turning eighteen; the age Mother was when she married Father. Marie will be sixteen and Anastasia fourteen. There will be no dancing and no orchestra this year. No soldiers for Anastasia from the Corps de Page.

"Mousier Bertrand is always a fine addition to a party," Mother says, hoping we will forget, if only for a day, that our father is fighting a war. Mother allows Peter to come up to the palace for the first time. François lends him a suit.

"It's a little baggy," Anastasia prepares us before he is presented, "and a little short, even though I let down the hem as much as possible." Although she doesn't say so, I know she hopes he will feel he is accepted here. She has chosen to wear one of Marie's old dresses instead of buying a new one. She keeps adjusting the bust line that had to be taken in.

"It's honorable that you all have chosen to save money by reusing dresses this year, but not necessary. Only our family will see, and I adore seeing my beautiful daughters in new dresses." Mother is uncomfortable with our decision to be conservative, but we stand firm by it.

"But it won't just be us," Marie reminds her.

Most of the guest list only includes our household, our extended family and a small number of close friends. Rasputin will be there with his new friend, our cousin, Prince Yusipov.

"I'm so grateful for the way your father's cousin has shown friendship towards Rasputin," Mother tells us that evening. The "friendship" has gone on for months now and Rasputin is as fit as ever. Maybe Stepan was mistaken in the role that the prince would play.

"Do they get on well? Is Uncle Makhail encouraging the friendship?" I've been watching, waiting to see what would happen since Stepan told me about it months ago. Any information I collect is third-hand, and maybe Mother has developed a false hope, but what I have heard from society, which isn't much, the prince is fascinated, almost obsessed with our healer. I'm not surprised. Our Friend has a captivating personality.

"As far as I know, your uncle doesn't even associate with Yusipov. Have you heard differently?"

That must be part of the plan, I think. If something happens that would upset Mother, it is

best if Father and Uncle are as far removed from it as possible.

"No, Maman, as usual, I hear nothing." I remain stoic, unfeeling.

But I watch, and Uncle Makhail seems to show no interest in Prince Yusipov. Instead he, his new wife, and stepson spend most of the evening with Alexei. Makhail has no interest in matter of state. His life has been a scandal itself in the past years, but now that he is finally married and his new family is settled, he seems to have put the past behind him.

Alexei seems to see our Uncle Makhail almost as an older brother, and clings to him when he's around. Uncle Makhail doesn't seem to mind. Because of the age gap between father and his one remaining brother, they haven't spent a lot of time together. But Makhail and Alexei have much in common. Uncle is number three to the throne as my brother is number two, and with all the rest of the men at war they are now both always surrounded by women.

My mother calls my sisters and brother and me into Father's office after the cake is served. She has a surprise for us—but me especially. She sits us down in the office chairs and turns on the radio. With much difficulty, through the static, we hear Father and Stepan's enthusiastic voices sing the birthday song. After Father has given us his love and Mother has shown me how to turn off the radio, she and the rest of the family quietly leave me to my future husband.

Tears stream down my cheeks, partly because the connection has gotten worse and I'm afraid I'll lose him, but also because just the sound of his almost indiscernible voice has put him in the room with me.

"Don't cry, don't cry," he begs.

My tears become laughter as I become overwhelmed with joy.

"That's better, baby. Wow," he exclaims. "You're eighteen! Not a baby at all, old enough to be a bride."

I start laughing and crying all over again. "No, no, don't cry again. The sound of your tears rang in my ears for months after I left you."

This time I speak out loud and clear. "Don't ever leave me again Stepan. I love you and I want to be in your arms forever."

His end is quiet for some time. I think he is also trying to regain his composure.

"I can't talk long. This line is supposed to be kept open. If I didn't have the permission of the tzar, I could be in big trouble," he softly chuckles, "Happy birthday, my love."

Now there are a hundred things I wish I could tell him. "Take care of yourself, Stepan. Always wear dry socks (something I learned working at the hospital). I want you to come back to me in one piece. My twenty children are going to need a father...." But the static has taken over. I sit back in the chair, listening to the static, straining my ears for sounds of the world he just came from.

When my tears are dry, I rise up from the chair and turn off the radio, like Maman showed me. When I get to the door I hear voices, a man's and a girl's, reminiscent of the drivel I heard while hiding in the bushes, years ago. Waiting for the maid to call, for Olga's soldier to leave, but this isn't Olga's voice I hear squealing with delight, it's Anastasia's. I want to open the door and warn her. This can't be good. Look at the heartache it has caused Olga, but I can't deny my little sister the greatest happiness I've ever felt, even if it can't last on earth.

In heaven, Stepan says, it can last forever.

I wait a minute longer, but finally push open the door. The blushing couple guiltily takes a step back from each other, and he reluctantly removes his hand from her hair. Though Mousier Bertrand's suit hangs off Peter like it were hung on a green willow branch, Peter has become a man, his face aged with worry. I cover my mouth to hide my smile and walk by without a word.

I don't get far, when I see Marie and François embracing behind a bookshelf. Marie's face is hidden, crying into his lapel. He's looking down on her, so I walk by unnoticed. I enter the salon and take a seat next to Olga.

"Here we are, the oldest sisters, and the only ones alone." I whisper to her.

Olga has a faraway look in her eyes. She places her hand on her heart. "I am never alone."

Feeling left out of whatever memory my sister uses to keep herself breathing, I sigh. My sigh brings her out of her dream. "How is Stepan?"

Hearing his name brings back the pain and the tears return. Olga comfortingly wraps her arms around me. "I know, I miss him too, but he will return to us safely soon—with Father."

For some reason I feel her words are prophetic and it brings me comfort.

****

There is gossip to be heard outside the palace. The relationship between Rasputin and Prince Yusipov has become quite scandalous.

"They had a fight." A nurse in the hospital whispers. They don't want us to hear their blather, but we hear.

"A lover's quarrel." The other nurse giggles.

Apparently my cousin, who is married, with children, thought Rasputin, because of his promiscuous past, might be interested in a little homosexual experimentation. This is odd and highly frowned upon by the church, but some aristocrats do strange things to amuse themselves. Of course this is only rumor, but I guess Our Friend was offended by the suggestion. There is no longer regard in their relationship. Mother says nothing on the matter, but word travels fast and far in this case. Soon after I hear the story, I receive another letter on the subject from Stepan.

> *My Darling,*
>
> *I realize that the last letter I sent may have been concerning to*

you, and since you have probably heard the rumors going around about your cousin, I felt it necessary to reassure you. Yes, there has been a disagreement, but it will not affect the outcome of the original plan. Prince Yusipov is more motivated than ever to complete his task.

We are within two hundred miles of Moscow now. This is not good for the war, but it makes me giddy with hope, that our time apart will be but a little longer and then no one, not Olga, not your father, not even God can keep us apart any longer.

*Love always,
Stepan*

I fold the letter and put it back in its envelope. A chill runs up my spine. Holding its contents to my heart, I look around to ensure I'm alone. Does he know? Does Rasputin have an inclination that there is an order out for his death? I know. Only I, in this house, know that he will soon meet this fate. I look guiltily over my shoulder, fold the envelope in half, rip it, and fold it again. This too will have to be burned.

Winter

Transportation has become a problem in Russia. Food and supplies are gravely needed. The country hasn't run out of food completely, but there is only one way to get what is left where it is needed, and that is by train. But the railroad is in complete disarray and there are no plans being made to resolve the problem

The cold has come early this year and by October, the railroad workers are overworked, hurting and tired without necessary compensation. A strike is inevitable. Hundreds of workers convene in Petersburg, demanding better working conditions, but the country is desperately in need of the services they provide. Without a transportation system there will be no food.

Father has his men stationed near Moscow now (about four-hundred miles east of Petersburg) but the supplies needed for them are no longer arriving either. He sends soldiers, hundreds of them, to help coerce the strikers back to work and to maintain peace if the striking becomes violent. To his dismay, the men that have been sent away from battle feel more loyal to the cause of the railroad workers than the cause they are fighting for. The men insubordinate and join with the railroad workers.

The Dumas reconvenes in November to discuss a solution. A new party, called the Progressives, think the Dumas doesn't recognize the implications of the rebellion. The leader asks, "Is this folly or treason?" The nation has lost its confidence in the government and my father's power to rule Russia.

Mother should have recognized that the people would lose confidence in my parent's rule when the soldiers became mutinous, and if she hadn't been concerning herself with other matters, there would have been consequences for the soldier's disloyalty, but her concern for Rasputin remain forefront in her mind. I too, am concerned.

Our Friend is acting strange, even for him. I can't fight the feeling that he knows that there is a plan to have him killed. He acts jittery, nervous, and his eyes…

When he looks at me, I get a sensation that he is looking into my soul, examining my every thought. I wonder if he senses that I know about the plan.

But by December, Mother's worries are eased. "The rumors about Our Friend and Prince Yusipov have been highly exaggerated. He tells me that he has been invited to a holiday gala at Yusipov's palace. The party is for men of prestige and high esteem. They will all be charmed by Our Friend, and he will be welcomed into Petersburg society."

Mother seems relieved, but I am not. It may just be my guilty conscience, but every time Rasputin and I are in the same room together, I feel his penetrating eyes on me.

Early one morning, as I'm washing for tea, I feel a presence in my room. Olga is gone, she always wakes before me, but I see that she has left the door open a crack. I scurry across the room in my petticoat and close the door tightly, so that I might put the feeling aside and get dressed. As I smooth my gown and look in the mirror, I see that the door is once again cracked open, and standing in the shadows, I see a dark figure. Terrified, I let out a short scream and Rasputin is immediately next to me, covering my mouth.

"You would not want to upset your mother." His voice is a harsh whisper. His words are slurred, his Siberian accent dominant. The foul scent of body odor and stale alcohol reek from his clothing. I don't know how mother can stand to be around this man.

Now I am completely appalled. How dare he be upstairs? He is not permitted—there is no need for him to be in this part of the palace. My soul stirs with anger, but before I can speak, I am silenced by his icy glare.

"Your father is not stupid enough to hurt me. He knows it would break your mother's heart, but your lover—well, he's as good as dead anyway."

Too surprised to react, I continue to stand motionless, but I tremble on the inside. Nothing this man has said makes any sense to me at all—is it a curse, or does he think Stepan won't survive the war? He shouldn't even be here. I stand frozen for a good minute after he leaves. I am struck with hatred for this man. How dare he? And yet, I choose not to say anything to Mother. He's right, this would be too much for her to handle right now and Olga would not let it alone if she knew. I will not mention this to anyone. Rasputin is as good as dead anyway.

December 17, 1916, while mother is praying at the Feodorov Cathedral, her usual routine during the forty-day fast, she receives a message from Rasputin's niece. She is worried because he didn't come home that night. She has questioned Felix Yusupov and he claims that Rasputin had not even been there the night before. His niece doesn't believe Yusupov, and neither does my mother. She calls the police and an investigation begins immediately.

When the police visit our cousin's palace, they find massive amounts of blood on his lawn. He claims that one of his servants had gotten drunk and killed his dog. The animal's body was found, but it didn't fully explain all the blood.

"Isn't it obvious whose it is?" Marie voices her opinion while Mother is with the police. I am in shock. I keep replaying the conversation with him in my bedchamber the other morning in my mind. I can't believe it's happening already. Almost as if his words were, once again, prophetic.

"Perhaps," Olga explains. "But they won't be able to prove anything until they find the body."

"Felix should just confess," Anastasia bursts out. "He will be proclaimed a hero."

On December 19, police began looking for a body near the Great Petrovsky Bridge on the Malaya Nevka River. A bloody boot had been found there the day before. There was a hole in the ice, but they couldn't find the body. After looking a little farther downstream, they came upon the corpse floating in another hole in the ice.

When they pulled him out, Rasputin's frozen hands were raised above his head. The police believe that he was still alive under the water, and froze trying to untie the rope around his hands.

When Mother is told, she goes into a fit of hysterics, demanding that Father come home so that an Imperial Funeral—something reserved for members of the royal family or senior members of the aristocracy or church—be held in his honor. Nothing can be done to console her.

On December 22, less than a week later, her demands are met. At the Imperial Train Station, impoverished Russian peasants watch, fuming, as the luxurious train pulls up, indicating I fear, that for our family a funeral for Rasputin is more important than our dying soldiers. I don't care what they think as long as it brings Father and Stepan home. But Rasputin's last words for me still ring in my ears. I am afraid. Afraid for Stepan.

They arrive from Moscow looking pale and thin, with Russia's troubles etched on their faces. I stand before my love, and trace the lines on his worn face. Aggravated onlookers melt unseen into the background. He reaches for my hand and smiles. My eyes are drawn to the familiar green orbs that dwell in my heart. It bursts with gratitude that I can see him, touch him again and for now, my fear of Our Friend's final warning are diminished.

I wish we could feed them—Father and Stepan—but Mother is still holding firm to her Christmas fast. We will eat something after dark. I wish we could let them sleep, but there is much to do the few days they are in Petersburg. The first item, arrest Rasputin's killer. There is enough evidence to charge Felix Yusupov.

"I'm sure there will be a trail." I finally pull Stepan away from his business and my father for a moment. He has arrived at the place after talking to the police and is still in his coat, so I take him out to the snow-covered patio.

"That's exactly what Felix wants. To be put before a judge so that he can brag about his triumph. He will be proclaimed Russia's hero—the man that rid the country of the powerful influence of Rasputin." Stepan chuckles a tired-sounding laugh as he puts his hands around my waist and pulls me to him. "Your father will never let that happen. If there were a trial, he might implicate your father. No, there will be no trial. Yusupov is to be exiled to Persia."

I burrow my face into his neck. I don't think he wants to talk anymore of Rasputin. But after a moment of nuzzling, I can't hold back any longer.

"He knew." I swallow the lump in my throat and go on. "Rasputin knew there was a death warrant out on him, and he knew it was you that initiated it."

Even though my voice is full of fear, Stephan's laugh is soothing. He smoothes back my hair from my forehead and looks into my eyes.

"Don't let his memory continue to haunt you, my love. There is no way he could have known, he was only a man, despite what he wanted your family to believe. A bad, bad man."

My fiancé wraps his arms around me to soothe away my anxiety. "This was my fault. I never should have burdened you with that information. I just wanted to share—I just wanted you to know, that you didn't have to worry…"

I have more questions, but the time we waste talking about Rasputin I will never get back, so instead I use this precious moment to savor every bit of Stepan being back in my arms.

Though Mother has declared it an Imperial Funeral, it is a relatively small affair. Rasputin's niece and her daughter are the only members of his family that are in attendance. Our immediate family and the necessary church officials round off the party. Mother is so beside herself, she doesn't notice that she's the only one grieving. Even Alexei's eyes remain dry. I never understood my brother's relationship with Our Friend, but I know Alexei has never been afraid of death.

Greggori Rasputin's body is laid to rest at Feodorov Cathedral in Tsarskoe Selo.

For me, the most upsetting part of the funeral is when it's over. It means I will have to send my father and fiancé off to war again.

"Let's get married," I insist. "We have the church, the clergy is here." Stepan holds me to his chest as I blabber on. "We could elope, like Olga. Then I could be sure that you'll never be taken away from me."

Stepan frowns. "Dmetri was taken from Olga for that very reason." He squeezes me one last time. "No, the war will be over soon—within the year. We will have a proper Russian Orthodox wedding, ensuring our children's future." With that promise on his lips, he leaves me again. He and my father board the train, back to the nightmare of war.

Within days after they leave, rumors of how Rasputin died are everywhere. The nurses at the hospital no longer seem concerned about what we hear.

"First, Yusupov tried poison."

This I had suspected from what Stepan had told me about the plan.

"I was told that he put enough poison to kill a man in each of the cakes Rasputin was served, and also in his wine. He ate every cake and drank the wine."

"It proves it," the second nurse replies, he was not human, but I thought he was shot. The blood found on the lawn at the Yusupov palace was matched to his. That's why Yusupov was arrested."

"I heard that after he had eaten and drank enough poison to kill five men, he stood smiling before Yusupov as if the poison had no effect."

"Oooo, that smile gave me the chills," the second nurse speaking shivers. I picture that smile in my mind and I shiver as well.

"Felix Yusupov was so frightened, he pulled out his pistol and shot him directly in the head, but Rasputin turned to run."

"The shot must have missed him." The nurse gapes in shock as her friend explains.

"No, the wound on his head was gushing blood as he ran, and while chasing him across the lawn he shot him two more times. The first bullet entered the chest on the left, hitting Rasputin's stomach and liver; and the second bullet entered the back on the right, hitting the kidneys, all potentially fatal shots. So, when he finally fell, The Grand Duke Dmitry Pavlovich caught up with him and was able to secure the angry devil by tying his hands."

"I hadn't heard that Pavlovich was involved." The second nurse's eyes are still large.

"Yes, he was arrested too—sent to Persia to fight the war."

My father has done this before. Using the war to inflict punishment on an offender he doesn't know what to else to do with. It makes sense that my cousin had an accomplice. Dmitry Pavlovich is also my cousin. His grandfather reigned as tsarevich under Alexander II.

The first nurse continues speaking. "Poisoned, shot with three fatal blows, and still, when his body was found, it was frozen with his hands in the air, trying to untie himself. The coroner found water in his lungs. The devil would not die."

I tune myself out of the nurses' conversation. I've heard enough. According to the coroner's report, no poison was found in the body, only alcohol, but maybe the poison was left out of the report my mother received to spare her, or maybe Rasputin was adhering to the laws of the fast, or as I have suspected, knew what was happening all along, and didn't really eat the cakes. Either way Stepan's warning rings in my ears. He truly was a devil.

Rasputin continues to haunt us from the grave. During their investigation the police uncover a message from Rasputin, addressed to my father. It contains another prophesy.

*"If I'm killed by my brothers, the
Russian peasants, you have nothing*

to fear. If it is your relations that have brought about my death, then none of your family will remain alive for more than two years. They will be killed by the Russian people."

Petersburg 1917—The Petrograd

Though we thought my parents' relationship with Rasputin was the cause of our weakened monarchy, the death of Our Friend seems to have come too late to reverse the damage. If anything now it looks as if our family used the aristocracy to kill a peasant. The people have no confidence in the Russian government. With no working transportation system in Russia, there is no food. All workers are on strike, and the people take to the streets in protest. My sisters and I are no longer welcome at the hospital. The Dumas reconvenes to discuss what should be done.

While my father is away meeting with Allied leaders to discuss future policies, a message goes out to the generals asking whether they think he is fit to rule or should be replaced. Uncle Makhail tells us that there has been some discussion in the family as whether or not Alexei could rule with a regent.

On March 12, 1917, while standing in line waiting for bread, an angry riot of cold, hungry men storm the bakery. There are thousands of people in the streets, and when police fire rings out it to stop the looters, everyone standing around is suddenly in danger of crossfire.

When the police realize their mistake, they go to the aid of the people, and some join the riot.

Soldiers are called to the street to help maintain peace, but seeing the crowds, they disobey orders and return to their barracks. All of the commands my father gives to restore stability at home are ignored or blatantly disobeyed. Many of the soldiers also join the rioters. They raid the city's arsenals and break into the prisons, setting prisoners free.

The terror in the streets is unrestrained as the Dumas meet to appoint a provisional committee that represents all of the political parties. The man they choose to lead the committee, Mikhail Rodzyanko, is a member of the Petrograd Soviet party. He is thought to be a good choice because he has many links with the working class of Petersburg. He sends a telegram to Father asking that he appoint a

Prime Minister that has the confidence of the people. We don't hear whether or not he ever received the request, but no Prime Minister is appointed.

Instead, rumors fly through the city that soldiers from the front are being sent to put down the disturbance. The newly elected provisional government perceives this as an expression that the tzar has no confidence in the new government. The Pertrograd Soviets vow to support the provisional government on the condition that it summons a constituent assembly and guarantees that civil rights are to be enjoyed by all.

In reality the provisional government has nothing to fear from the soldiers on the front. There are already many that have deserted. But still, they send word to the soldiers that if they are called out by my father, they should not obey him. He is caught between the war and Petrograd.

With all of the terror and confusion on the streets our household has been turned upside down. Mother is so overcome with grief from the loss of the man that she once called her savior, she cannot rule. Most of her advisors, as well as our household staff, lose hope in her ability to bring some kind of control to the chaos, and abandon her.

She even refuses to see us, her family, her children, and we are left alone to wonder what will become of us. We live in constant fear of a raid on the palace as the noise surrounding it gets louder and closer. We are left to fend for ourselves. Only twelve-year-old, Alexei seems to fear nothing. Marie tells us that he has confided in Bertrand, telling him that he has heard the rumors and feels ready and willing to rule if Father deems it necessary.

During this time of fear and despair, I receive a puzzling letter from Stepan.

> *Dear Tatiana,*
>
> *We have received word of a small disturbance in Petersburg and your father has gathered a group of his most loyal soldiers (me included) to join him in a march to disrupt it. I feel this could be the end of our part in the war. Your father is needed at home. I don't wish to falsely raise your hopes but I feel that we will be together soon.*
>
> *Your only love,*
> *Stepan*

I fear Stepan and father have been deceived or have not received proper communication if they are calling this a "small disturbance." What started out as a disagreement has now turned into a full scale rebellion. All hell has broken lose in the streets of Petersburg. Red banners fly from the streets stating, "Down with the Tzar, Down with the German Woman. "The German Woman" is my mother. I fear Father has no idea of its magnitude—the hate that has been stirred up by the people—or its political backing. But before his small army reaches Petersburg, they get caught in a snowstorm and have to stay in Pskov. It's there that my father receives a telegram from the provisional government, with the backing of his generals, asking him to abdicate his position as tzar of Russia.

Abdicate—abandon his reign, his responsibilities, his family heritage. It must have almost killed him, but I am told that with grace and dignity he accepted his fate and attempts to appoint his younger brother, Mikhail, to succeed him.

We are all in a state of shock, but Mother most of all. She receives the news via the radio along with all of Russia's other leaders. No telegram, no warning. When she hears, she comes out of Father's office, screaming like a banshee.

"Abdicate, abdicate? He would never. He has his home, his family to think of. What will become of us? Where will we go?"

The doctor goes to her, and as the children of a disgraced monarchy, we are left to deal with the implications with only each other to lean on. But after a few days she seems to arouse from her sickness and comes up with a plan of her own.

"England. We will go back to my mother country in exile, until this silly government destroys itself and they beg us to come back. But we will need to assure our safe return."

She insists we sew the royal jewels into our corsets. "There they will be hidden in case we need to sell them, Heaven forbid, but at least our family's heirlooms won't be looted by peasants

Most of the imperial household has deserted us already, but some stay loyal, including Peter, he takes over the stables. Our personal servants, Mother's lady in waiting, Father's valet, all stay, as well as Alexei's doctor and my mother's favorite cook.

Father arrives home, but not to a grand welcome. The streets are still covered with protesters singing "Down with the Tzar." Mother, still recovering from her near breakdown, is able to pull herself together when he gets home. He enters the empty palace with his head hung low, takes my mother in his arms and carries his own bags to his suite. My sisters and I stand around confused and a little disappointed.

He usually acts most happy to see us when he returns home after being gone for so long, but he seems to have forgotten about us this time. My sisters turn to the kitchen to help cook prepare a humble meal fit for a humbled tzar, but I hold back waiting for the man that has accompanied Father.

He opens the door to my awaiting arms, but his body sags and he doesn't hold me back as tightly as I am holding him. I look up into his forlorn eyes and he turns his head in shame. "I have failed you. All I ever wanted was to protect you, to keep you safe, and now our world is coming apart. All of my desires have been in vain."

I bury my face in his neck and sob for his broken heart. Mine too, breaks because of his pain. "How could you," the words get caught in my throat but I go on. "How could you think you have failed me? You have loved me more than any man could love any girl." His devotion to me and my family proves it more deeply than I thought possible.

I almost see a glimmer of hope cut through the clouds in his eyes and he puffs out his chest with resolve. "I can fix this. I will speak with the Dumas as soon as I possibly can. They will soon see that this has all been a mistake and we will fix this.

"I will go to the Dumas tomorrow. It is late in the game, but it is not over yet. Now that we have pulled out of the war, and our soldiers are coming home, the people will remember happier times. This socialism will be forgotten."

"You mean the provisional government," I remind him. "Much has changed since you've been away, and I fear it's too dangerous for you to be out, even on the streets. It would be much worse for you to be trying to persuade those men that they are wrong. You were the tzar's closest friend and ally. The position of tzar is not looked on so highly on as he once was." I want to be cautious of my father's feelings, but I also want to be assured that Stepan knows what he's up against.

"The representatives in the Dumas—the provisional government—know I respect your father, but they also respect my opinion. I have kept my relationship with him professional in the government's eyes and my relationship with you is known only by our social relations."

I see now that the delay of our engagement and marriage was a political move on his part.

"He's right." Father comes back down the stairs and joins the conversation. "Your future husband has high influence in our Dumas.

If the other influences haven't gotten too strong, he may have a chance. He may be our last hope."

Meanwhile, Mother and Father make plans for us to exile to the United Kingdom. They are our allies and have been loyal to us in the past, but a telegram from King George comes as a shocking disappointment to Mother. He has been advised that taking us in could cause an uprising.

So instead, things go on are as they usually do in Tsarskoe Selo. Well, not exactly the same, but we stay busy and stay relatively content in our new situation. Alexei, Anastasia and Marie study with Monsieur Bertrand. Olga and I help the cook keep house and prepare meals. And Father is always around. He has a much more difficult time keeping himself busy.

With spring blooming we would like to be outdoors, but mother's fear of snipers and terrorists is greater than ever, so instead we stay inside. Monsieur Bertrand is the only tutor who has stayed, but he has much to teach us. He teaches art and music, along with history, mathematics, and languages. Marie and François no longer hide their affection for each other. Anastasia is allowed to go to the stable to see her horse, but Peter accompanies her both ways. He also is no longer seen as an outsider in the household. He is frequently invited in and asked to stay.

The family no longer comes to visit in the evening, but my aunts don't leave my mother without a friend. They usually come to call during the daytime. The male members of the family are afraid that a conspiracy will be suspected. Of course Stepan comes to call every night after dinner. He waits till dark and parks his automobile in the back by the stables. He must be very cautious. If the other members of the provisional government were to find out that he was still in contact with Father, his plan could not possibly work. He always comes in with a worried look and talks to my father first. He tries to ease my father's concerns and give him hope. Then he still seems to make the time and energy for wooing me.

I become curious about what my fiancé does all day—what his platform is.

"Are we still lobbying for Makhail? Could he at any point take Father's place as tzar?"

When Father appointed Uncle Makhail to take his place, he refused saying he would only accept the throne if it was given to him in a vote by the people. At that point it was impossible.

"Your uncle was very smart when he suggested that an election be held. At the time he knew much more about the political atmosphere then your father or me." Stepan has gathered my hair up in his hands and is combing his fingers through it thoughtfully.

"Knew more about it?" I smile anticipating the answer to that question.

Stepan's green eyes twinkle. "I am a very quick learner."

"So do you think an election is a good idea?"

Stepan stretches and yawns indicating that an election is old news. I nuzzle into his shoulder. It pleases me that we understand each other so well.

"Things are changing fast. At first it was thought that the Soviets had the answers. They understand the working class. Then there are the Bolsheviks. Their party is smaller, but they won't be ignored. They are not to be trifled with. But the Socialists are winning over the representatives of the provisional government with their complicated philosophies and poignant speeches. Many of them are followers of Vladimir Lenin."

"Ah, Lenin," I interrupt. "I am familiar with him. I have seen his picture in the paper. He has written much propaganda on Marxism."

Stepan's eyes light up with surprise. "You have read some of Lenin's Marxist propaganda?"

I give Stepan a sly smile. "When Peter brought it for Anastasia. I was curious. We are not so isolated in this palace as it may seem."

Stepan tries to act as if he's not impressed with me and goes on. "While Lenin's writing on economics and the harsh lifestyle of a peasant may be both eloquent and painfully truthful, his suggestions could be very dangerous to your family. Though he has been in exile for the past eleven years, he has been invited back to share his wisdom and leadership. If the Socialists can get him back to Russia, I'm certain that he will be asked to lead the new provisional government. I think if I pose as an admirer of Lenin's, I can persuade the majority to listen to my arguments and in time I will show them that with a few changes, the monarchy is the best way. Then your father can demonstrate his loyalty to Russia and the church. Patriotism goes a long way in this country."

"That will take time," I frown. Stepan reaches around my waist and pulls me close, demonstrating to me that he understands my concerns about time.

"It does seem long, but, darling, we have forever."

We have chosen to make the most of our new predicament. In some ways this imprisonment at Tsarskoe Selo is better than our normal lives. We no longer have the responsibility of our position, and though we still have no idea what fate awaits us, we try to live as normally as possible. For our birthdays in June, we are all together. We don't need a ball or a big social event to celebrate. Instead our tutor has a surprise for us—a beautiful painting of the family, and a song he has written in our honor. Cook creates a smorgasbord of our favorite meals and Stepan, François and Peter join us around the table, as well as our family, for dinner. Even father's younger brother, Mikhail comes to wish us well. His handsome face and silly antics are a welcome change to the household. Olga teases me that at nineteen, I have joined her as one of the "old maids" of the family. I'm beginning to wonder if our future will ever be considered conventional, considering our choices are so varied. Maybe the new society that Stepan is helping to create will allow the tzar's daughters to choose for themselves, whether that be a soldier, a tutor, or a stable boy.

As the summer moves in, the palace becomes stifling. The heat, the boredom, the stress gets to all of us. We always thought that Mother was the unsteady one in the family, but the strain on Father changes him. Instead of being even tempered and jovial, he becomes short-tempered and paranoid. He demands that the curtains stay closed and refuses to let Anastasia out to see her horse.

Of course, this has never stopped her in the past. She begins to wake up early and leaves before Father gets up. With nothing more to do, he sleeps late and wakes up like an old bear that has suffered insomnia all winter. Mother tries to keep our living area quiet and dark. But Anastasia is still more a child than adult and forgets as she comes charging up the back steps into the kitchen with Peter in tow.

"He's my horse and I will take him wherever I like!"

"Hush Ani, you'll wake your fa—,"

But it's too late. The former tzar, standing in nothing but his undergarments and a worn robe, is blocking the entry to the living area. Red-faced, Peter stops abruptly, almost knocking over my little sister who stands with her arms folded, trying to match Father's stern expression.

"What is the meaning of this, young lady?" The question is directed at Anastasia, but he looks at Peter, who seems to know that his is coming next.

Her pout turns to a humble frown, "I'm sorry I woke you, Papa." She casts her eyes downward. This has always worked before.

"Waking me is one thing," Father clarifies, "But what's this I hear about the horse? Haven't I forbidden you to…?"

Anastasia's face goes white as if she has just realized she won't be able to sweet-talk Father this time and she knows she has something to lose. "No, Father you don't understand. I can't go on without him. He is the only thing that saves me from going insane in this place." She looks over at Peter, apologizing for her half-truth. Peter is the other half that keeps her sane.

Father looks almost sympathetic for a moment. The mention of the word "insane" rings true in all our ears, but he remains in control. "That horse may be the death of you, child. If you can't stay inside, maybe the temptation should be taken from you."

Anastasia makes no sound, but her heart screams in pain so that we all feel it. Her hands go to her face and she runs up to her suite. Marie follows her this time as Peter stands by to await his punishment. Father sits down hard in the nearest chair, as if all of the life has been drained from his body. Seeing the young stable hand out of the corner of his eye he turns to the boy.

"You," he says accusingly, but doesn't seem to have the energy to stay angry. "You have

been a good friend. You stay, even though you get no pay."

The young man hangs his head. I think this is the first I've realized that the servants that have stayed loyal are making such a sacrifice. "No one has any money, sir. I might as well stay where I am happy."

The sides of my Father's mouth turn up in a wan smile. "In this palace?" He laughs as if he has heard something absurd. "This palace makes you happy?"

"This family makes me happy."

The smile melts from Papa's face, and it becomes contemplative. Peter stands tall—waiting. When Father turns back to him he smirks. "You boy, may stay, but go out for now, my daughter likes you and she's in trouble."

I would like to say that he was enlightened by his conversation with Peter, but his bad temper continues for most of the rest of the summer. Носки stays for now, and Anastasia is much more careful about spending time with him, but Peter is welcome and Father even seems to find some joy in his company.

The Governor's Mansion—Urals, Russia

August is unusually warm the summer of 1917. Searching for a breeze that has eluded us all month long, I follow Stepan to the automobile waiting behind the palace as he is leaving to return home for the evening. This night, something tells me to hold him a little tighter, say good-bye a little longer. Moved by my need to have him near me, Stepan takes my face in his hands. He kisses my forehead, my eyelids, my nose, my chin, my neck, and then moves up to my lips. Sighing he pulls away, but as he takes me in his arms, he whispers in my ear. "This is going to work, My Little Tanya, it has to. No one has as much to lose as I do in this case, because no one else has you. I will succeed and we will be together—together forever, my love." He holds me back at arms' length, studies my face and seemingly puts it to memory. Then he kisses my nose one last time and climbs in the awaiting vehicle.

Still intoxicated by his kiss, I stay outside a little longer, watching until I can no longer see the trail of dust coming from his vehicle, but as soon as I walk in through the back, we hear a pounding on the palace's front gate and an authoritative voice.

"Это компьютерный перевод оригинальной веб-страницы. Он дает лишь общее представление о содержащейся там информации и не должен рассматриваться как полный или как точный."

A shocking chill runs through my heart as we are told to open the door, get our things and come with them. Maybe ten—fifteen men dressed in police uniforms invade our home. They are holding guns trained on my father and my brother. We have lulled ourselves into thinking this would never happen, but we are wearing the corsets with the jewels sewn inside. Mother has insisted that we wear them at all times. We took care when sewing them so that their course edges should not scratch our skin. But we can feel them whenever we move. We have gotten used to how they feel. We also have packed our most necessary things: our winter coats (it's hot now, but we don't know how long we will be away) a fresh change of clothing, a bar of soap and cleaning cloth have been placed in knapsacks for each of us. We have been physically prepared for some time, but there is no way we could be emotionally ready to give up this life we have become accustomed.

We leave with our eyes and our hearts turned towards the walls of the palace, trying to memorize every inch of them—there are so many memories—not knowing if we'll ever see this as our home again. As we follow the men to awaiting vehicles, I make sure my precious ring, coiled with diamonds, is securely on my finger on my left hand, and reach for the gold locket to affirm that it's snugly around my neck.

But some things must be left behind. Instead of going towards our ride, Anastasia struggles to break free from the guards, screaming for her horse. Peter comes running out of the stables.

"Носки," she sobs. "I can't leave him, I love him. What if I never see him again?"

Peter sees the uniformed men and stands aside, his shoulders sagging, tears streaming down his face, and waits for her to be finished, and then answers for Носки.

"He knows. He loves you too. I will take care of him and he will be here waiting for you when you get back."

The soldier holding her scoffs out loud as he tightens his hold, dragging her to the waiting wagon. She continues to struggle until the heel of her boot gets caught on a root in the ground and breaks off. With no time to grab another boot, she is left with the broken one. My brother rips away from his distracted escort and goes to our sister's aid. He gives her his arm as she hobbles along next to him; his head held high.

The trauma of the night settles as we are forced to board a train. We find that we are not being taken to prison as Father had feared, but instead that our destination is the Ural Mountains. We are to be taken to a place they call The Governor's Mansion.

It is not a palace, but certainly comfortable for our family and our remaining servants. Most of the household that has remained loyal has been brought as well, save the stable hand. There is no need for our animals in the rocky terrain of the Urals, and we have been given no means of transportation. The mansion is bigger than our living area at the palace, and since we are no longer in Petersburg, there is no need to fear our neighbors. There are a few men that have been assigned to watch us. Though they are always there, they give us our privacy, and don't seem to concern themselves with our daily activities

We welcome the cooler air and the coming of fall as we walk around the grounds freely. I believe Stepan must have persuaded the government to give us this act of grace.

Mother's main concern is our diet. We are no longer near a garden producing fresh fruits and vegetables and she worries about our nutrition. After talking to the guards, she finds that she is allowed to send messages to Petersburg. After sending a troubled note to her Romanov sisters, somehow, we receive a fruit basket every day. Although the fruit is a few days old, messages are easily sent in and out of the mansion with the basket. Daily I find a note addressed to me from Stepan taped to the inside bottom of the fruit basket. This is also how he sends encrypted messages to my father, hiding them in the same envelope.

Less than a week after we arrive, Anastasia receives an "anonymous" package from Petersburg—a pair of worn boots, at least two sizes too big. She wears them constantly and keeps them impeccably shined. I think she even sleeps with them.

I eagerly anticipate a note from Stepan every day and I am never disappointed though the messages he sends to Father are longer and more detailed. When mother sees my melancholy expression she tells me, "Chin up, this will not last forever. A woman can endure anything if she knows there's an end to it."

And she is right. I remember the conversations Stepan and I had back at the palace about how he predicted things would change. I see that he has been correct so far. If things continue to go in the direction he said they would, it will all be over with soon. We are not suffering as much as some. I remember the Grecian prince, Paul, talking of his family's exile and spending the winter in a hotel. It must have been much worse than this.

As the nights get longer and the air gets cooler, another concern sets in. The mansion is cold. The mountains surrounding it border the Arctic Ocean, and like Siberia to its east, the temperatures in Ural are known to be frigid. We have not been provided with anything for heat.

On October the 17, we receive word that the Bolsheviks have taken power away from the Soviets in the provisional government. We are told that the government run by the Bolsheviks is not as cordial as the Soviet provisional government, but nothing has changed for us so far. I hold out hope, because I think this is what Stepan suspected would happen.

As winter nears, there is still no change in sight. Father is watching closely and is as anxious to receive Stepan's message as I am. Our most important task of the day is to stay warm. Our coal and matches are rationed. Cook barely has enough to keep the oven warm to cook our food. We stay in the kitchen as long as she is cooking. We wear our winter coats all the time inside and huddle together, using each other as human furnaces. Marie and François take advantage of this excuse as often as possible and no one questions when they snuggle together under a blanket. The rest of my sisters and I hold each other, each of us wishing we had a man to hold on to as well. Olga celebrates her birthday with notes and well-wishes from family members and tchotchkes included in the basket.

The forty-day fast has begun and though we do not have a chapel or an altar, we all pray often and fervently. Mother is concerned that her children will be disappointed for Christmas, but as long as we have our lives and each other, we don't need new dresses or a Christmas dinner.

I do long for one thing for Christmas. Anastasia has a similar wish, but Stepan has already told me that this year, again, we must spend Christmas apart. My aunts can get us a basket because they are women and family and not a threat, but if he were to be caught trying to get in all of his efforts so far would be lost. I think that on Christmas, they can't be watching so closely, but I must yield to his wisdom.

It seems that this year, our family has become the charity project, as baskets containing Christmas decorations and treats are sent to us in honor of the twelve apostles during the twelve days of Christmas. One basket contains candles and a book of matches so we can continue the tradition started by François, placing the candles in the windows of the mansion, Father gathers bark and kindling from outside and attempts to start a fire. The house is warmer than it's been since August. Christmas day, Cook takes some of the items she has gathered from the basket along with the food we are provided with and makes a fine meal.

As we are in the parlor singing carols, hoof beats can be heard in the distance. We stop singing and brace ourselves. A horse can only mean one thing—military. But as we gather around the window, we find that we were mistaken. "Носки!" My sister squeals with delight. "Peter!"

We all follow Anastasia out the door, and before the boy can dismount the horse she has her arms around him, covering him with kisses—in front of my father. But Father only chuckles, grabs my mother by the hand, and takes her inside.

Peter is invited to stay. We crowd around him and hang on his every word as if he were a celebrity. He has news on everything from what has happened at the palace since we left, to the politics discussed in the streets.

"The protesting has slowed down, but the bread lines continue. A change in government philosophy doesn't change the fact that there isn't enough food. But the Bolsheviks are cruel. If a disagreement erupts and causes a disturbance, it is immediately put to a stop—by gun fire."

"Aren't you afraid that you will be punished for coming here?" Anastasia holds tighter to
his arm.

Peter grins. "What? I'm just a simple peasant. Can I help it if my horse ran off into the mountains and I was invited in by your charity so I could get warm before heading back home?"

Anastasia's stern looks tells us she doesn't think he's funny. Peter sighs, "It's Christmas. The Bolsheviks are more focused on making themselves merry, than they are worried about me. Would you deny me my Christmas present?" He bats his long dark eyelashes and we all "Aw," as Anastasia presents him with another Christmas kiss.

"So the Bolsheviks are in control now," Father sternly interrupts.

Peter scoots his chair closer to Father's and respectfully answers him, red-faced. "Yes, but the Socialists have sent for Vladimir Lenin. He is a very powerful man."

Father nods, pleased at what he's hearing. I smile too. Stepan's theories, so far, have proven to be correct. It may be only a matter of time, maybe in the summer, that his plans will succeed and we will be together. When I close my eyes, I dream of our future. I dream of a time when we will be together surrounded by our children and laughing at how impatient we once were to be married.

We keep Peter late, although I don't think he minds, with questions until it's much too late to travel back. He is assigned a guest room, but he and my sister fall asleep in the parlor, holding each other to keep warm. By morning, the guards have been alerted that we have an overnight guest. We hear hoof beats again, and this time it is not a stray horse.

Fortunately, when the soldiers arrive on our doorstep, Anastasia has left Peter and it look
as if he slept the night on the couch, something that might seem appropriate for a simple stable boy chasing a stray horse at Christmastime, but the police still take Peter and Носки into custody. Anastasia contains her emotions until after the police leave, and then she bursts out in angry sobs, running to her room to cry into her pillow.

We are all anxious to get Stepan's letter, hoping for news. He doesn't disappoint us. Insisting I read it in private first, I take it to my room to preview it before the family can see.

Dearest Tanya,

>*I hope your Christmas was merry.
Mine was not. I swear this
will be the last holiday we spend apart.
I am told that the stable boy Peter was
able to penetrate the protective fortress
that has been built around the
Romanovs. I am quite jealous, but I'm
sure you are all wondering what has*

become of him. Fortunately, he is not seen as a threat. The guards believed his story and he was let off with a warning. But it was discovered that the horse he was after once belonged to your sister. Peter has begged me not to tell you this, so don't mention it too Anastasia, the boy feels an obligation to keep the horse safe for her and he feels like he has failed in that promise. It has been turned over to the military and is no longer in Peter's care. I'm sure this loss will be felt strongly through your entire family, so it would probably be better if it remained a secret until you have secured your freedom and have regained your perspective.

I love you, my angel. You are and will forever be my reason for living.

Your Stepan

I fold up the letter, vowing to keep his secret. I share the news that Peter was let free, and though I try to finish it there, my face betrays me and Ani knows there is more.

"Носки?" She questions. I try to avoid her, but she corners me in the kitchen later when we are alone. "What happened to Носки?"

I shake my head, "Peter didn't want you to know. They wouldn't return the horse to him. He feels like he has failed you."

Anastasia quickly wipes the tears from her eyes with her palms in frustration. "I love the horse, but I love Peter more. He could never be anything but a hero in my eyes."

I am humbled at my sister's strength. I wish I could communicate her words back to Peter, so he would understand his importance to our family, but I have no way of getting a message back to Stepan. I hope that he feels, that he knows, that my love for him is never-ending, and that he is the light that I look to in the darkness.

As the weeks go on, the darkness seems to spread. First it is the cold. Fighting the cold has become a constant battle. We keep ourselves busy, cleaning, dusting, gathering tinder for the cook so she can keep the fire burning. We keep moving as much as we can during the day, and at night we have learned to rely on each other. Olga and I share a bed, Mother and Father, Marie and Anastasia. Alexei sleeps with his tutor, but the cook, the doctor, and our remaining loyal household can only hope that the spring will come early this year.

дом одноцелевого

"House of Special Purpose"

Yekaterinburg, Russia 1918

The awakening of spring brings an awakening of the Bolsheviks. They seem to have discovered that we have not been punished enough. Stepan has warned that it will probably get worse before it gets better. The first new orders we receive are for Papa. He enjoys wearing his old uniform. Besides being warm, it reminds him of a more fulfilling past, but it is apparently offensive to the new men that have been recently posted to stand guard. He is ordered that he cannot wear anything with epaulettes. Because of the style, and the fact that he was recently the imperial emperor, his clothing selection becomes extremely limited. Mother removes the epaulettes from his clothes as discreetly as possible.

Messages are getting harder and harder to sneak into the mansion. The baskets come less frequently and finally stop altogether. On the first of March, we are placed on soldiers rations. Meaning we are given the same amount of food as the soldiers that are fighting the war. For the first time since he has been part of our household, François Bertrand shows his anger. Taking Marie's face in his hands, he traces the bones protruding through the skin on her once plump cheeks with his thumbs.

"Haven't our woman endured enough?" He shouts in frustration to Papa. But Father is powerless to do anything. I twist my engagement ring around my boney finger. It has become out of place in this world that we have been forced into.

The last day of April I receive a rare message from Stepan, finally giving us some hope.

> *My Dearest Tanya,*
>
> *We have been saved from the Bolsheviks. Lenin has arrived and has been elected to head the provisional government by a large margin. He is aware of your situation, and has promised me that he will use his power to protect you. It will be easy to convince him that I am his ally; he is a*

> *man that is easily admired. Though I fear that it will be some time before he loses his popularity and your father can come back into his place, I think that I can convince him that you are not a threat to him and you may be returned with your family. I am giddy with delight. I know that the end of your misery is in sight.*
>
> *Yours forever,*
> *Stepan*

Father is also delighted with the news that the Bolsheviks are no longer in power,

but repeats Stepan's earlier warning that they will not back down easily and continue to be a danger.

That night I have a dream. I am in a beautiful place. Stepan comes to me and

takes my hands in his. My heart swells with light and peace—more love than I can ever

explain. He leans into me and kisses my lips. "I told you we would be together and this

truly is forever."

Disoriented, but happy, I look around. We are surrounded by children, pulling on my dress and climbing on Stepan. I've had this dream before, but this one is so vivid.

I can smell him, feel his touch. My heart quivers with joy like it's ready to burst, yet there

is a part of me that knows this can't be real and I waken with tears on my face. I get out

of bed and go to the window looking to the stars for the answer. Looking over at Olga's

bed, the memory of the night she lost Dmetri comes fiercely back to my mind. For a

moment I fear something has happened to my Stepan. The horrifying thought causes

me to shake, but the glorious feeling from the dream wraps around me like a blanket and

I am comforted. I say nothing to my family about my dream, but it stays with me all day

until that evening when we receive another message—specially delivered by a

uniformed soldier.

My father frowns as he hands me the envelope. It's Stepan's stationary with my name written on the front in his hand writing—just like every other message I have received from him at the Governor's Mansion. But when I open it I don't find a letter written in his crisp, neat penmanship. Instead I find a note written in quick long strokes that I don't recognize.

> *Princess Tatiana,*
>
> *I regret to inform you that your friend Stepan Karenin has been captured and taken prisoner by the Bolsheviks. Though I will do what I can, the Bolsheviks cannot be trusted and I fear for his safe return.*

I now fully understand the meaning of my dream.

> *I vow to do all in my power to keep your family*

safe.
Your Friend,
Vladimir Lenin

The last words spoken to me by Rasputin sear through my heart like a hot knife.

He's a good as dead anyway.

I gingerly place the note back in my father's hand and with all the dignity I can

muster I climb the stairs to my suite. I hear the cries of my sisters downstairs as Father

breaks the news to my family. I hear Mother try to hush their cries so I don't hear. I close

my eyes and pray for the comfort of the dream I was given last night. The room goes

dark as I wait. No comfort comes, but when Olga comes to bed she doesn't wait to see if

I'm asleep. She comes to my side and smoothes my hair against my tear-wet pillow.

"Did he come to you?" she barely waits for a nod before answering for me. "I thought I felt his presence here last night. I thought it strange until I saw you standing at

the window, and I knew. He's gone isn't he?"

Her understanding expression causes me to throw myself into her arms.

"At least we have Lenin's promise that we will be safe."

We both laugh at the ridiculousness of that statement, neither of us not caring if we are safe or not.

The next morning we are ready when the soldiers arrive to take us to our next destination.

A man in a grey uniform and a red scarf explains that where we are going, we will be safe. Wearing our specially converted corsets under our worn and faded dresses, we carry our meager remaining belongings, and our family, accompanied by our adopted family members—François, Cook and Dr.Fedorov, Father's valet and Mother's lady in waiting follow the soldiers. We are pushed towards a carriage, more like a cart for carrying animals. I have been drained of all life since receiving the letter from Lenin. I didn't sleep. Instead, I prayed all night most fervently for the dream of Heaven and Stepan. They are all I have now and I long to be there again.

The soldiers push and drag us in their haste to load us into the cart. A young man with fiery red hair and blazing green eyes grabs me from behind and I hear a slight "ting." I would not have even noticed it at all in our situation if I didn't know exactly what it was. My ring. Stepan's ring—my grandmother's ring, has slipped off my boney finger and fallen to the ground. It seems for a moment that time has stopped, or at least it has for me, and the clear morning air becomes silent. The "clink" has been heard by someone else. A large fat man with black hair and black eyes reaches down at the same moment I do, but the red-headed man tightens his grip on my arms. The black-eyed man meets my eyes and his face erupts in a smile. He snatches up my ring before anyone can see and puts it in his pocket. My legs, along with my heart, give out. I no longer have the strength to stand and I am thrown into the back of the cart like a sack of potatoes.

Even if I were unconscious, which mentally, maybe I am, the ride would be excruciatingly jarring as we travel over the mountain pass to The Ipatiev House, or the place the soldiers call "дом одноцелевого, House of Special Purpose." It's in the town of Yekaterinburg. Hours later, from my position in the cart, I look up at a tall brick building. Ipatiev House was once the home of the military engineer

Nikolayevich Ipatiev. It is surrounded by leafless trees and thorny bushes that have long overgrown their intended purpose.

The lifeless bushes pull at our dresses as we are escorted up the front steps. We are greeted by a man in a brashly decorated gray suit with a red scarf. He also tells us that here we will be protected from the Bolsheviks, and that Vladimir Lenin hasn't forgotten his promise. The man's scarf is the only patch of color in the gray room and loudly reminds me of the banners that waved down the streets of Petersburg shouting, "Down with the Tzar."

My brain is fuzzy from the surge of emotion that it has experienced in the last twenty-four hours. Here we feel as though we are prisoners, pushed and shoved like animals. Some of the guards are people we once trusted, Derevenko, one of Alexei's former doctors, and others. Some were once servants, or acquaintances of society. People we have invited into our home, and shown respect, and cordiality. No one returns the favor. If they are here to protect us, they have a funny way of showing it.

All of our belongings are taken from us save the clothes we are wearing. We are shoved into a room. I land on my knees and don't move out of that position, begging God to take me now. We have all tried to keep a stern face, but when the guards shut the door and leave, the tears start to flow. I'm suddenly acutely aware of the pain and the bruises that have been recently inflicted on my body, and the hunger that rips at my stomach, but I'm sure I'm not the only one feeling pain. Alexei has been very strong, but we have no idea how much he may be already bleeding on the inside. I fall asleep to the sound of my mother and sisters' weeping. My father and François are silent, unable to reassure them.

I awaken, just before dawn, and survey my surroundings. The small room has hard floors (but I already knew that) and a small window. I remember climbing stairs to get here, but I have no idea if we are still on the second floor or if we are in an attic or tower of some sort. My family's bodies are sprawled all over the floor and the smell of dirt and body odor fills the air. I fight my brain to shut off again, to go back into the semi-conscious state that has allowed me to endure the pain up until this point, but it is awake and aware of the aching now. With my nurse's trained hands I trace the pain and access the damage. My fingers are drawn to the chain around my neck.

It seems like an entire lifetime ago that it was placed there. Fear causes me to grip the heart-shaped locket tightly in my hand, and with some force I rip it from my neck, no longer caring if I damage the clasp. I open it and the sparse light of dawn comes through the window allowing me to see the enclosed picture. My finger traces Stepan's bearded face and in a prayer I tell him I'm sorry for losing our ring. I can almost hear his condescending chuckle. The ring is not where our love is, but our love is still in me.

I tighten my grip on the heart in my hand and I understand. We may have had everything taken from us, our home, our family, the ones we love, but there is one thing they will never be able to take from us—our spirits, our hearts. And soon, one way or another we will have our freedom too. I take the golden heart and tuck it into my corset with the other jewels that have been sewn inside, under my left breast, as close to my heart as possible. Something, at least will be protected here. I resolve to be bright, not bitter, optimistic, and strong like my little brother.

July 16-17, 1918

"The Bolsheviks are coming!"

We are awoken around midnight by the cries, and in a disoriented state, we are led down three flights of stair into the basement.

"There is sure to be gunfire, rioting in the streets, you will be safe down here," our guards reassures us. But it quickly becomes apparent that our safety is not what the soldiers have in mind as we are pushed and tied to chairs. Marie has to be torn from François' protective arms, but their chairs are placed next to each other. "So you can watch her die." The soldier's laugh is the last thing I hear before room goes completely black. Surrounded by those remaining who are most dear to me, we await our fate.

Safe. In the basement, bound by cords, surrounded by gunmen, until the word is given.

"Пожар!" The gunmen obey the order and shots ring out. I feel a pain in my ribcage, the kind of pain I imagine could kill me. But it doesn't penetrate. As I fight to stay conscious, I reach my hand through the cords and try to place it on the wound. There is no blood, just a torn spot on my dress where the locket was hidden. Every nerve is heightened as my skin checks itself. It feels like the locket is still intact.

A round of bullets buzz past and ricochet off the concrete walls. The room is filled with flying bullets, terror, and confusion. For some reason, the first round of fire was unsuccessful. Though the smell of blood burns my nostrils, I am not dead, and judging by the screams that follow, I am not the only one who has survived. Were the gunmen off their mark in the dark or were we protected by some unseen force?

The gunmen shriek in terror when they realize the bullets that were once aimed at our hearts are now seem to be flying around the room, looking for a soft spot to bed themselves in. Some of the guards are hit and injured, most try to escape. The door opens and light floods into the room through a haze of smoke. I look around and assess the damage. Father has been hit, more than once. Thick, black blood oozes from his head and chest. Maman is in the chair next to his, shaking, rocking back and forth. She too has been hit, not fatally, but she is bleeding profusely under her arm. She will certainly bleed to death if no one helps her. But I am frozen, my arms are bound. I can only move my eyes, which continue to scan the room.

Marie and Anastasia are still, but also alive. Olga's listless body is flailed across her chair. I see no blood, maybe she has fainted, or maybe her wound is hidden. For a moment it is silent. I hear only the soft sound of a young girl sobbing. François' lifeless eyes stare forward. He, also, is fatally wounded. There is nothing we can do, but still Marie fights her cords to reach for his hand. The last thing I see before the door shuts is my brother, sitting tall—the bravest man that I have ever known, aside from my father —Alexei faces death every day. Now with Papa dead, Alexei is the head of the Romanov family.

There is a lingering smell of gunpowder, so much of it that it suffocates me. It feels like we've gone to hell, but it can't be hell, for I am still alive. It's a miracle or perhaps another trick God is playing on my family. I think of Rasputin's prophecy—his curse. But this is worse than a curse—worse than hell. When death is the only thing left that can set us free, not even death will come.

Now the room is filled with the shouting voices of soldiers. "They are witches!" some say. "They are protected by God," say others.

The door is closed and for a moment—silence, darkness, and that putrid
smell of death. A lantern is lit to reveal the face of our enemy, the man who has sworn he will protect us. "They must be wearing some sort of protective device." Vladimir Lenin screams.

The jewels sewn inside our corsets—they have proven to be priceless after all.

"They are protected by God!" One man fervently steps forward.

"There is no God." Lenin flings his arm out and smacks the man in the face. "God is a device concocted by men to justify asserting their power. They must be wearing something—some protective clothing. The only way to kill them is to put a gun directly against their heads. I only need nine willing men. The rest of you can leave with the other cowards." He then takes his shiny revolver and approaches my brother. "The Tsarevich, God's so-called- 'chosen-heir' will be first."

As the arrogant man circles my brother, trying to intimidate him, their eyes meet. "Are you afraid young man?"

His question sends chills down my body. I cannot stand to see this evil person break my brother.

"I have no fear—only hope." My twelve year old brother's voice rings out with conviction.

"There is no such thing as hope—at least not for your family." The sound of Lenin's

laugh burns my ears.

"Then why do I see fear in your eyes?" The Tsarcavich's voice rings out with surety.

Lenin's eyes move from my brother to me. I see it too—fear—and though I am also afraid, my eyes momentarily meet my brother's and we smile.

"I've got Tatiana," an unknown voice whispers behind my head. As I feel the cold metal of the gun barrel press against my temple I close my eyes, and think I will finally know what it means to be free and whisper, "Together forever. Soon my love."

Epilogue

The tragic story of the execution of the last tzar of Russia and his family was big news all over the world. As early as 1920, rumors that some members of the family had escaped were rampant, and dozens of girls claiming to be the lost princesses came forward. Some were quite convincing. One girl, claiming to be Anastasia, puzzled the court for decades. She died in 1986 before her claims could be disproven

In the early 1970s, an amateur archeologist found an unmarked grave near Yekaterinberg. The remains were smashed into pieces and several bones were missing. Vials of sulfuric acid were discovered in the mass grave. The Red Army was known to pour acid on the remains of their victims in order to speed up decomposition. The archeologist suspected it was the grave of the Romanov family, but the remains of only nine bodies were found, spurring the idea that the rumors were true. He kept the discovery a secret until 1991, and the fall of the Soviet Union.

DNA testing in the 1990s proved that the remains were those of the tzar, his wife, four servants, and three of their daughters. Researchers used samples of DNA from Britain's Prince Philip, whose grandmother was a sister to Queen Victoria, the tsarina's grandmother.

More recently, in 2009, a second grave site was found near the first. The bodies were badly burned, but the preliminary analysis suggested that the fragments were from three people, a female aged 17 to 24 speculated to be Marie; a male aged 14 to 16, possibly Alexei; and another unrelated male aged 25 to 30. Using new technology that allowed the use of extremely small samples and DNA from a bloody shirt worn by Nicholas when he was attacked by a Japanese policeman while touring the city of Otsu that had been preserved in a museum in Russia, the mystery was finally solved. Six of the bodies matched the DNA of Queen Victoria, and six matched the DNA of the tzar. Of course the five that matched both were the children, and there were five other unrelated bodies found. They were later proven to be that of the doctor, the cook, the tsarina's lady in waiting, the tzar's valet, and Alexei's French tutor. The genetic evidence was overwhelming, the truth was made known. The family could finally rest in peace.

Bibliography

Brumsfeild, William Croft. <u>Gold in Azure.</u> Boston: David R Godin, October 1, 1983.

Gilbert, Paul The Russian Dynasty, Monarchy and Imperial Russia. Retrieved from http://www.angelfire.com/pa/ImperialRussian/index.html

Gilliard, Pierre. <u>Thirteen Years at the Russian Court</u>. Charleston: Forgotten Books, June 25, 2012.

Jenks, Andrew (November 15, 2014) History or Russia in World War 1. Retrieved from http://historyofrussia.org/russia-in-ww1/

Massie, RK. <u>Peter the Great: His Life and World</u>. New York: Balentine Books, 1986.

Massie, Robert K. <u>Nicholas and Alexandria</u>. New York: Dell Publishing, 1967.

Rasputin: The Mad Monk. A&E, 1997. DVD.

Rosenbery, Jennifer (November 15, 2014) The Murder of Rasputin. Retrieved from http://history1900s.about.com/od/famouscrimesscandals/a/rasputin_2.htm

Acknowledgements

Acknowledgements? What a stiff formal word for "These are the people who cared enough to help me make my dream come true!" Be-that-as it-may, here they are:

This time, since we just got home from a library visit where he helped and supported me, I'm gonna thank my husband Kyle first. And my daughters too, they are getting better at thinking it's okay to have a Mom who thinks she's a writer. This particular book took hours of research and years to become what it is now. My family has been very patient with me.

As always, and I usually list her first, because at birth she was second but in life, she always comes in first, and also because I wouldn't, couldn't do this without her, my sister, Jennifer Shaw Wolf. She's the one that first got me going in a historical direction when she asked me, "What happened to your teenage voice? What have you been reading?" I suppose I should thank Phillipa Gregory for making me want to read historical fiction in the first place.

I would like to thank Val Serdy, who was my friend first and then turned into my editor. I'm so glad I found you, for both reasons. My critique partner, Anngela. For being my shoulder to cry on and lean against when I wanted to just quit this whole thing.

I've had many "beta readers," but I want to thank my fellow author and SF Cougar, Becky Browning Bryan for never telling me she didn't have time to read, when I know she didn't. Also Katy and Neeley, and Faith— always willing to be my guinea pigs. Thank you Jenny and Mckenzie for helping me with my back blog.

My cover portrait was sketched by artist, Jessica Laskasky. Your going places girl! Thanks for letting me be a part of it, and her mother, my friend, Kim. You continue to share my artistic vision. Also my sister-in-law Candee (Candice Amrine), who also shares and makes possible my vision by organizing it into a medium that becomes my covers.

One last unusual thanks I would like to give is to the late Tatiana Nikalova and her family. As I have researched and studied these people, I tried to write them as realistically as possible. Though some events have been changed, and let's face it, made up, I believe they truly loved each other and tried to be the best people they knew how to be. Their circumstances were difficult, if not unbearable at times. They were strong and a great example to me.

Can't get enough of the Romanovs?

Find out how it all began. How the Russian Grand Duke, Nikolai and the German Princess, granddaughter to the iconic Queen Victoria of England, Alexandra found each other and against the odds fell in love in the prequel to The Heart of the Romanovs, The Tsesarevich coming in the Spring.

Made in the USA
Lexington, KY
22 December 2014